I0762938

PRAISE FOR *BONE OF MY BONE*

"Decadently atmospheric and deeply unsettling, *Bone of My Bone* delivers a deliciously disturbing tale about survival and the choices we're forced to make along the way. Johanna van Veen's sublime prose and world-building left me completely enthralled."

—Monika Kim, award-winning author of *The Eyes Are the Best Part*

"Exquisite and sumptuous like the most ornate bone-and-ivory casket, Johanna van Veen's new novel—perhaps her most compelling yet, fast-paced and surprising, and not without some mischievously funny moments—moves with cinematic assuredness through a war-ravaged hellscape and tackles big themes, faith and love and desire, with consummate deftness."

—Andrea Morstabilini, author of *A Blood as Bright as the Moon*

"*Bone of My Bone* is a holy sojourn of a novel. Fans of Christopher Buehlman's *Between Two Fires* will surely worship this blasphemous masterclass of sapphic historical horror. I, for one, am bowing down before Johanna van Veen."

—Clay McLeod Chapman, author of *Wake Up and Open Your Eyes*

"Johanna van Veen writes beautifully rich and daring horror, and *Bone of My Bone* is her finest novel yet. Every page thrums with desperation, hunger, and dread—this is a breathlessly twisted and ghoulish tale that boasts a fierce, gleaming flame of hope at its heart. Never shrinking from the bitter reality of life in the 1600s, van Veen keeps you happily wriggling on the end of a very sharp hook as she explores the kind of delicate, hard-earned courage that can conquer unspeakable evil."

—Josh Winning, author of *Heads Will Roll*

"A sapphic romance buried amid the gore of war, necromancy, and getting a little too familiar with the skull of a saint, *Bone of My Bone* is captivating historical horror at its best."

—Chelsea Conradt, *USA Today* bestselling author of *The Farmhouse*

"*Bone of My Bone* is a gripping folk-horror fable about love, loss, and loyalty that kept me up reading late into the night. Johanna van Veen vividly conjures a Bavaria blighted by death and dark magic in a tale that is sure to hold you in its spell."

—Carmella Lowkis, author of *Spitting Gold*

"*Bone of My Bone* is a gruesome, beautiful, and utterly unputdownable read. Johanna van Veen writes lovable characters and historical horror masterfully—I couldn't put it down."

—Tatiana Schlote-Bonne, author of *The Mean Ones*

"Captivating and unsettling from the very first page, this lyrical gothic tale will rip your heart out. A dark vision of a dark time in history, *Bone of My Bone* braids together love and death, hope and fear, suffering and delight as only Johanna van Veen can. Exquisite."

—Charlotte Cross, author of *The Brides*

PRAISE FOR *BLOOD ON HER TONGUE*

"Chilling in its intimacy, this tale of monsters and monstrous love is a gorgeous gothic treat. I drank up every delicious word."

—Jennifer Thorne, *USA Today* bestselling author of *Diavola* and *Lute*

"A new gothic masterpiece. *Blood on Her Tongue* is decadent, full of gore and rot, and viscerally, relentlessly engaging. I devoured this one. Once you've tasted a little, you'll need more, then more, then more."

—CJ Leede, author of *Maeve Fly*

"Dark, visceral, and deliciously disturbing—van Veen has woven a tale that feels like a brand new nineteenth-century classic, bristling with gothic horror and mounting dread."

—C. E. McGill, author of *Our Hideous Progeny*

"Johanna van Veen's artful and cunning use of the sublime will pull you into a sisterly web of terror, beauty, and horror, all of it sensual and dripping with the idea that death should be a kind of mutilation."

—Nicholas Belardes, author of *The Deading*

"Gruesome, at times unhinged, and deeply beautiful, *Blood on Her Tongue* is morbid in the best sense of the word. A vital addition to the gothic genre that will make you shudder with both pleasure and fear."

—Katrina Monroe, author of *Through the Midnight Door*

"Johanna Van Veen weaves a seductively gruesome horror yarn with *Blood on Her Tongue*. Every page is dripping with gothic dread and undead yearning, and I couldn't devour it fast enough."

—Brian McAuley, author of *Curse of the Reaper*

"Johanna van Veen embroiders a rich tapestry of dark secrets and disturbing monsters, then delights in smothering you with it. A chilly gothic horror story that begs to be read by a roaring fire while the wind howls outside your window."

—Josh Winning, author of *Heads Will Roll*

"A heightened experience for gothic horror fans. Johanna van Veen indulges the audience with atmospheric tension and deeply flawed yet emotionally compelling characters. The taste of blood becomes sharper with every page."

—Bram Stoker Finalist Vincent Tirado,
author of *We Came to Welcome You*

"Johanna van Veen takes up the mantle of Stoker and Le Fanu with this seductive tale of hunger, transgression, and the violent power of sisterhood. Sumptuous, disturbing, and sensual, *Blood on Her Tongue* is queer gothic fiction at its audacious best. A bloody and decadent feast of a novel."

—Elliott Gish, author of *Grey Dog*

"Gothic horror for the ages... Combining shiver-inducing horror with sharp-fanged social commentary, this more than merits comparison to *Dracula* and other genre titans."

—*Publishers Weekly*, Starred Review

PRAISE FOR *MY DARLING DREADFUL THING*

"Dark and decadent, with the haunting allure of a true gothic tale, *My Darling Dreadful Thing* is a sensation that horrifies as acutely as it delights. Johanna van Veen is a force to be reckoned with and will stain your thoughts a brilliant shade of crimson. I adored every page."

—Rachel Gillig, *New York Times* bestselling author of *One Dark Window*

"A sapphic seance of preternatural proportions, *My Darling Dreadful Thing* summons a stunning new literary voice to be reckoned with. Johanna van Veen reaches beyond the veil to conjure up a gothic shocker like no other."

—Clay McLeod Chapman, author of *What Kind of Mother*

"*My Darling Dreadful Thing* is a disquieting delight—an exciting and original gothic tale told with tremendous flair."

—Cherie Priest, author of *The Drowning House*

"*My Darling Dreadful Thing* is an unabashed gothic treat with a plot that propels you with restless, creeping logic toward its brutal conclusion. Van Veen's imagery is lushly cinematic, evoking the very best work of Guillermo del Toro. This is a delicious novel."

—William Friend, author of *Let Him In*

"This book got under my skin, all the way down to the marrow. It's as dark as a grave and throbbing with queer desire. I won't forget it."

—Kirsty Logan, author of *Now She Is Witch*

ALSO BY JOHANNA VAN VEEN

My Darling Dreadful Thing

Blood on Her Tongue

BONE
OF MY
BONE

BONE OF MY BONE

JOHANNA VAN VEEN

Cover design by Erin Fitzsimmons/Sourcebooks
Cover art by Dawn Xintong Yang
Edge art by Dawn Xintong Yang

Published by Poisoned Pen Press, an imprint of Sourcebooks
1935 Brookdale RD, Naperville, IL 60563-2773
(630) 961-3900
sourcebooks.com

Library of Congress Cataloging-in-Publication Data

Names: Veen, Johanna van author
Title: Bone of my bone / Johanna van Veen.
Description: Naperville, IL : Poisoned Pen Press, 2026.
Identifiers: LCCN 2025053655 | trade paperback | trade paperback | epub
Subjects: LCGFT: Fiction | Horror fiction | Lesbian fiction | Novels
Classification: LCC PR9130.9.V44 B66 2026
LC record available at https://lccn.loc.gov/2025053655

Printed and bound in Canada.
MBP 10 9 8 7 6 5 4 3 2 1

For Corinna,

who is the Scully to my Mulder, except for when it comes down to my writing because then she is the Mulder to my Scully

[Germany] is now become a Golgotha, a place of dead men's skulls; and an Acaldama, a field of blood. Some nations are chastised with the sword, others with famine, others with the man-destroying plague. But poor Germany hath been sorely whipped with all these three iron whips at the same time and that for above twenty years' space.

—Edmund Calamy, "England's Looking Glass" (1641)
(spelling updated by the author)

AUTHOR'S NOTE

Dear reader,

From the blurb of this novel, you may have seen that this book takes place during the Thirty Years' War (1618–1648). This war has gone down in history as one of the deadliest and bloodiest conflicts in the history of mankind. It has been estimated that around eight million people lost their lives as a direct result of it, either on the battlefield, at the hands of marauding soldiers,* or due to the famine and epidemics** it caused. That was almost a quarter of Germany's entire population, although it must be noted that these "three iron whips" did not hit all parts of Germany equally; in some areas, the

---

* It must be noted that the soldiers, in turn, were at times killed by groups of peasants, either when those peasants were defending themselves or their property, or in acts of revenge.

** Specifically the plague and a kind of typhus that people called either the "head sickness" or "Hungarian sickness." It's likely that the plague would have occurred during this period regardless of war—the Black Death seems to have occurred in cycles, with some years being plague years and then several years being plague-free—but it is certain that the war allowed the plague to spread more easily. This is in part because of the mass movement of people such as armies and groups of refugees, partly because people tended to crowd together in unsanitary conditions, and partly because people, when tired and hungry and stressed, are more susceptible to diseases.

loss of life may been as low as only a few percent; in others, as high as 50, 75, or sometimes even 90 percent.

Apart from the tremendous loss of life, the Thirty Years' War is also known for its brutality. Torture was common, as was sexual violence. As is unfortunately still common in wars nowadays, rape was used as a tool to brutalize the occupied population. Many women and girls suffered sexual abuse at the hands of soldiers; many more lived in near constant fear of it.

Though I have at times played fast and loose with historical facts—for more information on that, see my notes on the historical setting at the back of this book—the time and place in which this novel is set inevitably lead to the discussion and inclusion of some heavy topics, including but not limited to trauma, death, torture, sexual violence, hunger and famine, illness, looting, and being forced to flee your home. I have done my utmost to ensure that I have treated these topics with the sensitivity they deserve.

This book also talks a lot about religion. It specifically addresses Catholicism and Calvinism. Religion formed a vital part of people's daily lives in early modernity and was one of the primary lenses through which they tried to make sense of everything that happened to them, both the good and the bad. Religion is also a root cause of the Thirty Years' War. With this novel, I am not trying to make grand sweeping statements about Christianity, on whether it is good or bad, harmful or useful; rather, I wish to explore in a nuanced and sensitive matter what might happen to people with strong religious convictions when they encounter one horror after another.

I am telling you all of this in advance to allow you to take any necessary precautions before embarking on what I hope will prove to be a suspenseful, heartfelt, and perhaps at times even beautiful read. An alphabetized list of trigger warnings can be found all the way at the back of this book. Proceed with caution, but don't forget to enjoy yourself!

PART I

"Farewell happy fields,
Where joy forever dwells: Hail, horrors, hail."

—John Milton, *Paradise Lost*

Prologue

ELSEBETH

When I was a little girl, I saw three witches burned.

This was when the war was still young compared to what it is now, though we weren't to know that then. A lucky thing that was, because who wants to know that a war will last so long that there are now men and women alive who have known nothing else in their entire lives?

Nothing but soldiers who go plundering and torturing and raping and murdering.

Nothing but plague and the Hungarian sickness.

Nothing but hunger.

But we didn't know that yet the day my father and my grandmother took me to see the burnings. My mother did not come, for she did not care for violence. My big sister, Margarethe, would have liked to join us—she did always love any sort of excitement—but rheumatism had crippled her again, and so she had to stay home.

We followed the cart with the two women and the man in it

as they were brought to the pyres to die. People jeered at them and threw all manner of filth at them, rotten eggs and clods of earth and dung, for although Christ tells us that only he who is without sin may cast the first stone, to not cast out a sin when you know it is there is a kind of sin also.

After they were tied to the stakes but before the fire was lit, the three were allowed to say something.

The man said that he was no witch and that God knew.

The first woman claimed she was no witch either and would plead her case better if only her hands didn't hurt so much. They had tortured her for her confession, and her thumb had come clean off under the screw.

The final woman didn't speak of God and forgiveness. She didn't plead, either. Instead, she tossed her head and laughed, and when she spoke, she did so with a loud and pleasant voice clear as a church bell.

She said that she was indeed a witch.

She had met the devil at the crossroads one January afternoon when she was still a girl and looking for food, for she and her mother were poor and starving. He came to her in the shape of a hare. He smiled and called her by her name. He told her he had come to ask her for her soul and maidenhead.

She should have fled then, and if Satan had made it so that her legs no longer worked, she should have closed her eyes, stoppered her ears with her fingers, and prayed to God to save her, for Satan's might is great, but God's might is greater still. Instead, she proudly raised her head and asked him what he might offer her in return.

The devil told her he could teach her many of his dark arts, like how to make women barren and how to spread sickness that strikes both man and animal across the land so she might punish all who had ever mistreated her and her poor old crooked mother. He would also teach her how to steal babes and kill them by driving a needle through their brains so she could boil them into a salve that would make her fly and thus let her join the witch's Sabbath, where she would fornicate with demons and find a pleasure no mortal man could give her.

She said all of that sounded fine indeed, but she would be better served if he gave her a pot of soup that would never empty, and a pretty dress and a pair of good leather shoes as well, for she was hungry and cold, and her bare feet much bruised and cut.

The devil smiled and agreed to her terms, then transformed into a handsome man with bare, hairy feet dressed in an embroidered coat of green. He had her on the cold, dark ground, and afterward it was as he had promised.

Did she regret any of it?

She spat on the ground. Pah! Of course she did not, for this was a cruel world, and poor women such as herself should grab any crumb of power they could get their hands on. For this reason she had thrown in her lot with the devil. Seeing as she had given herself to him and he owned her body and soul, he was welcome to fetch her home now.

When the pyres were lit, the man tried to pray, but his words soon slurred into screams. The woman with the missing thumb only sobbed. Both soon choked to death; someone had added green branches to their pyres, that they might die from breathing the smoke before the flames reached them.

Not so the witch. She didn't pray or scream or sob, just bit her lips with such force, blood slicked her chin as the flames raced up her skirt. Soon, the air smelled of cooking meat, and my stomach growled, for the harvest had been bad and my meals lean.

The witch burned so bright, my eyes ached to look at her, but I could not tear them away. One of her arms fell off, yet still she lived. She did not scream, but she writhed and somehow managed to wrench herself loose. As soon as the ropes no longer bound her, she leapt out of the flames and into the air.

I caught her eye as she hung, for a moment, suspended. I thought mayhap she might fly away; mayhap she had managed to rub some of that salve she had made from all those poor little unbaptized babes on her body before she was brought out to die.

She had the strangest eyes, round and yellow, not the eyes of a woman but of a hare.

I knew then what it was like to be so afraid your heart stutters in your chest, the blood thrums in your ears, and you go cold all over as if someone has upended a bucket of water over your head.

Time stretched and stretched in the way a clump of wool stretches impossibly long as you spin it into yarn, and still she floated, still her flaming hare eyes bored into mine. It seemed to me she could see straight into my soul. She must have liked what she saw, for she began to grin.

I shuddered once, but with such violence, it was almost a convulsion.

Just when I thought I'd run mad, or I'd faint, or something else would happen to me, for standing there held by a witch's spell was more than I could bear, she finally fell and was trampled to death by the crowd.

Not in my dreams, though.

In my dreams, she flies.

1

URSULA

Bavaria, 1635

THERE IS NO WARNING. ONE moment, the road is just that: a humble country road in the Bavarian countryside on which travel a dozen people, all of them looking pinched and starved and miserable. The next, it is a slaughterhouse.

Had she been turned into a pillar of salt as befell Lot's poor wife, Sister Ursula could not have stood stiller than she does when the soldiers swarm among them with their swords and knives and guns raised, their faces contorted with hatred. She doesn't mean to freeze, but terror has suffused her limbs and won't let her move them.

Those soldiers must have lain in wait at the edge of the forest, where the shrubs and the trees hide them from our sight but not us from theirs, she thinks. It's the last clear thought she has. After this, fear makes her mind gutter like a candle in a draft, so that later, she only remembers the ambush in flashes.

An old man trying to gather his steaming entrails in order to push them back into his belly.

A soldier grunting on top of a woman, whose hands fist uselessly into the mud.

A child lying motionless with eyes glassy like marbles, their skull horribly dented just above their ear, which turns pink and orange and almost see-through where the light hits it, like a seashell. She can't stop staring at it.

Such horror.

Such beauty.

She only breaks out of this trance when a skinny peasant girl takes her hand and roughly pulls her off the road and into the forest. They run as if the devil himself is on their heels, which Sister Ursula supposes is true. Those soldiers are in thrall to Satan, possessed by rage and lust and greed. The farther they leave them behind, the better.

Get thee behind me, Satan, she thinks and has the sudden urge to laugh. She has no breath to spare, though. The peasant girl may look half starved, but she is strong, and she is fast, her grip on Sister Ursula's hand relentless.

They crash through the woods, not following any path that Sister Ursula can see. Branches snatch at their clothes, rake through their hair. Are those soldiers after them? She can't hear over the pounding of her blood and her ragged breathing.

Someone grabs her cape. The cord that fastens it around her throat tightens like a noose as her body is yanked backward, ripping her hand from the peasant girl's with such strength that her arm feels half wrenched out of its socket.

A soldier throws himself on top of her. He smells of sweat and blood, so strong that she would gag if only she had any breath to do so, but her cape, now caught underneath her body, is still strangling her so that she is scrabbling uselessly at her throat rather than fending him off as he tears at her clothes.

He only manages to rip off a button before the peasant girl launches herself at him, knocking him off Sister Ursula. Silently they roll on the ground, trading punches and trying to bite at each other.

Sister Ursula tears at the fastening of her cape, manages to loosen it enough to allow her to breathe. The cool, damp air does not soothe her wounded throat; rather, it makes it feel as if it is on fire, but it is sweet all the same. Gasping, she struggles to her feet.

The peasant girl and the soldier are still at each other's throats. Sister Ursula hesitates, approaches without knowing what to do. Until today, she has never been in a fight before. She feels for the little knife in her belt that she always carries to cut bread, but her hands tremble so much that she daren't pull it out for fear that she'll drop it. When she draws closer to the two with the intention to somehow help the girl, the soldier's booted foot connects with her right knee. This time, she can cry out, and she does so as she falls to the ground, clutching her knee.

Her screaming is just the distraction the peasant girl needs. As the soldier falters for only a second, no doubt spooked by the ragged sound produced by her bruised throat, the girl grabs a broken rock and smashes it against the side of his head. With a grunt, he falls to the side, where he lies twitching and foaming at the mouth. The smell of urine fills the air.

The peasant girl spits at him, then wipes her mouth with the back of her hand before adjusting her little white cap, which, although much dirtied from all that rolling around, has remained on her head. This done, she pulls Sister Ursula to her feet.

They keep running. The ground is littered with branches and twigs, deadwood torn from the trees in past storms. They snap easily underneath her feet, the sound so loud that Sister Ursula mistakes them for gunfire at first.

Soon, her knee throbs and her side hurts with each breath. It feels as if someone is driving a needle into her flesh, trying to stitch something there clumsily, like a child who has yet to learn how to sew. She welcomes the sensation. It's better than being terrified out of her mind.

Once, there is a high-pitched scream close by, but it cuts off before she can tell whether it is human or animal in nature.

When they reach a little stream, they don't pause to wash the mud from their feet and legs, or even to drink, but only to hitch up their skirts, and, in Sister Ursula's case, to take off her shoes; the girl has none. The water is cold as the touch of a dead man.

Sister Ursula makes to cross, but the girl shakes her head. "We must wade upstream. That way, we will be harder to track," she pants and points to their footprints, which are clearly visible in the earth all soft from the recent rain.

They wade upstream for as long as they can stand, then clamber out and continue running. They only stop when neither can run anymore. Sister Ursula thinks she might be sick from the pain in her side, which no longer feels like a needle stitching, but a knife repeatedly stabbing her.

An image rises in her mind, of a soldier sitting astride a little boy and knifing him over and over again. She can hear the wet, meaty sound of the knife as it cuts through skin and fat, can see the boy jerk with every stab, can smell the blood and the shit.

This is not some dark thing her mind has conjured on its own. *I just saw that*, she thinks, *and if it wasn't for this peasant girl, that could have been me.* She begins to heave. She hasn't eaten all day, though, and so when she bends over, all she brings up is a mouthful of bitter bile.

The girl helps her wipe her mouth with a dirty handkerchief, then pulls her along. "We must find some place to hide in case they come this way," she whispers.

They find a spot in the undergrowth where the branches don't grow so thickly, almost a kind of nest, with soft moss. They crouch there, holding each other close.

Sister Ursula wraps her cape around them to try and make them invisible. It's made out of coarse brown wool, and though it almost strangled her earlier and even on its best days rubs her throat red and raw, Sister Ursula knows to be grateful for it, as she is grateful for the humble dress she wears and her plain shoes, even though they are too big and she must stuff them with straw or else risk blistering her feet. They keep her warm, don't they? And they keep her safe; no one who sees her dressed like this will suspect she is a nun.

Ever since the war began and reports of unspeakable violence done to nuns and monks by the Protestant armies reached Sister Ursula's convent, the sisters have worn laywomen's clothes when forced out onto the road. It's a sad world in which she must hide that she is a bride of Christ, but it could be worse. How many poor people has she seen on the road who have nothing to wear but rags, and sometimes not even that? Like the peasant girl beside her, who doesn't have any shoes to protect her feet from the cold and all the sharp, cruel things on the road.

It's a miracle that the two of them are unharmed, at least for now.

What if the soldiers find them?

If they find them, they...

If they find them...

She works her free hand—the peasant girl still has a firm hold of the other—underneath the collar of her dress until she reaches her rosary. *Ave Maria, gratia plena, Dominus tecum*, she prays, clutching wooden beads with such strength she knows her fingers will come away with little red dents. There's no dousing the inferno of fear inside of her; she learned that when she and her sisters stayed in the castle of Eichstätt whilst it was under siege by the enemy. The shooting went on for two weeks. But though prayer can't kill the fear completely, it makes it more manageable, and so she prays and prays until the cramp in her legs makes it impossible.

She sits down on the moss, wincing at its dampness, then gingerly stretches out her legs. Her right knee throbs and burns. No doubt that soldier has badly bruised it, even though her knees have been hardened, calloused, even, by years of kneeling in prayer. It'll probably be black and blue tomorrow, but she doesn't think she has damaged it beyond healing. Her throat, too, hurts abominably and will likely be sore for days to come, but surely that won't have any lasting effects, either?

If only Sister Junius was here! She would know. As their infirmarian, she tends to all their ailments. But Sister Junius chose to stay behind at the convent when they were ordered to flee, together with the handful of sisters too old or too sick to leave.

As Sister Ursula should have done, and would have done, if she weren't a coward.

The peasant girl is still clutching her hand; the other is balled into a fist. Sister Ursula strokes her fingers gently to get her to let go.

The girl blinks. One eye closes a little before the other, which gives her an owllike appearance. Her mouth is pinched shut in fear as tightly as a closed book. With her fingertip, Sister Ursula draws a line on the girl's cheek to soothe her. Her skin is almost translucent; the veins at her temples and around her eye sockets are clearly visible and different shades of blue and purple.

Sister Ursula takes out a waterskin and offers it to her companion, who sips at it gratefully. Giving water to the thirsty is one of seven corporal acts of mercy and thus pleasing to the Lord, though Sister Ursula would have watered this girl even if it hadn't been. When the girl gives it back to her, she drinks a little herself. She lets the water slosh around to wet the inside of her mouth, which is painful in its dryness. The sound of her subsequent swallowing is obscenely loud.

"Do you have something to eat? I haven't eaten in two days," the girl whispers.

Sister Ursula has only a stale crust of bread. She tears it in two, gives the bigger half to the girl. She may be a coward, but she's not ungenerous. Besides, to feed the hungry is another corporal act of mercy.

The girl stuffs the crust into her mouth straightaway, but Sister Ursula says grace first, then makes the sign of the cross over the bit of bread to bless it. They take a long time to eat, not because the meal is particularly fine—though if you are hungry, any type of food tastes heavenly—but because the crust is so tough, and in Sister Ursula's case, it hurts to swallow.

When they are done eating, Sister Ursula whispers, "Do you think it's safe for us to come out of hiding now?"

"I don't know."

"What soldiers were they, did you see?"

The girl's gray eyes lock with hers. They flash cold and hard as knives. Sister Ursula feels a thrill run through her. Nuns are encouraged to keep their eyes lowered; they call it "keeping custody of the eyes."

The girl says, "Does it matter? They meant to rape and murder you. Soldiers aren't men. They are beasts." She speaks with such fire, Sister Ursula knows that these are not the first soldiers she has met, and whatever they did to her, they weren't kind.

A phantom ache spreads through Sister Ursula's belly. She has had this ever since she was a child: When she sees another suffer, she wishes, more than anything, to ease that suffering or to be part of it. She has been told often that she is too sensitive, but no matter how she strives to shear herself of it, it has never gone away entirely. She would like to embrace this girl, as if touch can draw out whatever has been done to her like a leech can draw out corrupted blood, but she daren't for fear she will overstep or offend.

Instead, she says, "You must think me ungrateful. I haven't even thanked you."

The girl blinks again in that slow, owlish way. "For what?"

"For taking my hand and bringing me here. For fighting that soldier." She remembers the ammonia stench of urine after the girl hit him with that bit of broken rock, the way his eyes rolled back. "Do you think you killed him?" she asks.

"I can only hope so," she replies, anger roughening her voice.

Sister Ursula gingerly touches her throat, at the ring of bruises made by her cape. "It was a brave thing to do, and selfless, and charitable."

A harsh laugh punches out of the girl, hoarse like a crow's caw. She wraps her arms around herself. "No it wasn't."

"But it was!" Sister Ursula perseveres. "If you hadn't dragged me to safety, and if you hadn't beaten that soldier with a rock, he would have...he would have done exactly as you said, would have murdered me and... Well, praise the Lord that you were there. I don't know why I didn't run, why I didn't fight."

Liar, she thinks. *You know well why. It's because you are so cowardly.* With the cuff of her dress, she wipes at her eyes, which burn with tears of shame.

The girl says gently, "You mustn't be angry with yourself about that. Fear takes people in different ways. Some grow quarrelsome, some flee, and some, like you, grow dazed." She has balled her hands into fists again, so tightly that her knuckles stand out like little hills, the tendons taut and yellow.

A fighter, this one, Sister Ursula thinks. She is suddenly grateful beyond words that she is no longer alone. Ever since Sister Hildegard died some three weeks ago, leaving Sister Ursula all alone, the fear inside of her has grown so oppressive as to be almost choking. Now, with this hardened farm girl next to her, it finally lets up a little.

Sister Ursula takes the girl's hands and uncurls the fingers, then strokes them gently with her thumbs. No one can fight all the time. "What's your name?"

"Elsebeth."

"How old are you, Elsebeth?"

"Nineteen." That makes her six years younger than Sister Ursula, who turned twenty-five this Christmas.

"What were you doing on the road?"

"Traveling. I'm trying to reach my aunt." Elsebeth hesitates, then says, "She's married to a parson."

A Protestant, then, Sister Ursula thinks, and though her heart doesn't harden, exactly, for she believes that to love often and selflessly is as close as she may come to true divinity, she does feel herself draw inward.

It's not because she inherently mislikes Protestants, although their views are heretical and there would never have been a war if the Protestant nobles of Bohemia and Austria had not risen up in rebellion against the Holy Roman emperor. Her personal experiences with Protestants, though limited, are not bad. When the Swedes occupied large parts of Bavaria two years ago, Sister Ursula's convent came to be under the protection of a group of Protestant officers. They—and their wives as well—generally behaved in a manner exemplary of all Christians, full of kindness and courtesy.

But not all Protestants are alike, and so Sister Ursula must be careful.

"Last thing I heard," Elsebeth goes on, oblivious to this change in her companion, "he had a parish north of here. And you? What is your name?"

"Ursula. I'm traveling to reunite with family, too, also north of here." It's not a lie, exactly.

"Let us travel together then, at least for a little while. It's safer than traveling alone, and even if it weren't, I've my belly full of being alone," Elsebeth decides.

"You were alone on that road?"

"Yes." Elsebeth is quiet, then adds in a curiously flat voice, "My aunt is all the family I've left. That is, if she's still living."

Sister Ursula's heart aches. She, too, has known loss, but nothing so obliterating as this girl's. She gives Elsebeth's hands a firm squeeze. "I'm so sorry. I am sure the Good Lord knew what He was doing when He called them home to Him, but that doesn't mean it's not a heavy burden to bear. I hope the knowledge that you shall be reunited with them in Heaven consoles you. I shall pray for their glorious resurrection."

"You're very pious, aren't you?"

Sister Ursula flushes.

Now, it is Elsebeth's turn to squeeze Sister Ursula's hand. "I don't mind," she says softly.

They sit and wait for hours, and it's like Eichstätt all over again, only a little better in that there is no shooting now. It never fails to amaze Sister Ursula how terrifying war can be, yes, but also how incredibly boring, and sometimes both at once.

Finally, Elsebeth crawls out of their hiding place, dusts off her skirts, and says, "Those soldiers must have gone the other way, or we would have seen them by now. Let's walk back to the stream. You can refill your waterskin, and I saw some dandelions not yet gone to seed that we could eat. That crust of bread of yours has woken my hunger."

Because Sister Ursula doesn't know what else to do, she trails after Elsebeth. Her knee throbs with every step. Once at the stream, they drink water cold enough to make her teeth and jaw ache. Along the bank they find a clump of dandelions, exactly as Elsebeth said they would. The girl has a good practical head on her shoulders; when they were fleeing, all Sister Ursula noticed was the stitch in her side and the fear clawing in her breast like a cat in a sack.

They dig the dandelions out, wash them carefully, then eat them. Together with the cattail shoots that Sister Ursula cuts down with her little knife, they form a passable meal.

"Look at us, two little cows chewing our cud," Sister Ursula says as she hands Elsebeth a piece of cattail, which she has blessed with a quick sign of the cross. It tastes like cucumber.

"Better a cow than hungry," Elsebeth says.

"That indeed. What shall we do now? Traverse the woods, or make our way back to the road?" Sister Ursula asks. She realizes it's silly to defer to this peasant girl, who is younger than she is, as well as a Protestant and virtually a stranger, but Sister Ursula is not used to making her own decisions; one of the three vows she has made as a nun is a vow of obedience, which in practice means she is to listen to her superiors and do as she is told without complaint and without question.

Elsebeth chews slowly on the cattail as she thinks. "The soldiers might still be there, lying in wait for the next group of travelers." She rips apart a dandelion between her fingers, puts the leaves in her mouth. "Besides, there's food to be had here but none on the road."

"But we can't spend the night here," Sister Ursula frets.

"Why not?"

"It might freeze tonight. The days of the ice saints have not yet passed. But if we start a fire, those soldiers might see the smoke."

"Worry not. We can walk through the woods for a while, then enter the road far away from where those soldiers attacked us."

Sister Ursula brightens at this. Perhaps they'll find a kindly farmer tonight who will put them up in his barn. Cities and towns may switch from Catholic to Protestant and back again depending on what army occupies it, but at its core, Bavaria is loyal to Rome, and thus its people shall be eager to help a nun.

"Do you know the way?" she asks.

Elsebeth nods as she licks the dandelion juice from her fingers. Her mouth and hands are stained yellow. It makes her look young, like a girl almost.

As they walk, they find more dandelions, as well as some oyster mushrooms and plenty of nettles that, once cooked, will make a decent dinner. For the first time in weeks, Sister Ursula feels something akin to joy, and it is so sweet that she is almost light-headed with it. How good God is, to send her food to fill her belly, sunshine to warm her face, and a companion to protect her and to talk to!

Around noon, He sends them a dead man.

2

URSULA

WHAT ALERTS THEM TO HIS presence are the flies. There are so many, their buzzing forms a steady droning that is felt almost as much as it is heard. Sister Ursula makes to go around it, for any meat that has become a feast for flies and maggots brings nothing but sickness, and sickness is what killed Sister Hildegard—*only that's not really true, now is it?*—but Elsebeth moves straight to the source of the sound, her dirty handkerchief pressed to her face.

"What is it?" Sister Ursula asks, her voice high with fear as Elsebeth bends over the thing that lies propped against a tree. It's hard to see through the heaving sheet of flies that covers it.

"A man," Elsebeth says. She doesn't get up, and so Sister Ursula has no choice but to come closer and see for herself.

The man's mouth hangs open. His swollen tongue, strangely pale because it is coated in dried spittle and plaque, protrudes from between his lips like a grub.

"From the smell of him, he must have been dead a while," Elsebeth says.

Indeed, he reeks of rot. Sister Ursula presses her face to the crook of her elbow and takes little sips of air through her mouth, but even so she can taste the decay, sweet and meaty and horrible. The flies are the worst, though. They crawl all over him, mating, filling him with maggots. It makes Sister Ursula's stomach roil.

She has always been squeamish. The first time she saw the crucifix in the refectory with the corpus of Christ on it, His wooden hands seeming to strain against the nails beaten through them, His face contorted with pain, His whole body liberally splashed with bloodred paint, she fainted dead away. It is for this reason that Reverend Mother Regina has chosen her to assist Sister Junius in the infirmary: They are always assigned some post that they have no affinity for, because singularity, even when it is accompanied by excellence, is the enemy of monastic life.

"But don't worry," Sister Junius told her the day she was assigned to be her apprentice, her eyes twinkling, "give me a year or two, and with Christ's help, I shall make an excellent infirmarian out of you yet!" Dear Sister Junius, always confident, always quick to reassure, always merry. Of all her fellow nuns, Sister Ursula has found Sister Junius the easiest to love.

Elsebeth shoos away some of the flies, revealing something that looks like a box wrapped in dirty cloth tucked under the man's arm. She reaches for it.

Sister Ursula takes hold of her sleeve to stop her. "You don't know what killed him. It might be sickness. That would explain why no animal has touched him. We should follow their example and leave him be. I don't want you to fall ill."

Like poor Sister Hildegard, who you then killed, a voice inside of her head sneers. It is a sharp voice, rough and mocking, not at all like the gentle, burbling voice of Christ her Husband, who murmurs sweet things to her on those moments she opens her heart and soul completely to Him. An ugly voice, this, and thus likely from the devil.

"He didn't die of any sickness. He's been stabbed, see?" Elsebeth says and points to the man's belly. Through the rips in his shirt and the teeming flies, Sister Ursula spies a festering wound the length of her little finger just left of his navel. The sight of maggots wriggling in the inflamed flesh makes her feel faint. She strives to love all creatures because all have been created by God, but if she's honest, she can muster nothing but hatred and disgust for the humble fly and its squirming progeny.

Elsebeth reaches for the object held in the crook of the man's arm again. Sister Ursula tightens the grip on her sleeve.

"It might be food," Elsebeth says.

"If it is, it will have spoilt by now."

"We don't know that. Come, let me at least take a peek. Whatever is in there won't do him a lick of good, but it might serve us well. Or do you want for so little that you may turn up your nose at this unexpected bit of luck and be sure you'll not come to regret it?"

"No," Sister Ursula has to concede. Then, she adds, "It just doesn't seem a very godly thing to do, to rob the dead."

"How do you know God didn't send this man to us? You're a pious woman. Surely you see His hand in everything around you. Why then not in this?" Elsebeth asks, smiling.

Sister Ursula doesn't know whether the girl is mocking her or simply trying to disarm her with that smile. Before she can retort, Elsebeth has already pulled her sleeve free and picked up the bundle. She pinches the edge of the cloth between two fingers, begins to pull.

The man's hand shoots out and grabs Elsebeth's wrist, causing her to jerk back, mouth twisting into a snarl, her other hand balling into a fist.

"Water," the man gasps.

"Sweet merciful Christ, he's still alive!" Sister Ursula cries out. Her first instinct is to freeze, as if this man cannot sense her if only she doesn't move. Then, that phantom pain in her belly that always throbs quietly whenever she sees another in pain roars to life. It is strong enough to conquer her fear and revulsion. She drops to her knees, grabs her waterskin, and carefully pours a bit into the man's mouth, as Sister Junius taught her.

He lets go of Elsebeth, clasps Sister Ursula's wrists instead. He drinks only a little. Then, exhausted, he sinks back against the tree, his head drooping. He doesn't even swat at the flies that still swarm him.

She props him up a bit more to stop his head from lolling so horribly. He whimpers, presses a hand against his belly.

"I know, I know," she says. "You poor thing. Let me help you." She turns to Elsebeth. "Can you see what he has inside his pack, please?" There might be something in there she can use. At the very least, that bit of fabric he has wrapped everything in might be cut up and used as bandages to dress his wound.

Elsebeth nods and sits down, drawing his pack into her lap. Her bare feet are dirty and bruised, her heels covered in a thick rind of calluses. How long has she been going around without shoes for her feet to look like that?

Sister Ursula wets her handkerchief, uses it to clean away the filth that has gummed the man's eyes shut. He barely seems to notice. With every breath, something wet rattles inside his chest. She has heard that sound before.

He will be dead before sundown.

"Can you tell me what has happened?" she asks.

For a while, it seems the man is beyond talking. The only sounds are his labored breathing and the rustling of Elsebeth's deft hands as she rifles through his possessions to look for fabric. When he finally speaks, Sister Ursula has to bring her ear close to his mouth to make out the words. His voice is no more than a hoarse whisper. His breath reeks of death. "Soldiers," he murmurs. He swallows, which seems to pain him, then continues. "I was stabbed. I ran into the woods until I could run no more. Then I hid."

"How long have you been here?"

"Three days, I think. It might be more. It rained once. I know that. I opened my mouth and caught the drops."

Sister Ursula looks over her shoulder to Elsebeth to tell her that the soldiers who have stabbed this man may well be the very same ones who ambushed them, but the words die on her lips. Elsebeth has unwrapped the bundle.

Inside is a box made of glass and wood.

Inside the box made of glass and wood is a skull.

Sister Ursula doesn't remember getting to her feet, but one moment, she's at the dying man's side; the next, she is taking the box from Elsebeth, careful not to jostle it. Through the panes of Venetian glass set carefully in rosewood, she can see the skull, which has been wrapped in silk gauze. Someone has stitched locks of reddish hair to the gauze and given the skull eyes of painted glass.

Sister Ursula has seen remains like this before. Her own convent has the incorruptible body of one of her fellow nuns, Sister Anna, on display, who must surely be a saint, because she obtained stigmata in the wrists and feet when still a postulant and made a deaf boy hear again after praying with him. Then, after death, her body did not rot.

Elsebeth, clearly, is not familiar with such holy relics. "What in Christ's name…?" she mutters, her lip pulled up in what is half a sneer, half an expression of fright.

"It's the skull of a saint," Sister Ursula explains. "The gauze is to keep the bones together and to protect them against dust and vermin."

"How do you know?"

"Our beloved Sister Anna wears a wax mask over her face. The gauze keeps it from sticking to the skin underneath and staining it."

Elsebeth stares at her. "A wax mask?"

"To show what she looked like when she was found to be incorruptible, which is a possible sign of sainthood."

"If that's a saint's skull, shouldn't it be in a nunnery somewhere, for the papists to fawn over?"

Sister Ursula winces. Yet despite Elsebeth's brash way of wording the matter, she is right. A skull such as this belongs in a convent or a church, where it can be given the honor and love it is due, and where it can be preserved. Otherwise, vermin, dust, light, and other common things will eat away at it until nothing but grit remains, and that is no way to treat something that was once human.

Perhaps the man has a legitimate reason to be traveling with a saint's skull. He might well be a monk wearing layman's clothes to stay safe on the road, as she is doing now.

Or perhaps he's nothing but a common thief who took the skull when a cloister was sacked by the Protestants and hoped to sell it and make a tidy profit.

Still, Sister Ursula tries not to judge lest she be judged, and so she hands the box back to Elsebeth, crouches down next to the man and asks, "This is a saint's skull. How did it come to be with you?"

"I didn't steal her," he murmurs.

"Are you sure about that?" Elsebeth asks, one eyebrow quirked.

"I am! I won her from a soldier in a game of dice two weeks ago."

"And you have kept it all this time for what? You thought it would make a fine traveling companion? You are lying. Mayhap you dressed up this skull yourself so you could sell it to some gullible papists and make money from the dead."

"No, no," the man moans. "I speak true. I swear it, on Christ and the Holy Virgin and all the saints above. This is the relic of a saint. The soldier told me that if you reunite the skull with the body, she will grant you a wish. I've been looking for her body ever since."

Sister Ursula asks, "Do you know how the soldier got it?"

"No. I didn't ask. It's better that way. He was a mercenary. A man who knows only war is no man at all, but a beast. The things some of those mercenaries have done..." He shudders, which causes a bout of pain to rack him. He moans through gritted teeth. The sound is pitiful.

Sister Ursula passes her hand over his face to brush away the flies. It's little use, the flies crawl back as soon as she removes her hand, but she can't bear to do nothing. "What can I do to ease your suffering?"

He clasps her hand with all his might. It would not even break a twig. "You must take the skull and reunite her with her body. She yearns to be whole." He smiles, causing a sore at the corner of his mouth to weep yellow pus. "I've never known such longing."

"Of course," she says to soothe him. "Where must we take her?"

"The cloth that was wrapped around the box," he rasps. "There's a map embroidered on it. But if you lose it, not to fear. She'll show you the way."

"Show us?"

He nods, smiles. "She shows me things all the time. She's an eager one. I think she must have been lonely before she came to me."

Sister Ursula's skin ripples with gooseflesh, though from fear or wonder, she doesn't know. Can it be that Elsebeth was right and God has indeed placed this man in her path? Daily she prays for her sisters' welfare, for forgiveness for her many sins, for the strength to overcome her many faults. Has God heard her prayers and given her this miracle, not only to allow her to conquer her cowardice and to atone for what she did to Sister Hildegard, but also to ensure that her sisters are safe and well?

If it is indeed so, then I thank you, my Lord; your love and mercy truly know no bounds, she thinks and tightens her hold on the man's hand. "What things has she shown you?"

"Things of great beauty and bliss," he says. Suddenly he begins to wail, his mouth a dark cavern. "Forgive me, but I don't want to die!"

The sound distresses Sister Ursula more than she can say. She feels tears spring into her eyes. "Don't be afraid!" she pleads with him.

He smiles again. Something inside his mouth has begun to bleed. It paints the lines between his teeth not red or pink, but a horrible brown color, as if the blood has begun to fester in his veins. "I'm not afraid. How could I be, after all the wonders she has shown me?"

"What upsets you so, then?"

"I have failed her, and I am ashamed."

If he had any tears, she would dry them for him. There are only the flies, though, and so she brushes them away, her hatred for them surging as they settle in the same spots again after mere seconds. "Peace, my son," she says. "You have done all you could. The saint knows this, as does God, who sees all. Now rest. I shall take this burden from you. Would you like to pray with me?"

He shakes his head, coughs weakly, grimaces. "Please just let me hold her one last time."

They do as he asks. He strokes the box like one would a cat, coos at it. Not wishing to intrude upon something that seems strangely intimate, Sister Ursula averts her eyes and goes to stand with Elsebeth, who is studying the cloth with the embroidered map. It's crude work, perhaps done in haste.

"Can you read it?" Sister Ursula asks.

"I believe so. This might be the Bavarian Forest; this the river Donau."

"Her body is close, then?"

"If the map is to be believed, it's only three weeks of travel or so away from us, less if we travel hard, and mostly to the north, too."

A sure sign that this is a godly endeavor, a chance for her to repent for her many sins and to show herself worthy of being a bride of Christ. Excitement fizzes through her veins. She can't help but smile.

Elsebeth isn't smiling. A frown like a thumbprint has appeared between her brows. She is hugging herself again, restlessly shifting her weight from one leg to another. She steals a glance at the man, then lowers her voice and says, "If you ask me, that soldier played him for a fool, filling his head with stories about wishes."

Sister Ursula feels her smile growing tight. "Do Protestants not believe in miracles, then?"

"They don't believe in saints."

"What do you mean, 'they'? Are you not a Protestant?"

Elsebeth's cheeks stain such a violent red, it's as if someone has spilled wine on a tablecloth, yet she still meets Sister Ursula's eyes with a boldness that Sister Ursula should find unseemly but instead rather thrills her. "I was raised as such, but lately, I have found it difficult to believe."

Sister Ursula is instantly filled with tenderness toward this peasant girl. "You are not alone. It is common to struggle with faith in trying times. Maybe that is why God has sent this man to us: to show you that He is real and that His love for you is boundless."

With her fingers, Elsebeth plucks at a loose thread of the map. "I don't see God anywhere around me. If anyone sent this man, it's most likely the devil."

What horrors has Elsebeth seen that makes her speak so? Oh, but how it breaks the heart! Perhaps Reverend Mother Regina was right after all to assign Sister Ursula to the infirmary, because in this moment, she wants nothing more than to heal and mend. "You mustn't speak like this!" she says and reaches for Elsebeth's hand to still it. "If you come with me and we bring back this skull, you'll change your mind about that. If—"

"What does it matter to you whether I come along?" Elsebeth says, her gray eyes hard and dry as dusty stones. "This morning when I woke, I didn't even know you. If you want to travel around with that skull, I'm not stopping you, am I?"

Sister Ursula feels as if she might cry. Distress makes her bruised throat ache as if at the onset of a cold.

Why this strength of feeling? she wonders. She cannot say. All she knows is that to be separated from this girl would be unbearable. Besides, wouldn't this journey give her the chance to restore this girl's faith and instruct her in the ways of the Lord, both of which are spiritual works of mercy and thus godly?

She clasps Elsebeth's hand, strokes the velvety bit of skin on the inside of her wrist where the veins cluster like tangled yarn. She can feel the girl's pulse jump like a bucking horse. "Please don't be angry with me. I mean well. I am not forcing you to come with me, but I would be glad of your company. I can't... I don't..." she stammers. How can she put into words these feelings she does not understand herself?

"I daren't well travel alone, not after what happened this morning," she finishes lamely.

But that is not what I meant at all!

"I'm no papist," Elsebeth says.

"I know that, and I am not asking you to do anything against your conscience, though I do have to wonder: Do you want for so little that you may turn up your nose at this chance and be sure you'll not come to regret it?" she asks, echoing Elsebeth's remark from earlier.

Those words hit their mark, as she knew they would.

Elsebeth flinches, bites her lip. "I want for a great many things," she whispers.

"Then let us seize this chance!" Excitement makes her tighten her grip on Elsebeth's hand. How delicious it is to touch her! She licks her dry lips as she thinks on what else she might say to convince the girl to come with her. Elsebeth seems to her pragmatic above all, and so she says, "At worst, you and I will have kept each other safe on my fool's errand, though even then, we will have done some good, for we will have fulfilled a dying man's wish and restored a dead woman's disturbed rest."

"And at best?"

"At best, that poor wretch spoke true, and we get to wish for anything that is in God's power to give."

"How prettily you speak," Elsebeth murmurs. She rocks on her heels, almost close enough to kiss. She sighs, rubs her eyes with her free hand, smearing her calloused palm with tears. When she looks up, her eyes are steely with resolve. "God take me for a fool and a sinner. I shall come with you."

"God bless you, you darling creature! You won't regret this!" She brings Elsebeth's hand to her mouth, kisses the jagged knuckles. "Why don't you study that map a little longer whilst I tend to that poor man?"

Elsebeth's eyes dart anxiously from left to right. "It's no use. He won't live, and we should keep moving. It's better not to stay in one place too long."

"I know that, but if there's anything I can do to comfort him in his final hours, I must." Yet when she crouches down next to him, she finds she is no longer needed. He lies slack-jawed, his eyes not quite closed but definitely unseeing, the glass box hugged to his chest.

She realizes she never even asked him his name.

3

OTTO

WE SHOULDN'T HAVE TOSSED THAT *fucking farmhand down the well*, Otto thinks as he walks to the barn. The thought is old by now, and no longer sends him into a fit of rage, though it does leave him feeling sour.

Poisoning a well with a corpse is all fine and proper unless you and your fellow soldiers need that well's water. Any fool knows that.

Then again, they didn't expect to be here long, now did they? This was supposed to be a quick raid to secure food and drink, and it would have been, if that fucking farmhand hadn't stabbed Karl in the belly with a shit-smeared pitchfork. Now the farmhand is dead, his body corrupting the water, and Karl is dying slowly, his wounds corrupting his blood.

If it were up to Otto, they'd just put him out of his misery already. You wouldn't let a dog suffer like this, let alone a brother in arms. But it's not up to him. Wolf and Fergus the Irishman are deeply religious and would never stain their souls with the murder of a sick man, never mind that they have no problem stabbing, gutting, and maiming on the battlefield. Gottfried is a Protestant mercenary and therefore doesn't much care who he fights for as long as he gets to eat, but he, too, would rather not bloody his hands if it isn't necessary. And so, because Karl is too sick to move, and they can't leave him behind because there's no saying what the farmer's family might do to him then, they are stuck here until Karl decides to hurry up and die already.

Otto enters the barn, inhales the smell of wood, hay, and manure, then grabs a stool and a pail, and sits down next to the goat. They ate her kid last night, and if no one milks her, her udders will become infected. In time, such an infection will kill her. That would be a waste of good milk and good meat, neither of which are particularly abundant right now.

Otto scratches the goat between her horns, chuckles at the way she tosses her head and rolls her eyes at him. Goat eyes never fail to remind him of the coin slot in the collection box at church.

As he milks her, he finds himself growing calm. Here, he doesn't need to listen to the farmer's daughter weeping. The sound is incessant, like the droning of a hive but with just enough variation to make it impossible to tune out. Last night, he smacked her in the mouth to get her to shut up. His hand came away all bloody, the knuckles marred with the impression of her teeth, two of which have now blackened and will soon fall from her gums, but even that would not quiet her.

Otto prays that Gottfried won't take this peasant girl back with him like he did the last one. He doesn't want to be confronted with her agony at the camp, though if Gottfried keeps treating her the way he has, she probably won't last long; there's only so much the body can take. A good thing that other girl ran off, or she'd probably be dead by now.

You're a lucky man, Otto Donatus Kreuzler, he tells himself, for unlike Gottfried and Wolf and Fergus, Otto has a wife. She's a real treasure: skilled, nurturing, and quiet by nature, even when he's inside of her and makes her spend. He can only tell he's brought her to bliss by the way her brow creases, then smooths until it's like a piece of alabaster.

Otto feels in his pocket for the delicate golden necklace with a small crucifix at the end. He took it from the farmer's wife. How she screamed when he ripped it from her throat! His Frieda would never scream so. He imagines brushing away her dark braid, then clasping the chain around her slender neck. She might shudder against the cool bite of the gold, the flesh of her throat rippling like a horse's flank. Once the shiver has passed, she will smile at him, grateful to wear such a jewel around her neck. It'll look much better adorning her queenly throat than the neck of that ugly farmer's wife, who should have known better than to wear something so costly.

A smart man can grow rich from war. The world is full of precious things ready for the taking. Just this past year, Fergus the Irishman found a beautiful ivory statue of the Mother Mary, and Wolf a book of hours bound in deerskin and decorated with gold leaf.

By far the strangest thing they've found has to be Gottfried's skull, though. He found a Swede clutching it when the miserable wretch really should have been clutching what was left of his leg. There could be no mistaking this skull for anything but a saint's. Yet looking at it had made Otto feel profoundly uneasy. It was a strange thing, that skull, not yellow like the bone relics he has seen in churches before and has prayed to, but a chalky white. And that hair… Don't they say the devil's hair is red? Thank God it's gone now, lost to a peasant in a game of dice.

The goat bleats suddenly and backs away, kicking over the pail of milk.

Otto curses, springs to his feet. He rights the pail, but most of the warm milk has been spilled already. He raises his hand to hit the goat. The animal doesn't even cower. It stands frozen, panting, looking at something behind Otto with its coin-slot eyes.

Otto's nape begins to tingle, and he knows that he's no longer alone. He whips around, ready to give Wolf or Fergus or Gottfried a tongue-lashing, but it's not one of his comrades he finds.

A man he doesn't know is leaning against the wall. He's tall and gaunt. His dark hair and eyes and clothes, sober but well cut and made of fine materials, make him look extraordinarily pale, the sort of color you'd expect to see only on a sick man who hasn't been outside in months.

Or one recently dead.

Like a corpse resurrected by the devil himself to dance at a witch's sabbath, Otto can't help but think. The tingling at his nape spreads like the spilled milk, rapidly and relentlessly.

"Who are you?" Otto demands to know. He feels for his

Katzbalger, realizes he has left the small sword inside the farm. No matter. He has killed men with his bare hands before and will do so again, if pressed.

The man looks up, smiles. It's a hungry smile, all teeth. There's something wrong with his face, though Otto can't say what, exactly. He doesn't like that. He rushes the man, grabs him by the throat, and pushes him hard against the wall. "I asked you a question," he hisses.

The man's smile never falters, which is decidedly unnerving. Otto has encountered men who have gone mad before. Some laugh without cause and with the abandon normally only found in children. There's nothing childlike about this man's grin, though.

His only answer to the fear that rises inside of him now and makes the sweat prickle under his armpits is to smother it with violence. He elbows the man hard in the face, causing his head to snap back and crack against the wall.

Blood as bright and thick as sealing wax slowly rolls out of his nose. The man touches his nose, then looks at his bloodied fingertips. Still he grins, as if his face is fixed in this position, like a death mask made of wax. "My turn."

At last, Otto realizes what it is that has unsettled him about the man's face. It's not the chalky color of his skin nor his too-wide grin, but his eyes.

Like the goat's, the pupils are horizontal slits.

Before he can let this sink in, the door to the barn flies open. For a moment, Otto is too blinded by the sudden light to make out more than the shape of a person standing in the doorway.

He squints against the pain of his pupils contracting rapidly. If this man with his goat's eyes has brought an accomplice, and that accomplice has a pike, a halberd, a sword, any type of weapon, really, then Otto could be in serious trouble, but if he can alert the others, then he might…

His eyes adjust to the light, and he can finally make out the face of the man darkening the doorstep.

It's the dead farmhand.

Otto has seen dead men before. Of course he has. He's a mercenary, isn't he? Though a Catholic in name, it is really at the altar of war that he worships, and has been worshipping for twenty years.

He is also intimately familiar with the workings of the human body. How else can you torture a man for information without killing him, without having him lose consciousness, without his mind snapping? There's an art to it, one that Otto has mastered. He can keep a man alive for days and reduce him to nothing more than a weeping sack of meat and shit ready to renounce his mother, his name, his God, anything to please make it stop.

And because he has seen so many dead men before, and because he knows the limits of what the human body can take before it buckles, he knows instantly that the farmhand is dead, very much so.

Yet somehow, he has crawled out of the well and is standing in front of Otto now on his shattered legs, dripping water polluted with rot everywhere. He lurches toward Otto. His movements are strange and jittery, like those of a wooden puppet being tugged to and fro by an inexperienced hand.

Though Otto's brain has trouble making sense of what he sees, his body's response to the sight is almost instantaneous. His hands turn stone-cold and his heart beats with such force, he can actually feel his eyeballs bulging.

But he hasn't survived twenty years of war by freezing when an enemy approaches, and he doesn't do so now. Lacking any other weapon, he grabs the pail that had contained goat's milk and swings it against the farmhand's head. It connects with a sickening crunch.

The farmhand grunts. His breath is so putrid as to make Otto's eyes water and his stomach contract violently. Vomit rises up his throat. He swallows it down. There's no time to be sick, not when the farmhand doesn't buckle, even though Otto is certain he swung the pail with enough force to bash in his skull.

Wiedergänger, he thinks. A revenant.

The farmhand grabs him by the throat. His hands are much rotted and feel cool and horribly gelatinous. The bones are still strong, though, strong enough to clench his windpipe shut.

In a reflex, Otto grips the farmhand's wrists and tries to pull his hands away. His skin has the texture of wet paper. It splits, then comes away altogether, dangling from his arms in marbled strips.

The farmhand opens his mouth to laugh as he chokes Otto. Perhaps a vestige of who he used to be remains, and he remembers how Otto used a hammer to break his legs as his comrades egged him on. He certainly seems to relish this moment, opening his mouth wider and wider until his cheeks rip and his tongue protrudes from between his teeth. It's dark and swollen like a slug.

Think! Otto screams at himself. There's not much time. Dark spots swarm his vision like flies. His eyes feel ready to plop from their sockets, and the pain in his throat is atrocious.

The way to kill a *Wiedergänger* is by beheading them or setting them on fire, preferably both. Only Otto has no sword, no dagger, not even a spade. He doesn't have anything on him to start a fire, either, though even if he did, the farmhand is too wet to burn anyway.

What he does have is the pail, still held in his shaking fist.

He clasps it in both hands, begins to raise it. It feels as if it's filled with lead. His arms soon shake from the effort.

Oh God don't let me drop it please don't let me drop it if I drop it I'm done for…

He doesn't drop it.

The lip of the pail connects with the farmhand's chin, causing his mouth to snap shut. His tongue gets caught between his teeth. Instinctively, he lets go of Otto's throat to touch his mouth.

Gasping and choking, Otto staggers out of reach. Every breath is both bliss and agony.

Accompanied by the strange man's laughter, the farmhand comes at Otto again with outstretched hands.

This time, Otto is ready. He smashes the bottom of the pail against the farmhand's face. The stink that bursts forth is so overwhelming, he can't stop himself from vomiting after all. He opens his mouth and lets it pour out, splattering on his shoes and getting stuck in his beard. Through streaming eyes, he clobbers the farmhand, whose shattered legs can't hold him. When he goes down,

Otto sits down next to him and slams the pail against his face until all that's left is a mass of slimy meat dotted with bone shards.

And still the fucker tries to rise.

Otto realizes he's sobbing. The sound of it mixes with the goat's terrified bleating.

Why is it that bleating sounds so much like humans screaming?

The *Wiedergänger* only grows still once Otto manages to tear off his head.

When it's done, Otto bends over, vomits again, then wipes the sick from his chin, the skin burning from the acid. He sobs, then stops; it makes his throat feel flayed.

All the while, the man with the goat eyes has been laughing, shaking as one with the falling sickness might when brought low by an attack.

"Why do you laugh?" Otto rasps, every word like a piece of glass he has to cough up.

The man—*but he is no man he is a necromancer he's a witch one who consorts with demons and devils and Satan himself*—straightens, wipes the tears from his cheeks with the heel of his hand, and says, "Did you not think that amusing? You just killed the same man twice."

"What do you want?"

"You have something of mine, Otto Donatus Kreuzler. I want it back."

How does he know my name? Otto thinks wildly. A shudder tears through him with such violence, his teeth clack together. A piece of cheek gets caught, filling his eyes with tears and his mouth with blood. He digs into his pocket, then holds out the golden chain with the crucifix he had intended for Frieda. "I'm sorry. I know stealing is a sin. Please forgive me," he groans.

For a moment, the necromancer's yellow eyes widen in surprise. "Whatever makes you think I care about your sins or your silly little necklace?"

Otto folds his hands, the small cross held firmly between his fingers, as if the sliver of gold can protect him. "What is it you're looking for, then?"

"A skull."

Otto's stomach feels as if the bottom has just dropped out of it. "A skull? One with hair as red as the devil's and glass eyes?"

The man is still smiling that horrible wolfish smile. "That's the very one."

Now it is Otto who wants to laugh. He has to swallow it down; if he begins now, he thinks he might never stop. "You have the wrong man. I never had your skull. That would be Gottfried."

"And where is this Gottfried?"

"Inside the farm. But he doesn't have it anymore. He lost it in a game of dice."

The man sighs and rubs his face. His hands are like pale spiders, thin and with long fingers. "How unfortunate. I had hoped this would be quick and easy. Oh well. Come along, you."

Otto stays where he is.

At the door, the necromancer turns around, frowns when he sees Otto has not followed him. Then, his death mask of a face splits apart as he laughs again. "Oh dear. I forgot you aren't dead yet."

In one fluid motion, he takes a knife from his belt and flings it at Otto. It all happens so fast, there's no time for Otto to even raise his hands. The knife catches him right in his bruised throat.

There is no pain, not at first. There's only a sense of disbelief. He swallows, causing the weapon to move under his hand. The pain arrives then, hot and mean, radiating out so that the wound feels much bigger than it is.

Otto swallows again. He doesn't mean to, but his brain knows there is something lodged inside his throat and wants it out. Blood trickles from the cut, warm and soft as a woman's caress.

Frieda, Otto thinks. He wraps his fingers around the hilt, then tugs the knife out. A fountain of blood bursts from his ruined throat, coming so thick and fast that it overpowers the scent of shit and rot.

Otto sways. He feels cold and weak. It's as if a rock has fallen on top of him, pressing him down, down, down, and he needs all his strength to keep standing, but it's not enough, he's so weak, and so cold, and the blood keeps coming, and—

4

ELSEBETH

URSULA IS A PAPIST.

Worse than that, I think she might be a nun.

Oh, she's tried to hide it, but she's not good at it, not at all. I've seen the rosary around her neck made of pretty wooden beads all shiny from use, and I have seen her make the sign of the cross twice already with her dainty hands.

White and cool as lilies those hands are.

How could I not look at them?

And if I hadn't seen that, well, then I would have known when I saw her stare at that skull as if she's half in love with it. When she told me how they wrap the skulls in gauze to keep them clean, I knew for certain that she's a papist all right, a papist through and through, and mayhap a nun to boot, or she wouldn't be saying "we" and "us." No Protestant handles bones like that, and no Protestant would believe the fairy story that poor dying wretch told us about a saint granting those who give her back her skull a wish, either.

Wish granting is for God alone.

If He even exists, that is.

Lately, I have begun to think He does not, for what all-good, all-powerful, and all-knowing God would allow for such horrors as we encountered on the road to be visited upon His flock? Surely no sin can warrant such a correction? As a girl, I felt His presence everywhere. Now, I just feel alone.

If I were the godly woman Ursula believes me to be, I would turn my back on her now and try to forget all about this, for it can only lead to tears and more suffering.

And yet for all that I know this is a fool's errand, I cannot leave her. Ursula seems to know so little of this world, I might have thought her an innocent if she didn't speak so prettily. If I am not there to guide and shield her, I know in my heart something dreadful will happen to her, and although the papists are to blame for this war, for the tyrant emperor left the nobles of Austria and Bohemia no other choice but to rebel when he tried to force Catholicism on all of us, that doesn't mean she deserves to die. The thought of any harm coming to her makes my belly squirm as if it has been filled with eels.

And if there is indeed a wish at the end of all of this, then I may wish for my grandmother, my father, my mother, my big sister, Margarethe, and my little brothers, Friedrich and Johannes, to…

I may wish for them to…

I dare hardly think it, for if I let this hope into my heart only for it to be dashed to pieces…

Well, that would mutilate and maim me, would ravage and raze me.

Mayhap Ursula's manner of talking is like the devil's, pouring pretty prattle into my ear and filling my head with vain hope. I may no longer be certain in my belief in God, but I have seen too much not to believe in Satan.

I look at her as she sits with that dead man, praying for his eternal soul, her head bowed meekly, exposing the pretty curve of her neck. All white it is, that neck, even whiter than her hands. Don't nuns wear wimples that cover their necks, keeping them marble white even when they toil in the fields?

How pretty she looks, how pious!

But looks can deceive.

If she is of the devil, she will lie to me, and then I shall know her for what she truly is.

I smile as I think about this. The devil may be crafty, yes, but then so am I, or I would've been dead three times over, wouldn't I?

And so I ask, "You are a nun, aren't you?"

She freezes, like she did on the road, and looks at me all frightened from the tail of her eye, like a rabbit being hounded, her folded hands shaking.

"Aren't you?" I press.

She squeezes her eyes shut.

"Aren't you?" I say, for three is the Lord's number and shall compel her to answer me, as indeed it does.

"Yes," she whispers.

"Why did you lie to me? Don't you know lying is a sin, or do they teach you nothing in those convents but worshipping bones?"

She winces, and I know I am being mean, even cruel, for what strife do I have with her? But since I have already promised to throw in my lot with hers and travel these godforsaken roads with her whilst carrying that ghastly skull done up so horribly with hair and embroidery, I am to know who and what she is.

"I was afraid," she tells me. "I've heard of what horrible things might be done to me if the wrong people discover what I am."

I have heard such tales, too. I find myself softening, so much so that I almost reach for her. I have known her for scarcely a day, and already I find myself craving her touch. Mayhap it's because I have been lonesome for too long, for my grandmother did always say that a lone woman is easy prey for the devil.

Ask I, "You said you were traveling to see family. Was that a lie as well?"

"No, no!" She reaches for me, hesitates, then lets her hands fall to her lap, where they lie like doves, and my traitorous heart feels heavy with disappointment that she did not touch me. It has been such a long time since anyone touched me with love that I can't well remember the last time it happened.

"I didn't lie," she says softly. "My fellow sisters are my family, and it is them I'm braving the roads for. Our guardian ordered us to flee because of the approaching troops. He feared we might be killed by the soldiers, or worse, if we stayed behind. But some of my sisters refused."

I cock my head. If I knew soldiers were coming, I would run like the wind. "Why?"

She looks at her hands as she speaks. One of her fingers twitches. "They were too old or too sick, or they were tired of fleeing. Our order is a cloistered one. Once we become nuns, we are not supposed to ever leave the grounds. I asked Reverend Mother Regina what I should do, because we made a vow of obedience and must heed her in everything we do. She told me I was free to choose."

"And you chose to run?"

It's just a question, not a reproach, but she looks up from her hands as if stung, her eyes glistening with feeling. "I was afraid, so horribly afraid, of what might be done to me if I stayed..."

She swallows, then winces. There's a circle of bruises at her throat left there from that soldier's attack. I remember the crunch as I bashed that rock against his head, and I can't help but feel satisfied with myself, for from the fit he had straight after, pissing himself and gnashing his teeth, I am sure he will never hurt another again.

"We went to a sister convent," Sister Ursula goes on. "It was only a small one, and we were with too many, so the Reverend Mother had us split up. Sister Hildegard..." Her breathing hitches, and she makes this strange raw sound, half a gasp and half a gag, as if the name of her fellow nun is a fish bone that has lodged itself into the soft flesh of her throat.

Again she swallows. Something inside of her throat clicks. "Sister Hildegard," she goes on, her voice raw now, "and I were to travel to a Carmelite convent. She was our choir mistress. She had this heavenly voice, so pure and strong..." She falters.

"You were to travel to a convent," I say, gently leading her back to her story.

She wipes at her cheeks, all silvered with tears. "Yes. Yes, we were, but on the way, she became sick. It was some sort of infection of the belly, and then I… Well, she died, leaving me all alone. I didn't know what to do then." She works her hand under her collar to clutch her rosary for comfort.

I know she is not telling me everything, but I know better than to press. I have things I don't want to talk about, too, don't I?

(Like my big sister Margarethe, like the soldiers.)

"So you decided to go back to the one place you knew?" I ask.

"Yes."

She looks up at me, her brown eyes large and pleading. "Please, Elsebeth, don't be angry with me. I did not mean to lie; I know it is a sin. Please tell me you shall come with me still, if only for your own sake. Even if you don't believe you shall be richly rewarded, it's not safe, traveling all alone."

Is this what those soldiers see every day: a beautiful woman on her knees, her face pale with fright, beseeching them to have mercy?

There is a kind of dark pleasure in it. No wonder that witch I saw burned sold her soul to the devil to have such power always at her fingertips.

A fly tries to land on my face, filling my ears with its disgusting droning sound. Don't they say that flies are attracted to those who are corrupted by sin?

I am disgusted with myself then. I grab Ursula's hands, roughly haul her to her feet, slap at her skirts for her to dislodge the crumbs of earth and the maggots that cling to the brown fabric. "Don't be daft," I grumble. "I told you already that I'd come with you, didn't I? And I never break my word unless I can help it, for that would be dishonest, and there's little I hate as much as dishonesty. Now come. Let us take care of this man's body and then get out of these woods."

We can't bury the man. For all that the ground is soft, we have nothing to dig with. Sister Ursula tries for a while with her hands, for she says burying the dead is a corporal act of mercy, whatever that may mean, but it's no use. If she keeps going that way, we will be here for days. Instead, we say a prayer for him, close his eyes, fold his hands, and place two pebbles on his eyes to keep them shut, for looking into the eyes of the dead brings bad luck. I also bind his jaw shut with a bit of cloth torn from his shirt. I take care that no fabric touches his lips so he won't become a *Nachzehrer*.

"What are you doing?" Ursula asks me when I place some more pebbles in the dead man's hand and strew them around his feet.

"If he wakes as a *Nachzehrer*, this will keep him shackled here," I explain. "*Nachzehrer* must count small things; I know not why. They can't count beyond three, though, because the devil moves through them, and he fears that holy number, and so they must remain where they are, counting and recounting."

"What is a *Nachzehrer*?" she asks as she crouches down next to the man, her arms laden with branches she has collected to cover his corpse with. Some of them are rotting because of the rain; I can smell it, this bitter, earthy scent, much preferable to the stink of the dead.

"A sort of revenant," I explain. "When you bury a corpse with fabric touching their mouth, it awakes a hunger in them. They eat their way through their shroud and coffin, then claw their way out of their grave and eat their family."

Ursula shudders, making the branches click together. "Those aren't real, are they?"

I help her arrange the branches. "My grandmother says she saw one when she was just a little girl. One of her playmates died. Kathe Müller, she was called. They couldn't bury her because the ground was hard as stone with frost, so they wrapped her body in a shroud to keep it from leaking, and then they put it in her coffin and the coffin in the shed. When the Müllers didn't appear at church that Sunday, everyone knew something evil had befallen them, so some men from the village went to the Müller farm to see."

My grandmother described the horror in great detail, but from the look on Ursula's face, I don't think I should tell her, so I simply say, "They were all dead, and their bodies much mangled. Not little Kathe, though. She was still snug in her coffin, only her shroud was all torn around the mouth, and she was fat and bloated as a tick, so they cut off her head and burned her body, then threw the ashes in the river. It's the only way to kill a revenant, be they *Nachzehrer* or *Wiedergänger* or *Aufhocker*." I wipe my hands on my dress, for the branches are covered with dirt and some of them have gone soft and pulpy.

"What on earth is an *Aufhocker*?" Ursula asks, her voice shrill.

"A restless corpse who wanders from their grave. When the rot sets in and they can walk no more, they'll jump on the back of an unsuspecting passerby and demand to be taken back to their grave." I begin to arrange some of the pebbles in the sign of the cross, which servants of Satan dislike also.

"You are teasing me."

I push a pebble into the soft earth with my thumb. "Not at all. Satan loves to command the dead, didn't you know? He plays with corpses in the way a little girl might play with her dolls, and he teaches his followers to do the same. My grandmother said that the most powerful witches sometimes murder people and shackle their souls in their rotting bodies so they are forced to serve them."

"But that is awful," Ursula says, sounding close to tears now.

I look up from my pebbles. "Fret not. I will protect you if ever we should meet a revenant," I promise.

This seems to calm her down a little. "Sister Hilde—" she begins and again makes that horrible choking sound.

What, I wonder, did Ursula do to Sister Hildegard to turn her very name into a curse?

"One of my sisters," Ursula corrects herself, "told me that Satan can give special powers to women so they can spread sickness with a simple look, and that he gives men a belt that'll allow them to turn into wolves when they wear it, but until you told me all about revenants, I had never heard of Satan puppeteering corpses before."

They really don't teach them much in those convents, I think but say not, for I don't want to offend. Instead, I suggest putting a stone in the man's mouth and then placing him face down with his feet pointing west, but Sister Ursula tells me it's bad enough that we can't observe the proper funeral rites without making an active mockery of them, so we leave him lying on his back with his face looking east, his body covered with branches.

Then, we walk, and walk, and walk.

Whenever we see a plant we can eat, we stop to gather it. We have both known the bite of hunger, though me more than most, and would be fools to leave food when we find it. Ursula teaches me their Latin names, which sound both pretty and sinister to me.

I find myself talking to her without pause, telling her more about revenants and my grandmother's stories, about the work on the farm, about the weather. I don't mean to. My father did always say that a good woman is a quiet one. I can't seem to help myself, though. It's as if every thought I have inside my head rolls out of my mouth. I pluck some daisies—*Bellis perennis*—and braid a crown in the hope that giving my idle hands some work will quiet my tongue, but my hands are used to carding wool, spinning, and a hundred other tasks besides, so it doesn't do much at all.

"What will you ask the saint if it's all true and we get to wish for something?" I ask Ursula after I have placed my crown of daisies on her brow. She looks very fetching, even though her face is pale and a little drawn.

"For my living sisters to be safe, and that the souls of those who have died may be lifted up out of purgatory and sent to Heaven if they are not there already," she says promptly.

"How selfless of you. Is there nothing you want for yourself? A knee that doesn't pain you, mayhap?" She has tried to mask how she favors her left leg, but I'm no fool. I saw that soldier kick her very hard as I fought him, saw her touch her knee and wince when we were hiding in the bracken. It makes me regret not hitting him with that rock a second time.

"I won't slow you down, I promise!" Her eyes have gone all large with fright, her voice high as she pleads for me to believe her.

I tuck a daisy behind my ear. "Peace. I am just twittering on. I mean nothing by it. So you'll spend your wish on your sisters, not on yourself?"

"Wishing my sisters well shall gladden my heart and give peace to my troubled mind, so in a way, I am spending it on myself, I'm sorry to say." A low-hanging branch almost knocks her crown from her head. She pushes the branch to the side so I can pass by unencumbered, though really, there's no need; she is much taller than I am.

"Why are you sorry?" I ask.

"I shouldn't want things," she replies, her brow all wrinkled, like a piece of muslin fretted by a rough hand.

"Wanting things is only normal."

"Desire is at the root of all evil."

"You can give your wish to me, then, and I shall spend it for you, if there is a wish at the end of all of this, mind," I tease, flicking a flower at her.

I try on the second crown of daisies, but I have made it too tight, and so I open the wooden box with the skull that Ursula holds so carefully and place the crown on the skull's red hair instead. The effect pleases me; it makes her look girlish and gay.

When I look up, Ursula's brow is smooth again as a fresh piece of paper, and that pleases me, too.

Beauty always pleases me.

There are filth and rottenness in this world; I've been forced to contemplate plenty. But I've found that, if I see something of great beauty and I look at it for a long time until I have a clear picture of it in my mind, then I can call up that picture whenever there's filth and rottenness, and that makes it easier to bear.

That is why my eyes landed on Ursula's face when those soldiers ambushed us, and why I clasped that cool white hand with such force, I felt the little bones move under the skin. A good thing it was, for she would have surely died or worse if I hadn't, like my big sister, Margarethe, who couldn't run when the soldiers came...

I rub a daisy to pulp between my fingers, and the yellow smear left by its heart and its good green scent, which is a kind of beauty also, help to ground me amid the dark thoughts and memories that always lie in wait, ready to pounce and ensnare me. When they do, there's no saying how long I will be lost for.

I couldn't save Margarethe, but I did save Ursula from the soldiers, and in doing so, did I not take responsibility for her? Did I not make her my charge in a way?

And if that is true, then she is now mine.

Mine to protect.

Mine to cherish.

Mine to love.

5

URSULA

WHEN THEY REACH THE ROAD again, darkness is already stealing over the land. By now, Sister Ursula is limping badly. Her knee is much swollen; the skin is taut and pearlescent in some places, various shades of angry red and purple in others. She chewed some willow bark to help with the pain, but the joint still throbs and burns with every step. Elsebeth kindly found her a stick she can use as a cane and offered her a shoulder to lean on, but even so, Sister Ursula is ready to weep with relief when they spot a farm in the distance, smoke curling from its chimney.

By the time they arrive at the farm, which is dilapidated, the fields untilled and the stable empty, although the smell of manure still lingers, it has gone fully dark. The night sky is a beautiful dark velvet speckled with stars, the moon a buttery smear. Unfortunately, a clear sky means a cold night; already their breaths plume from their mouths, and their hands and feet have cramped with cold.

Sister Ursula limps to the front door and raises her cane to rap on the wood. Elsebeth's hand shoots out and stops her.

"What is it?" Sister Ursula asks.

"I've heard no dog or goose."

"Is that unusual?"

Elsebeth blinks in astonishment, then says, "Yes. Dogs and geese guard their homes well. For a house this close to a road plagued by plundering soldiers to have no animal to warn them…I don't like it."

"Perhaps they had one, but they've eaten it. The harvest was bad last year, and a farm this close to the road has probably seen a great number of soldiers come by and demand food and drink. We haven't heard any sheep, cows, or chickens, either."

Elsebeth chews her lip. "Mayhap."

"I understand that you are wary, and I understand that you are afraid. I am afraid, too." She almost laughs at this pathetic attempt to put into words the bone-deep dread that has dogged her all these years, so persistent and so often present that it sometimes oppresses all else she feels.

She clears her throat. "I am more afraid than I can say, but I am also cold, and I am tired, and my knee pains me. We can't stay outside much longer. Besides, God provides."

"Not for me, He doesn't," Elsebeth mutters darkly.

Sister Ursula turns her hand so that her palm presses against Elsebeth's. Their hands are so cold as to be almost without feeling, but still, there's comfort in the touch. "He will provide for us, truly," she says, because if the poor girl has lost her faith, Sister

Ursula shall need to believe for the both of them. "Come. Let us chance it."

With her stick she knocks on the door. Although there is light inside and a fire in the hearth, no one comes. Sister Ursula tries the handle, but the door is locked fast against them. She knocks again, harder this time, keeping it up until they hear someone moving in the hallway.

"Hello?" she calls out.

"Who is it? Who are you? Make yourself known!" a man barks.

"My name is Ursula, kind sir. My companion, Elsebeth, and I are looking for a place to spend the night."

"Go away! There's nothing for you here!"

Sister Ursula blinks at the man's vehemence. "We could sleep in the barn, if that pleases you? We won't make any trouble for you. All we need is a place out of the cold to rest our heads."

The man says something she doesn't quite catch. She asks, "Will you please open the door? That'll make talk a little easier, and then you might see me and know that I speak true."

This time, fear makes the man loud. "Do you take me for a fool? Come hell or high water, I know better than to open my house up to the likes of you!"

Sister Ursula looks at Elsebeth in astonishment. The girl, confused, shrugs.

"Please! If we find no shelter, we might well die of cold. Can you not hear our teeth chatter?"

"You won't trick me, you demon!"

Demon? Sister Ursula thinks, feeling her brow wrinkle. Her poor face is so cold, she fears the frown might split the skin. "We aren't demons, just two women looking for a place to stay. Have you no mercy in your heart?"

"This is a good God-fearing household, and you shall find no shelter here. Now get you gone!"

Sister Ursula makes to say something about how godly people should be charitable and hospitable, but Elsebeth gently pulls her away. "There's no reasoning with people as afeared as this, and we grow colder the longer we stand here. Let's try our luck elsewhere," she says.

"But I am so cold, and my knee... I don't know how much longer I can keep going," Sister Ursula confesses.

Elsebeth takes out the skull's map and moves her fingers across the stitching, squinting at it in the weak light of the moon. "According to the skull's map, there should be a village not much farther from here. We can find a place to sleep there."

They make their way to the village, though how, Sister Ursula can't say. She is freezing; a wind has risen that tears through her clothes and cuts her with cold.

The village is so small, it barely deserves the name; it's no more than a cluster of houses around a well, some of them quite grand, made out of stone and wood, others mere shacks.

It is also deserted.

No smoke comes from the chimneys, and no lights have been lit. The only sound comes from the wind whistling between the buildings. If Sister Ursula's skin was not already pimpled with cold, gooseflesh would ripple over her limbs and the hairs on her nape would rise at that sound, so mournful and eerie.

They knock at the door of the largest house. When no one comes, they try the handle and find the door unlocked. Inside, Elsebeth manages to light a lamp with a bit of flint.

"Oh," she breathes.

Inside, everything is untouched, as if the house's occupants have only just stepped out. A coat is slung carelessly over the back of a chair; an open almanac and a bit of sewing are lying on a little table near a window; in a different room, the table is laid for dinner.

Yet whoever used to live here has left a long time ago; spiderwebs are draped between the furniture, and all flat surfaces are gray with dust. When Elsebeth lifts the lid off one of the pots on the table, the earthy stench of mold wafts out. She gags and quickly places the lid back.

"I don't like this at all," she says. "Whoever lived here left in a hurry. Why?"

"Maybe they saw soldiers coming? This village has no wall to keep them out," Sister Ursula says as she carefully places the reliquary down on the table. The tablecloth has yellowed.

Elsebeth shakes her head. "If that were the case, then why is everything exactly as they left it? If I were a soldier out on the prowl, I would have taken the food and the candlesticks and much more besides, and then I would have smashed and sullied everything else. Such is their nature. They can't see a plate without wishing to break it."

Sister Ursula knows this well. Her convent has been looted close to five times over the past few years. She says, "I don't know why this town wasn't plundered. Perhaps it wasn't soldiers that caused the people here to flee, but something else. Whatever it is, it's likely gone now."

"If it's gone, then why did no one come back?"

Her flesh crawls as if it is covered with flies. She shudders. But unease is not all she feels; she is exhausted, too, and cold and in pain. It clouds her mind. She begins to cry a little. "I don't know. All I know is that we can't leave, not tonight. It's too cold outside, and even if it wasn't, I can't walk."

Elsebeth comes to her and wipes her tears away. Her hands are cold, and so Sister Ursula chafes them and blows on them to bring them back to life, only her own hands are too cold to do any good. To warm them, Elsebeth starts a fire; whoever lived here left a neat stack of firewood next to the hearth and a little twist of paper for them to light it with.

Sister Ursula picks up the reliquary—she can't bear to have it out of her sight—and places it on a little table out of the way of any stray sparks, then sits down heavily in a chair, hissing at the pain in her knee.

It doesn't take long for their fingers and toes to throb as the blood forces its way through their cold-tightened veins, and for a while, they both sit panting and crying. Soon, the pain becomes bearable, then fades altogether, leaving them feeling pleasantly warm and drowsy.

Elsebeth yawns till the tears run down her face, then knuckles her eyes roughly and gets to her feet. "I'm going to make us something to eat. If I don't do it now, I don't think I'll ever get up again."

"Do you need any help?"

She places her calloused hand on Sister Ursula's shoulder, gives it a squeeze. "You stay here and rest that leg of yours."

Sister Ursula mutters a halfhearted protest, then slumps back in her chair and stares at the fire dancing in the hearth. She has always loved fire. There's something mesmerizing about the flames licking the wood, leaping this way and that.

Though you'll soon lose your love for it when you burn in purgatory, as poor Sister Hildegard is doing now, she thinks.

She hoists herself up from her chair and kneels in front of the fire, hissing from the hurt in her knee. She places the poker into the fire until it glows. Then, she pushes up the sleeve of her left arm and presses the hot iron to the skin on the inside of her wrist. She cannot bear it for more than a second; already the pain is so horrible it drives out all thought.

Back home, at the convent, one of her sisters suffers from cankers around her throat. Sister Junius suggested trying to cut them out, then packing the skin with herbs to stave off infection, but Sister Valentina wouldn't hear of it. "Suffering brings us closer to Christ our Husband, and so I rejoice that God has seen it fit to send me this affliction," she said and wears the evidence of her illness with the same pride a rich woman might a necklace of gold. Or wore, perhaps. She might be dead now.

Like Sister Hildegard, who burns because of you.

Keening softly to herself, Sister Ursula sits back in her chair, her wrist throbbing and burning. If only she could be more like Sister Valentina, who offers up her suffering so gladly! But she has always been too sensitive, too cowardly.

Too weak.

Too sinful.

"When I was a little girl," she whispers to the skull, because if she doesn't talk, she'll go mad, "I wanted most desperately to be a saint." She licks at her wounded wrist, hisses at the hurt. "I know I'm not and never will be. I think saints are strange and unknowable. I am common in my weakness. All the same, I shall do everything I can to serve you."

She opens the glass reliquary so she can touch the saint's skull. A delicious thrill runs through her as soon as her fingertips touch her red hair. There's a smell to her, sweet and heady, like incense or precious oils. She bends over the skull and presses her mouth to the soft, cool bone.

"I like to think I would serve you even if there was nothing in it for myself, but I don't know if that's true. I'm only a weak woman, filled with shame and sin. Please won't you make me better than I am?" she murmurs, the gauze and the bone underneath growing warm and damp with her breathing. Her teeth graze the skull's brow, and she suddenly is overcome with the almost irresistible urge to bite down and consume her, to take her into herself. She tongues the glass eye, licking the rim of bone around it. She tastes something cool, dusty, and slightly sweet. The gauze is rough against her tongue.

Her burned wrist brushes against the edge of the table, bringing

Sister Ursula back to herself. She wipes away the spit from the skull with her sleeve, then closes the reliquary's glass door and prays fervently for her sisters, both alive and dead, which is just another way to please the Lord.

Despite the pain, she must have dozed, for the next thing she knows is Elsebeth handing her a mug with frothing beer. She takes it, then glances at the skull, which is snug within its glass box as if nothing has happened, and perhaps it hasn't; when Sister Ursula looks at her wrist, there is no mark.

Dream or miracle?

"Drink up," Elsebeth says, gently pulling her out of her muddled thoughts. She has been industrious; she has toasted the mushrooms they have gathered in the woods, chopped the greens into a salad, and made broth from water drawn from the well and some ingredients she found in the pantry.

"Most of the food has spoilt," she explains as she blows on her bowl of soup to cool it, "but I have found some cured meats and plenty of beer. There might be more in the other houses. Better we don't eat the meat just yet. It would probably make us sick on account of us not having eaten much these past days."

Sister Ursula sighs with relief. "We can stay here a while then, at least until my knee is a little better."

"Mayhap," Elsebeth says. In the flickering firelight, her gray eyes appear much darker, her face much gaunter.

What have those dear eyes seen? Sister Ursula wonders. She briefly has to close her own eyes to force down the images that rise in her mind unbidden. They are half-formed things, but dark and full of power. When she opens her eyes again, she makes herself smile at Elsebeth. "Come, let's not dwell on bad things. There's no end to them; we would be dwelling until the Second Coming. I'd much rather we speak of something nice instead."

Elsebeth blinks in her owlish manner, which, even though Sister Ursula has known the girl for less than a day, already feels familiar. "Will you tell me a story?"

Sister Ursula launches into the miracle of the loaves and the fishes, but Elsebeth raises her hand to stop her and says, "Something that isn't religious. I've my belly full of religion."

"Oh," Sister Ursula says. "Well, I don't know any other stories."

Elsebeth exclaims, "No other stories! Did your mother never tell you any?"

"I don't remember."

"Do they not let you see her because you're a nun?"

"She died when I was still little, before I became a postulant."

Elsebeth grimaces. "I am sorry to hear that. It's hard, losing someone you love. But did you not have a father to tell you tales?"

"I only saw him once a week, when he visited my mother and me, sometimes less than that if he was traveling."

"Visited?"

"They weren't married." After all these years, she still feels herself flush with shame, as if her parents' sin is her own. She laughs awkwardly, says, "That's why my father thought it prudent I become a nun. I would be safe and looked after, and I could intercede with God on his and my mother's behalf. Adultery is a terrible sin."

As is murder, but then you know all about that, don't you?

"Let's not talk about sin," Elsebeth says. "I shall tell you another story then as we ready ourselves for bed, seeing as you don't know any."

There are two bedsteads and three cots, the former for the master and mistress of the house and their children, the latter for the servants and apprentices. Elsebeth has made up one of the bedsteads for their use. "Unless you'd rather sleep apart?" Elsebeth asks.

"No," Sister Ursula says. She'll be grateful for the girl's warmth in the night, and for her presence when a nightmare inevitably comes to torment her. How can it not, after everything that has happened today?

As they undress and comb their hair—though there's not much to comb, for Sister Ursula's is only chin-length, and Elsebeth has hers cut short, too—Elsebeth tells her a strange story about a servant who eats a white snake and can then talk to animals. She uses voices for the animals: She honks for the goose, which makes Sister Ursula laugh, squeaks for the raven fledglings, and gulps for the three fish.

By the time they have crawled into bed, Elsebeth has reached the part of the tale where the servant must complete an impossible task in order to marry a princess. Sister Ursula tries to concentrate, but her lids keep fluttering shut, as if someone has threaded them and is now tugging hard on the string.

The story ends with the servant happily married to the princess. "And if they didn't die, they're living on today," Elsebeth finishes solemnly. She's lying on her side, her body firmly pressed against Sister Ursula's, which is both startling and pleasant. At the convent, each nun sleeps alone in her own cell. Sister Ursula loves her cell, which is her sanctuary and her bridal chamber, but lying here now with Elsebeth stirs something deep inside of her, a memory, perhaps, of when she was very little, and her mother was still living, and physical touch was sweet, safe, and easy, not this loaded thing that must be thought about carefully lest it lead to lust.

Sister Ursula knows she should get up and kneel and pray before sleeping, but the thought of putting pressure on her knee makes her feel this funny sensation at the back of her head where the skull is jointed to the spine. She has wrapped a cold cloth around it to help reduce the swelling. Once again, she wishes Sister Junius was here. With her perpetual smile and quick, deft hands, her presence alone would be a balm to Sister Ursula's troubled nerves. Of all her sisters, she misses the infirmarian the most.

Please, Almighty Father, she prays with her hands folded on her chest and her eyes closed, *ensure that Sister Junius is safe and well, and has everything she needs to tend to my other sisters. Please care for them as well, and forgive me for loving Sister Junius just a little more than the others when I know that I should love them all equally. As for Sister Hildegard, please...*

Elsebeth brushes against the wet cloth on Sister Ursula's knee and squirms, pulling Sister Ursula out of her prayers.

"I'm sorry. It mustn't be pleasant, to share a bed with me like this," Sister Ursula murmurs.

"I don't mind that. All I mind is that your knee pains you."

"Only a little, and suffering purifies. All for Jesus." That's what Sister Valentina says, or signs; they are not allowed to speak during the time of the Great Silence and use gestures instead. Besides, the cankers in her throat sometimes rob her of her voice.

Elsebeth turns toward her. Her eyes catch the light of the sole candle that still burns, and for a moment, it looks as if her eyes are aflame. "Would you rather I sleep somewhere else?" she asks.

Sister Ursula shakes her head.

"It's quite all right if you do. My sister, Margarethe, had rheumatism. Sometimes, her feet would swell so much, she couldn't get her shoes on, and her legs and her knees would pain her horribly, as if she was being stretched upon the rack. She couldn't stand the feel of the blanket, let alone my touch."

"I shall teach you how to make a poultice for her. It might bring some relief," Sister Ursula says, having to stifle a yawn behind her hand.

"Don't bother. She's dead," Elsebeth replies.

Sister Ursula winces, her faux pas creating an almost physical pain. "Oh, Elsebeth, forgive me. I am so tired; I wasn't thinking. I shall pray for her, and the rest of your family, too."

Elsbeth shrugs. "It happens. Even I sometimes forget she's dead. I see a hare dance at dawn, or I smell fresh bread baking, and I turn to her to tell her, as if she has been walking behind me all this time." Her voice, so animated when she tells her stories, is a hollow thing now, as stilted and stiff as her body.

Sister Ursula wants to reach out to her and in this way soothe her, but she isn't sure whether her touch will be welcome. Instead, she says, "It's a common feeling. When my mother died, I felt the same way."

"It's cruel, is what it is. Why should I sense her walking around when she couldn't do so in life? When the soldiers came, she couldn't run. She..." Something catches in Elsebeth's throat. She makes a soft choking sound, but she doesn't cry.

Sister Ursula's heart seems to clench in her chest. "You poor, poor thing," she murmurs.

"I wanted to stay with her," Elsebeth manages to say, each word sounding half strangled. "She told me to run, but I wouldn't. I clung to her. I was always stronger than she was, and no matter how she pried at my fingers, she couldn't make me let go. She took her clog then and bashed it against my head till the blood ran down my face, blinding me. The pain weakened me so that she could push me from her. She told me again to run, and this time, I did. God forgive me, but I ran, and I left her."

"She wanted no harm to come to you, and obedience is no sin," Sister Ursula tries to soothe her.

"It was no virtue, either. And then, after she was dead, I was all alone and so hungry, and I...I did what I had to survive, but now I often wish I hadn't, for I am so ashamed. It gnaws at my belly like a rat."

Sister Ursula doesn't know what to say.

Her own secret, her shame, her sin, always burning, always pressing, as if she has swallowed hot coals, throbs inside of her. She has not yet been shriven of it, for she has not met a priest who may absolve her these past few weeks. Though even if she did repent, she isn't sure she will ever be free. Some sins stain the soul too deeply.

That is, if she can even confess. Every time she tries to speak of what happened, it's as if an invisible hand closes around her throat, softly choking her. It's all she can do to push it from her mind; if she doesn't, she fears it'll drive her to madness.

Elsebeth asks, "Are you repulsed by me?"

"No, no!"

"Then why have you gone quiet?"

"Because I was contemplating my own vices."

Elsebeth scoffs; her breath is hot against Sister Ursula's chest. "What vices would those be?"

"I have many."

"I don't believe it." Elsebeth raises herself on her elbows. "You are much too sweet and pretty."

Sister Ursula blushes. She is not used to getting compliments, which surely only lead to vanity. "I have committed grievous sins," she says.

"What sins would those be? Wanting more bread, coveting another nun's rosary, thinking uncharitable thoughts of your prioress?"

No. I have committed murder, she thinks. Again she is choked by the horror of what she has done. She tries to push it down, to forget, but then Elsebeth's flinty eyes are boring into hers. If this Protestant peasant can offer up her shame and, in that way, humble herself so sweetly, not just before Sister Ursula but also before God, who after all sees everything, then why can't Sister Ursula do the same? An eye for an eye and a tooth for a tooth, yes, but doesn't a good turn deserve a good turn in return as well?

And so she forces the words out. "I killed Sister Hildegard," she whispers and tastes blood at the back of her throat.

It takes her a while to find the words she needs. Elsebeth doesn't rush her, for which she is grateful.

"She was sick," she finally manages to say. "Some sort of infection in her belly that Sister Junius may have known how to cure, but I didn't. We were traveling, looking for some place to stay after the Carmelite convent turned us away. Soon, she was too weak to walk, so I dragged her to the side of the road and tried to tend to her there, but her belly was so inflamed that she couldn't bear to be touched."

Sister Hildegard's face had gone all red as a fever raged through her, which made her writhe and gnash her teeth. Her voice, normally so strong and pure, soaring to the heavens, was now reduced to a guttural groan. During her more lucid moments, she had cried and asked God why He had forsaken her, why He didn't spare her this pain. Sister Ursula had tried to soothe her, to tell her that it was not for them to understand the ways of the Lord and that they only had to trust in Him, that He knew what He was doing, but she wasn't sure whether Sister Hildegard had even heard her.

"And then some men came down the road. I don't know if they were soldiers, farmers, or bandits; it was dark, and I couldn't see. But they were loud, and they stank of blood, sweat, and drink, and

I was terrified that they would find Sister Hildegard and me, and do unspeakable things to us."

Elsebeth offers her a bit of the blanket to wipe her eyes with, but Sister Ursula doesn't need it; she hasn't been able to shed a single tear since it happened. They are all locked inside her throat, sending out little tendrils of hurt.

"I tried to move her into the underbrush so we would be safe, but she began to scream with pain when I touched her, and when I tried to hush her, she only screamed louder. She was raving mad with fever at that point, so perhaps she mistook me for someone else, someone who meant her harm. The men were close now, and so I had no choice; I had to… She was making so much noise, and I… It's my fault she's dead."

She presses her palms against her burning eyes.

Elsebeth gently pulls them away. "You had no choice. If you hadn't left her, those men would have murdered you, too. What use would that have been?"

But I didn't just leave her, she means to say, but is not given the chance, because Elsebeth keeps talking. "You're a nun. Surely you were taught that your soul is sacred. That is why we may not do ourselves an injury. It would be offensive to the Lord. If you hadn't run and hid, then you would have placed yourself in harm's way knowingly. That would have displeased God."

The girl speaks sense. All the same, Sister Ursula killed Sister Hildegard. She died without receiving the last rites. That means she did not die in a state of grace, which in turn means her soul is now in purgatory, where it will be cleansed through suffering before it can ascend to Heaven. Sister Ursula explains all this to Elsebeth, who, as a Protestant, does not believe in purgatory and so must be taught.

When she is finished, she says, "So you see now why it's so dreadfully important we reunite the saint's skull with her body: I can use my wish to intercede on behalf of Sister Hildegard and ensure that her soul will enter Heaven if she has not done so already, and in that way repent for my crime against her. You could wish the same for your sister."

"Indeed I could, and for revenge on those soldiers who used her so."

Sister Ursula could tell her that there's no need, for to kill another willfully is a mortal sin and thus damns the perpetrator for eternity, but instead she allows herself the brief pleasure of kissing Elsebeth's forehead to let her know she understands.

Some wrath is rightful and godly.

Elsebeth must read all of that in her eyes, because she says, "What a pair we make, you and I! Of all the people I pulled off the road, I chose the one who can understand me best. Surely such a godly woman as yourself must see the hand of God in this?"

This instantly lifts Sister Ursula's spirits a little. Elsebeth is right; what else is meeting Elsebeth and being sent a saint's skull if not Divine Providence? God has given them a chance to redeem themselves. "Maybe so, yes," she says.

They are both quiet then. Sister Ursula can't speak for Elsebeth, but she herself feels relieved, strange, and raw.

Elsebeth drags a hand through her hair, so pale that it is almost luminous in the dark, then yawns. Her cheeks have pinkened beautifully and are now almost the same shade as the inside of her mouth. "You still owe me a story," she murmurs.

Whatever awkwardness Sister Ursula may have felt vanishes. *I couldn't save Sister Hildegard, but I might save this girl*, she thinks, and feels a godly fire burning in her chest, suffusing her with warmth, love, and protectiveness.

Whatever stories her mother has told her have long fled and been replaced with parts of the Bible, but she does remember the lullaby her mother used to sing to her. Not the words, but the melody, and the feel of her mother's voice vibrating in her chest. She hums it now, a feeling of love and melancholy spreading through her like wine.

Soon, Elsebeth is asleep. She twitches a little, whimpers once, but hushes and grows still when Sister Ursula gently touches her cheek. She continues with her prayers for her sisters, but the events and emotions of the day have drained her, and sleep comes for her as fast as a shot fired from a musket.

6

OTTO

AND THEN, OTTO IS WALKING alongside the necromancer toward the farm. He has no memory of getting up and leaving the barn, only of the knife in his throat, and the blood, and the darkness. Panicked, he looks down at his hands. They are covered in blood, as are his shirt and trousers. He feels his throat. There is a cut, which feels cool and wet, and doesn't pain him nearly as much as it should, not even when he thrusts his finger inside up to the second knuckle, though it does make him gag.

"Don't do that, please," the necromancer says. "You'll rot fast enough without putting your grubby finger into that wound and widening it, and then I'll have to find you another body, which is altogether more trouble than I need."

Otto finds his hand moving away from the wound of its own accord. He tries to stop walking, to turn around and run back to the camp, where his Frieda is waiting for him, because she is a soldier's wife and as such comes with him wherever he is sent, but his legs won't obey him. He is bound fast to this he-witch and must do as commanded.

"Please, please, please," Otto pleads, then hushes because he doesn't know what it is exactly he is begging for. He begins to cry like a child, he is so afraid. He tries to resist whatever sinister influence this devil has over him that makes him follow like a leashed dog, clutching the little crucifix with such might, the gold splits the skin of his palm, and is resisting still by the time they have entered the farm.

Wolf, Gottfried, and Fergus the Irishman are all seated around the table playing cards. The farmer's daughter sits on Gottfried's knee, wincing whenever he moves, sobbing softly to herself. The capillaries in her eyes have burst, turning them pink.

"You took your sweet time," Gottfried says.

"Who is this?" Wolf asks, barely glancing up from his hand of cards.

The necromancer places a hand on Otto's shoulder and says, "Go on, dear Otto. Tell them who you think I am," as if Otto is a shy boy who must be encouraged to speak up in front of his elders.

"A witch," Otto chokes out.

The men look up, ready to laugh and joke. When they notice the gaping wound in Otto's throat and his shirt sodden with blood, the smiles fall off their faces faster than overripe fruit from a tree.

Wolf is the first to speak. "Otto, what happened to your throat?"

He claps his hand over the wound as if to hide it. It stings. "I think he killed me," he says, the horror of it all compelling him to simple honesty.

"But why?" Wolf asks.

"For a laugh," the necromancer answers, and giggles, the sound high and strangely girlish.

Gottfried stops jiggling his leg, clears his throat, and asks in a voice that is remarkably steady, "What can we do for you?"

"Shut up!" Fergus hisses. "Don't you know you shouldn't converse with witches, you stupid Protestant?"

"He's come for that skull of yours, Gottfried, the one you took from that Swede. I told you not to take it. I told you to leave it, that nothing good would come of it, but you were greedy, weren't you? And now we are all damned," Otto moans. His voice sounds hoarse. *Maybe the necromancer damaged my voice box when he threw that knife and killed me, oh God oh God oh God...*

Gottfried keeps looking at the necromancer. His bearded face betrays no emotion, but from the set of his jaw and the way he grips the farmer's daughter's waist, Otto can tell he's afraid. "I don't have that skull anymore. I used it as a bet during a game of dice, and I lost. That was about a week ago. I can tell you—"

With a roar, Fergus jumps to his feet. In one smooth motion, he vaults over the table and draws his sword. "Get thee behind me, Satan!" he screams, raising the sword to decapitate the necromancer.

"Be a dear and kill him, please," the necromancer whispers in Otto's ear, his breath so soft, it's almost a caress.

Otto snatches a knife from the table and plants it into Fergus' neck.

For a moment, Fergus stands still, his face so full of shock and betrayal, it looks like an open wound. He feels for the knife, tugs it out. Before it can clatter to the floor, the blood is already bursting from the cut in a brilliant crimson jet. He staggers, then falls heavily.

Did I look like that, too? Otto wonders as he kneels down next to him. The blood just keeps coming, hot and sticky, coating his hands and drenching every bit of his clothes not yet soaked. "I'm sorry. I'm so sorry, Fergus. He made me do it. You saw, didn't you? Saw how he whispered in my ear? I didn't want to do it, I swear." He knows he's babbling, but he can't stop.

Fergus grips Otto's arm and squeezes it hard enough to bruise. He tries to say something, but all that comes up is more blood, first in thick globs, then as a fine mist whilst he chokes. His body tenses, then grows slack.

"What the fuck did you do that for? Are you in league with the devil?" Wolf asks. He has gotten to his feet and is holding his rosary in a shaking fist.

Otto looks at him helplessly. "He made me."

"We know," Gottfried says without ever taking his eyes off the necromancer.

Fergus's body begins to jerk. Otto leans over him, thinking that perhaps he's still alive, but when Fergus rises in that juddering way that characterized every move the farmhand made and the necromancer cackles as roughly as a dog's bark, Otto knows what's truly going on.

The necromancer makes Fergus dance a jig, his head lolling, the wound in his neck opening and closing like a mouth. In a guttural voice unlike his own, he begins to sing.

"There once was a family living on a farm.
All day they worked, doing not one bit of harm.
Five little soldiers came to them in the field one day
And took their health, maidenhead, and life away.
Five little soldiers, up to their usual tricks
Of rape and torture and feeding off others like ticks,
Five little soldiers knowing no other way to get by
Than through sucking the peasant population dry,
Not knowing that with every little thing they took,
They signed their names over and over in Satan's book
For there is not a sin the devil doesn't see.
Watch out, little soldier boys, now he is coming for thee..."

Wolf has begun to pray to drown out the sound, tears streaming down his ashen cheeks. Otto can't do anything but whimper. Even Gottfried has lost his calm; he is shaking. "Please," he says, and his voice trembles as much as his body, "there's no need for these devilish tricks. I'll tell you anything you want to know."

The necromancer titters. "Now where would be the fun in that?"

For the first time in three days, the farmer's daughter stops her weeping. Through her dead black teeth, she begins to laugh.

7

ELSEBETH

I AM DOG-TIRED, YET I dream.

I am at the execution of those three witches who were burned to death all those years ago. All the people from my village are there, but they look awful, killed by plague, hunger, and soldiers in their homes or on the roads when they fled. It's well possible that, of all of them, I am the only one still living.

Margarethe is there, too. She's sitting in the dirt. Her legs are all twisted, and her dress is sodden at the lap and chest with blood. Her hair, fine and beautiful as spun gold, has been cut away in great hanks, exposing her scalp, which is porridge pale.

I am afraid of her and ashamed of my fear, for she is my sister, and it is because of me that she looks thus, so I force myself to take her hand. It's the hand of a corpse, stiff and cold. I fret at it to warm it as the condemned say their final words, but it remains a dead thing.

In my dream, when the third witch escapes her bonds and

jumps, she doesn't fall to the ground to be trampled to pieces by the crowd. Instead, she rises slowly in the air, her hare eyes fixed on me, grinning like a demon.

I watch her, feeling fear swim up and down my back like a minnow in a stream, so cool that it makes me shiver.

Next to me, Margarethe squeezes my hand as best as she is able with her death-hardened fingers. When she opens her mouth, a glistening centipede crawls out and falls into her lap. It's the same color as her clotting blood.

I begin to whimper. I can't help it. I am so afraid, so desperately afraid…

"Run!" Margarethe croaks, and this time, she doesn't need to clobber me with her clog to get me to move. I am not one to grow dazed and still when afeared, like Ursula. No, no, I am like the rooster protecting his flock, ready to fight, maim, and kill, and when that does not work, I am like the rabbit: I bolt.

I run, but the witch floats after me, filling the air with the smell of burned meat, making my stomach cramp and saliva flood my mouth, because my body is too stupid to know that this meat is forbidden.

I run till I taste something foul at the back of my throat, till I am too out of breath to take another step, and still she's after me. I curl up in a ball, my hands over my head. The fear is no longer a minnow then, for those creatures are swift, small, and slippery. This feeling of terror is an ox, faster and stronger than I am. If I am not careful, it shall trample me.

It'll kill me.

How can I be so afraid and yet live?

The witch drifts to me, so close I can smell her breath, this foul stench of singed hair and charred flesh. "Elsebeth," she whispers, and for all that my hands cover my ears, I can hear her very well.

I begin to shiver like one struck down with the palsy.

"Be not afraid," she whispers.

"Leave me be, you witch," I moan. My teeth chatter so fiercely, I fear they might dance out of my jaw.

"Open thine eyes, sweet child."

I shake my head.

"Open thine eyes," she repeats, her voice threaded through with annoyance.

"No, no! Begone," I groan.

"Open thine eyes, thou vile little wretch!" she screams, startling me so much, I instinctively obey. It's not the burned witch whispering in my ear, but the saint's skull. She is still wearing the crown of daisies I knotted for her, and that seems to me so silly, I forget to be afraid. "What are you doing here?" I ask.

"I've come to warn thee, for thou and the nun are in grave danger," she says, her voice all soft once more. As she talks, she bobs like an apple in a barrel, her hair floating slowly in the way of water weeds. "A necromancer pursues you. He has with him a hireling who has been wetting his sword even before thou were budding inside thy mother's womb. Both delight in cruelty."

I know then this is no dream, for I don't know some of the words she speaks to me. "What is a necromancer?" I ask.

"A witch who makes the dead walk."

"What does he want with Ursula and me? What does the hireling, for that matter?"

She tosses her hair back. "They care not a whit for the pair of thee, only for what thou carriest: me. Whatever may happen, thou must not let me fall into his hands."

Her daisy crown has fallen in front of her eyes. I hesitate, then reach up and brush the crown up so it rests on her white brow instead. She flinches at the contact. "Why do you tell me this? Why not Ursula, who is a nun?"

"Why would I, after she licked me in the manner of a dog? Also, I cannot talk to one awake."

"I don't understand," I say.

She has no throat, and yet I swear she clears it. When she speaks, it is once more in that lofty way. "Thou hast been here a while. 'Twere better if thou wakest now. The nun has a need of thee. I am afeared that she is close to death."

I sit up with a great gasp. My legs feel like wet cloth, all weak and just as damp; I'm covered with sweat. I turn to Ursula, I know not why—*you do know why it's for comfort you want her to comfort you with those cool white hands of hers*—and my heart trips.

Ursula is gone.

I begin to tremble. The fear from my dream is still upon me, and all sorts of dark things form in my mind. Didn't the skull tell me she's close to death?

Don't be daft, I tell myself sternly. A dream's a dream, no more. There's no such thing as talking skulls. Ursula must have a good reason for being up. Mayhap she got hungry or thirsty; mayhap she had to relieve herself.

I light a candle. "Ursula?" I whisper, but she is not anywhere in the room. Her clothes and shoes are gone, too, and for a moment, I am certain she has abandoned me, and I fear I shall run mad again, as I did after Margarethe. But no, the box with the skull is still here, and she would not leave without it, she loves it so. It's not as if she can get far with her bad knee, besides.

Then where is she?

I dress hastily, then search the house, the candle sputtering not because the house is drafty, but because my hands aren't steady, no matter how often I tell myself I had a nightmare, no more. Wax runs down the slender stem, pooling in the little pocket of skin between my thumb and index finger. It burns, but I hardly feel it, I'm that anxious.

I need not search long.

The front door, which I had fastened carefully to keep us safe when we slept, gapes open.

I go outside. Almost immediately, the wind snuffs out my candle. In the dark, I walk from one edge of the village to the next, looking for Ursula.

As I walk, I try to think of the Latin names for flowers that Ursula taught me yesterday in an effort to calm my thundering heart and still my palsied hands. I never learned how to read, but

I've a good memory and a good ear. "*Taraxacum officinale*: the common dandelion. *Bellis perennis*: daisy," I whisper.

Yet these strange words, so like a spell, hold no power here. With every step, I grow more afraid, until my breath comes out in shallow pants, my mouth is bone-dry, and the fear is like a minnow again, flicking up and down my spine.

When something crunches under my shoe, I jump as if someone has shot at me, then dash toward the nearest house. I crouch against the wall and cower there until I realize I am still hale, hearty, and unharmed. It takes a few minutes to convince my body of this, too. Then, I creep back to see what it was that startled me so.

It's Ursula's rosary.

I pick it up. The cord has snapped, which might explain how she came to lose it, for she would not have left it behind willingly.

It doesn't explain why some of the beads are sticky with blood.

For a moment, I go quite mad.

I run around screaming Ursula's name, pulling on my hair with my free hand, because the burning pain as I rip it from my scalp is easier to bear than the horror of being alone again. I only stop running once I reach the graveyard, for what waits for me there is so vile, it manages to pierce through my panic and shock me into sanity.

The coffins have been dug up and broken into, and the dead are scattered everywhere. Here lies a skeleton draped over a tombstone like a forgotten coat; there a woman sits propped up against the fence, so much rotted I only know she is a woman from her clothes.

I crouch down next to a little girl whose corpse lies close to the gate. She's lying on her belly, one arm trapped underneath her, the other flung out, as if someone has tossed her aside. She stinks, though not as much as the man in the woods did, but then it's much colder now, and she may have been dead for longer. Her lips and gums have rotted away, revealing four rows of teeth. It's a monstrous sight. I never knew before that the marriage teeth sleep inside the gums and jaw like that, waiting for the day the milk teeth fall out and they can push their way up like daisies.

I grab a hank of her hair and make to drape it over her cheek, so she won't be grinning at me so. In lifting it, I reveal her throat.

It has been torn open to the bone.

Scavengers, I think desperately, dogs, crows, and mayhap even pigs, for everyone knows pigs will eat anything, even each other.

But I've seen enough dog and pig bites to know that the tooth marks visible on what is left of her throat weren't made by an animal.

To be sure, I bring my hand to my mouth and bite at the pad of my thumb, not hard enough to break the skin but hard enough to leave a mark. The seamed line left by my teeth is almost the same as the one on her neck.

I know then why everyone here has fled, and why the farmer thought us demons and would not let us enter his home, and why the skull told me Ursula is close to death.

This is no longer a village.

It's a *Nachzehrer*'s hunting ground.

8

URSULA

SOMEONE IS RATTLING THE FRONT door handle.

The sound of it awakens Sister Ursula, who has always been a light sleeper.

Maybe I imagined it, she hopes, yet knows that she hasn't.

There is someone outside who wants desperately to come in.

She turns to Elsebeth to ask her what to do. The girl is sleeping soundly. To wake her now would be no kindness, so Sister Ursula slips out of bed, hissing at the pain that lances her right knee as soon as she puts any pressure on it. She can't see very well—the fire has burned low—but when she touches the joint, she feels it is still very much swollen despite the cold cloth she has wrapped around it.

No matter. The body may clamor all it wants, but that does not mean she needs to heed it, not when there are more important matters at hand. She quickly puts on her clothes and shoes to keep warm and preserve her modesty from whoever is outside, makes the sign of the cross over the skull, says a quick prayer begging for the saint's assistance, then limps to the front door, which is moving softly in its frame as if someone is patting it, looking for a crack.

"Who is it?" she asks. The words come out all strangled by her fear.

The voice that responds is not easily defined as male or female on account of it being very hoarse. "Have you milked the cows?" it asks.

She blinks in astonishment. "Excuse me?"

"Barbara needs new shoes. I don't want her to go around barefoot like some urchin. We are better than that."

"I'm sorry about Barbara and her shoes, but I don't think I understand. Who are you, and why are you here? It's much too cold a night to be out."

The voice begins to babble. Perhaps it's the thickness of the door and the howling of the wind, or perhaps something is desperately wrong with the person outside, because no matter how Sister Ursula strains her ears, she can't make sense of what they are saying. It's not that the words are unintelligible, though they sometimes are, but that, when strung together, they don't make much sense.

"It looks like rain and...Maria burned the bread this morning. Holy Father, please preserve us... What if it is the Hungarian sickness? No, no... Do you think your wife knows about us? I heard that...Nikolaus caught a bullet to the stomach. If you go to the market, you must remember to bring black thread, or I shall have to mend your dress with the blue. This bloody cold!"

And all the while, the person outside keeps rattling the doorknob and scratching at the wood.

Fear drags its icy finger along Sister Ursula's spine, sending forth ripples of gooseflesh. It makes a pain rise in her throat like sap in spring. She is tired, so very tired, of having to play handmaiden to terror, but for all that it sickens her, she is powerless to stop it. Not all bodily sensations can be ignored.

"I'm sorry, but I truly don't understand," she says during a lull in the person's constant chatter. She still isn't sure whether they are male or female; the talking has only further hoarsened their voice.

"You are a sinner, aren't you?" The question turns into a giggle that makes the hair on her nape rise so fast the skin aches, because how could this person know about Sister Hildegard?

For a moment, she remembers the terrified farmer and his insistence that she and Elsebeth must be demons trying to trick him into letting them into his house. What if there was truth to his words, and whoever is standing beyond this door is neither human nor benevolent? And now that she has engaged them in conversation, they know that she is here...

Yet she does not turn around and limp back to bed. Instead, she rubs her sore nape, then lays her cheek against the cool, smooth wood of the door to hear better as she thinks about what to do.

For all that she believes in Satan and his legion of demons, Sister Junius also taught that there are much simpler things that can make a person talk so incoherently. They could be delirious from fever, like Sister Hildegard was in her final hours; they might have grown so cold that they have begun to hallucinate; they may have seen something so horrendous that it has temporarily disordered their mind.

The poor wretch outside babbles on. "But stay awake at all times, praying that you may have strength to escape all these things that are going to take place, and to stand before the Son of Man. Oh God, oh God oh God oh God have you seen its face oh dear God!" the person outside screams.

She flinches away, her heart beating as fast as a battle drum. Her belly clenches, though from fellow feeling or fear, she doesn't know.

The screaming peters out, turns into soft sobbing. "Hail Mary, full of grace, the Lord is with thee. Blessed art thou among women, and blessed is the fruit of thy womb, Jesus. Holy Mary, Mother of God, pray for us sinners, now and in the hour of our death."

That decides it. If Satan moves through this person, then the holy words of the *Ave Maria* would surely turn to burning coals in their mouth, blistering their tongue, cheeks, and lips. She lays her hand on the bolt, the iron shockingly cold, then slides it aside and opens the door at a crack.

What stands on her doorstep may have been human once but is now human no more. It is incredibly tall but in an ill-proportioned way, as if whoever this revenant used to be in life has been stretched upon the rack. Its skin is gray, the eyes luminous in the way of nocturnal animals. The lips have shrunken and peeled back, revealing overly large teeth in blackened gums.

Sister Ursula can do nothing but stare at it in horror. Just as happened on the road, panic possesses her. It makes her mind and memory flicker. One moment, she is standing in the hallway of the deserted house, staring at the revenant on her doorstep, trying not to gag at the scent of rot and freshly turned earth that clings to its desiccated skin and the remnants of its clothes; the next, she is being dragged through the empty street. "Please," she babbles over and over again, "please don't hurt me."

She only snaps out of this state of fear-induced madness when she stumbles over a bit of broken rock and hits the ground with her wounded knee. She can't even scream, the pain is so intense. It batters her and sickens her. For a moment, there is nothing else.

When she comes to, the revenant has hoisted her to her feet.

The agony of her knee has broken the choke hold panic had on her, allowing her to think.

"In the name of our Lord and Savior Jesus Christ, I beg of you: Please stop whatever you are doing and let me go," she pleads.

"I'm sorry, but I truly don't understand," the walking corpse answers, perfectly echoing Sister Ursula's earlier remark. Its face remains slack, its eyes empty and dead.

It doesn't understand what it's saying, she realizes. *It just mimics what it has heard its victims say in order to lure the living close so it can eat us.* She knows then that her begging is useless.

But she can't just let it drag her away to God knows where to do God knows what. If she has learned one thing since meeting Elsebeth, it is that doing nothing will get you killed.

What did Elsebeth tell her again about revenants? All the different ones are blending together in her mind, but she said they are often the playthings of Satan, didn't she? If that is true, then perhaps she can cast him out and in that way return this revenant to being a simple unmoving corpse.

She reaches for her rosary, raises the little cross at the end of the chain, and begins to pray the rites of exorcism. She does not know them fully—only priests are allowed to perform them, and she has only attended two exorcisms in her entire life—but she is desperate.

Soon, the revenant repeats the sacred words back to her in the way of some birds: perfect in pitch yet empty of understanding.

Tears of anger and frustration burn in her eyes. She knows this devil's puppet doesn't consciously mean to make a mockery of her prayers, but it's still atrocious. She digs her heels into the wet ground, gritting her teeth against the daggerlike pain in her knee, and hisses, "Begone, thou demon!"

The revenant only cocks its head. In the dark, its eyes shine bright as newly minted coins. It says, "Seven already dead from the Hungarian sickness. How many more will you take, oh Lord?" Then, it tears the rosary from around her throat. The chain cuts into her skin before it breaks. The creature drops it into the dirt.

"No!" Sister Ursula wails. She reaches for her beloved rosary. The beads are as familiar to her as her own hands. The exorcism may not have worked, but if she can take hold of it and undo the knots that keep each bead in place, she can scatter some of them in front of the revenant, just as Elsebeth scattered the pebbles around that poor peasant's corpse. It will be compelled to count them, but because it can't count beyond two, it will soon get stuck, and then she... Her fingertips brush the cord, but before she can grip it, the revenant roughly hauls her away.

For a beat, despair and panic drown out all other thoughts again, though this time, it's not long until the pain in her knee carves out a space in her consciousness. Perhaps Sister Valentina was right to thank God so passionately for her suffering after all.

Everything for Jesus, she thinks and laughs, or perhaps sobs.

By now, they have left the village, and the revenant is taking her down a rutted road, the black earth hard as stone due to frost. She wishes she could fight it, could flee, but her body, ever the traitor, won't obey her, and so she lets the revenant lead her as if she is a dog and it her master.

A bead of blood from the cut her rosary made as it was torn from around her neck rolls down her spine. She shivers.

I am going to die, she thinks.

All nuns are taught not to fear death but to embrace it. Upon their death, all their sin and all suffering too shall die, and they will live in eternal bliss with their Husband Jesus Christ in Heaven.

Yet for all that she is supposed to welcome death with good cheer, Sister Ursula finds herself balking at it now, for what will become of the saint's skull if she does? Perhaps Elsebeth will manage to reunite the skull with the body by herself, but then who will intercede for Sister Hildegard's soul? She cannot expect Elsebeth to use her wish on behalf of a dead nun she has never met, not now that she knows what has become of Elsebeth's sister.

Poor Elsebeth, who has suffered so much in this sordid war already. It's not to be wondered at that her faith has faltered.

If I die, she shall be all alone in this world.

This thought more than anything electrifies Sister Ursula. She begins to struggle. The revenant grunts as she rakes her nails across its wrist; the skin has dried and toughened like jerky. But it doesn't loosen its grip on her, and it doesn't slow down.

Next, she makes herself drop to the ground like a stone, but the walking corpse simply keeps dragging her along as if she's nothing more than a sack of spuds.

She opens her mouth and screams, spits, and rages. No meek sacrificial lamb, she; she has turned into one of hell's own demons, kicking, scratching, and punching.

The revenant stops dragging her. It looms over her, hisses. She bares her teeth at it.

It opens its mouth, and then the true horror begins.

It unhinges its jaw until it touches its throat, the skin bunching like a gray scarf. The smell that wafts from its mouth is the stench of the grave. Threads of saliva stretch between its teeth like spiderwebs.

Through all the horror and the fear, Sister Ursula thinks, *All the saints and angels above, please save me now.*

Her prayer is answered. The night splits apart in sudden heat and light. The revenant screams, this infernal screeching that is all its own, for no human being has ever sounded like that. It lets go of Sister Ursula and staggers back, its arms raised to shield its eyes from the light. Its lower jaw dangles like a piece of meat from a hook.

Elsebeth is there then, standing over Sister Ursula with a torch in hand, her mouth twisted into a snarl, looking exactly like what Sister Ursula imagines the early saints and nuns looked like, those who defended the faith with a Bible in one hand, a sword in the other.

"Touch her again, and I shall set you on fire, you fiend!" Elsebeth snarls.

"You found me," Sister Ursula says. She laughs, then sobs, then laughs again.

Elsebeth says, "Of course I did. Now get up and lean on me. I don't know how long this torch will burn for, and *Nachzehrer* fear neither God nor man, only fire."

Sister Ursula gets to her feet with difficulty. Her right leg is utterly useless; resting even the slightest bit of weight on it makes her knee feel as if shards of glass are being driven into the flesh.

Yet fear makes her fast. She hops on her good leg, her teeth gritted against the dull pain that soon blooms in her hip. Elsebeth has a hold of her, and that helps.

The revenant follows them all the way back to the house, gibbering and wailing. It lunges at them when they are near the well, and Sister Ursula fears her mind will buckle and break from sheer terror, but Elsebeth jabs at it with the torch, driving it back.

Once back inside of the house, Elsebeth slides the bolt home, then extinguishes the torch by dunking it in the bucket of well water she fetched before they went to bed. The smoke that rises stings Sister Ursula's eyes and throat. She coughs softly to get rid of the feeling, then opens her mouth to ask Elsebeth whether they should bar the windows, only the girl doesn't give her the chance. She grabs Sister Ursula by the throat and presses her hard against the wall, her thumb digging into the soft place just below Sister

Ursula's jaw joint. "How *could* you?" she chokes, as if it is she who is being half strangled. "How could you be so stupid? To open the door to a *Nachzehrer*!"

"I'm sorry. I didn't know it was a *Nachzehrer*." As she speaks, her throat moves painfully against the web of skin between Elsebeth's thumb and index finger. "I thought it was someone sick and confused who needed help."

"And you went to give it without thought!"

"I meant only to help. It pleases the Lord when we clothe the naked, feed the hungry, heal the sick, water—"

"You meant to be selfless," Elsebeth spits, as if the word is somehow dirty.

"Yes. I must be, don't you see? After what I did to Sister Hildegard—"

"You put yourself in danger, heedless of the cost! What might have become of your dead sister if you and I had died here tonight? Or of your fellow sisters in that nunnery you call home, or the saint's skull for that matter? When others depend on you, endless selflessness is not a virtue!"

Tears veil Sister Ursula's eyes. "I didn't…" she tries, but Elsebeth talks right over her.

"And did you even think of me, and what I might think and feel when I woke to find you gone?" She swallows thickly, then suddenly wails, "How could you leave me?!" She buries her face against Sister Ursula's abused throat and sobs.

For her to rail at me thus, I must have wounded her horribly, Sister Ursula thinks; a girl as stubborn and proud and fiery as Elsebeth does not easily admit to vulnerability. The guilt, the shame, and the pain of it draw the tears from her eyes. They roll down her cheeks, big and fat as drops of summer rain.

She winds her arms around Elsebeth and holds her close, and oh, what a pleasure it is to finally hold her! She wants to tell her how the thought of her was enough to make her fight the *Nachzehrer*, but all that comes out are the words that she has been taught as a girl. "*Mea culpa, mea culpa, mea maxima culpa.* Forgive me my trespasses against you," she murmurs, wincing at how stern yet hollow it all sounds. She tries to soften the words with kisses she drops on Elsebeth's pale hair.

Elsebeth looks up, her puffy eyes furious. "I don't want your papist prattle."

Just a few days ago, Sister Ursula would have recoiled at such anger, or would have frozen as she always seems to do in times of fear and emotional turmoil. But Elsebeth does not mean her any harm, and so she lays her hand against her sodden cheek, all pink and hot from fury. "Then what do you want from me?"

For a moment, neither woman says or does anything. There's only the sound of their breathing, and of the *Nachzehrer* outside murmuring words it doesn't understand as it keeps patting the door, looking for a way inside.

Then, Elsebeth grabs Sister Ursula's collar with both hands, pulls her close, and crushes their mouths together.

Sister Ursula has kissed her sisters before. When she was still a girl, she and two other postulants practiced kissing one afternoon so they might better imagine what the love of their Heavenly

Husband would feel like, giggling all the while. Besides, physical affection is not entirely forbidden if it is innocent, and kisses can be chaste.

There is nothing chaste about this kiss, though. It snatches the breath from her throat, makes the place between her legs, that furry, damp place she has no word for, clench.

Though nuns should be virgins, Sister Ursula knows the joys of orgasm. It's the only known cure for chlorosis, a condition common to young virgins and therefore common among nuns. Whenever she feels listless and her heart beats much too fast, Sister Junius wets two fingers with a bit of oil and gently strokes her until everything in her contracts and warm waves of pleasure wash over her.

"There is no sin in this," Sister Junius told her after that first time, wiping her fingers on a bit of cloth, "not when it is done for love, and what greater act of love than making you well again?" She had kissed her forehead, and Sister Ursula had felt safe and loved.

As Elsebeth kisses her now, Sister Ursula shakes as she does when she's close to spending. How can this girl's touch inflame her so? Everywhere Elsebeth touches her burns, throbs, and clamors for more, more, more. She wants to crawl inside of her, devour her, inhale her, like she did with the saint's skull, only more desperately.

She hitches up Elsebeth's skirts, places her hands on the back of her thighs. They are hot as a child's fevered brow, and soft as sin. She runs her fingers over them until she reaches her buttocks, firm from all her hard work on the farm. She strokes the gentle curve, lightly at first, then presses harder, dimpling the flesh, feeling the taut muscles and hard pelvic bone underneath. There's not much to hold. She's so thin, so sadly starved…

Elsebeth sobs, her fingers digging hard into Sister Ursula's shoulders to keep from falling. She's trembling all over. "Ursula," she whispers.

Her name has been many things: a weapon wielded to obliterate the sinful bastard child she was before; a gift to mark the start of her new life, one of hard work but also of great purity and spiritual bliss; an aspiration, because the virgin saint whom she was named after was a courageous martyr.

In Elsebeth's mouth, it is none of these things. It is both a curse and a benediction.

Yet when Sister Ursula moves her hand to stroke between Elsebeth's legs, wondering if the slick hair there is as pale as the hair on her head, Elsebeth recoils.

Sister Ursula stands panting and confused. Bereft of the joy and the glory of Elsebeth's touch, she feels both cold and sorrowful. Her lips still burn, as if Elsebeth has branded them. "Have I hurt you?" she asks softly.

"No."

"Then why did you draw away?"

Wordlessly, Elsebeth shakes her head, her eyes downcast.

"There's no sin in this," Sister Ursula counters, "not when it is done out of love."

Elsebeth rubs at her eyes, sniffs. "We should be abed," she says, still not looking at Sister Ursula. "You should be resting that leg of yours, and there's nothing else we can do now. *Nachzehrer* have no love for the light. Once the sun is up, we should leave. It's better if we keep moving, and the sooner we know whether there really is a wish waiting for us, the better."

"Elsebeth!"

"What?" she pants.

"I... We..." she stammers. She briefly closes her eyes, looking for the words to express all she is and all she feels, all the longing and the hurt and the sadness and the joy, but finding none.

"What?" She snarls the word this time. Her hands are balled into fists again, her body all taut and ready to fight, but there is a softness to her voice.

Sister Ursula opens her mouth, hesitates, then takes the coward's way out by asking, "Shouldn't we do something to make sure the *Nachzehrer* won't come in?"

Elsebeth blinks in her slow, owlish way. Then, the tension leaves her body, rounding her shoulders to a slump. "No," she says eventually. There is neither anger nor want in her voice now; the words are flat as pebbles. "*Nachzehrer* don't think. If the one outside knew how to open a window or work a door, it wouldn't be outside still, and this door is thick and sturdy. Its teeth will break and its fingers rot off before it'll come through."

"Very well," Sister Ursula says.

In bed, Elsebeth turns her back to Sister Ursula. Soon, her breathing becomes deep and regular.

Sister Ursula can't sleep. Her throat aches with all her unshed tears. She has done something wrong, yet knows not what and knows not how to make it right again. She turns to look at the saint's skull lying safely on its velvet pillow within its reliquary. The flames from the fire in the hearth are reflected in its glass eyes so that they seem to have fire for pupils.

"Please, sweet saint," she whispers, "won't you intercede for me and set to rights whatever it is that I have done that has upset and displeased Elsebeth so?"

The saint remains silent.

She feels for her rosary, remembers that the *Nachzehrer* broke it.

It takes an eternity for the sun to rise.

PART II

"The mind is its own place, and in itself can make a heaven of hell, a hell of heaven."

—John Milton, *Paradise Lost*

9

OTTO

In his twenty years as a mercenary, Otto has found that there is a trick to surviving war with both your body and mind intact: You must try not to think. If you are on the battlefield, thinking will only get you killed. Afterward, dwelling on all the horror will make your mind crack like an egg.

Otto does his best not to remember what happened at the farm: the knife that went in his throat and killed him, thus making him a necromancer's plaything, and everything the necromancer made him do to Gottfried and Wolf after he was forced to kill Fergus, and poor dying Karl…

Otto has tried to run from the necromancer, of course he has, but his feet won't obey him and simply lead him back. It's the same for his hands; whatever spell this sorcerer has spoken won't allow Otto to hurt him, or himself for that matter. The best thing he can do to protect himself now is to think nothing. There are ways to make your mind as empty as an upturned jug, such as coupling with a woman or drinking till you can't walk straight. Neither are options here, and so Otto simply focuses on the tasks the necromancer gives him instead: cooking supper, finding water, building a fire.

The necromancer owns a leather pouch with bits of bone, all shiny and smooth from being handled so much. Every now and again, he fishes a few of them out of the pouch and throws them in the air, then catches them on the back of his hand. It reminds Otto of a children's game he used to play with sheep's bones, though Otto suspects these bones are not animal in nature.

They travel hard and soon reach the Bavarian Forest. Such woods never fail to make Otto nervous. There's no saying who or what might lurk in there: demons, the restless dead, werewolves, witches, hungry peasants armed with pitchforks.

Fucking farmers. Nowadays, a soldier is more likely to be struck down by a peasant than by a fellow soldier. That is, if the hunger and disease don't get him first.

Though I am already dead, so what does it matter? What could be worse than this? Otto thinks. He knows not whether to laugh or to cry. He does neither. Though the necromancer has sewn up the wound in his throat, he is afraid that too rigorous a movement such as those produced by hysterical laughter will cause the stitches to rupture. Dead bodies don't heal. Any abuse his body suffers now will be permanent.

When the necromancer has once again played with his bones and has made them follow a gurgling stream afterward, Otto asks, "What even do you want that bloody skull for?" Although he has tried not to think at all, it's been on his mind a lot these past few days. Otto knows what he will wish for once they have reunited the saint's skull with her body, of course he does, because he plans to live a long healthy life with his beloved Frieda, but what on earth could a witch who already holds power over both the dead and the living wish for?

The necromancer smiles and says, "I have my reasons."

"Dark and disturbing reasons no doubt."

The necromancer tosses one of the bones into the air, catches it lazily. "Why do you say that?"

"Because you are in league with Satan."

"Why do you revile Satan so?"

Otto blinks, then realizes the necromancer's question is genuine. "Satan turned against God, who is good and all-powerful. For this, he was damned to Hell, and now he tries to corrupt us and have us turn away from God that we too may be damned."

"Suffering shared is suffering halved and all that?"

Otto has found that this is the way of the necromancer; he will remain pensive and silent for long stretches of time, almost as if forgetting Otto is unwillingly trudging along. Then, he will suddenly become talkative.

"This way, my dear Otto," the necromancer says, and Otto's feet move without his permission, following the necromancer's lead.

"How do you know what way to go?" Otto asks.

"The bones tell me so."

"Not very good at it, are they? We still haven't found that bloody skull."

The necromancer toys with a bone, letting it jump from knuckle to knuckle. "The bones tell me where to find her, but we still have to close the distance between us and her ourselves." He tosses the bone back into the pouch, fishes a different one from it, and rolls it between his fingers. "Now, as to the matter of Satan. Might it not be possible that Satan is actually God's most beloved angel, given the holiest of tasks: to tempt people to sin? Only if you are tempted and reject that temptation can you truly call yourself virtuous."

"That's blasphemy," Otto retorts.

The necromancer grins. "Perhaps, but that does not make it untrue. Ask yourself this, Otto Donatus Kreuzler: If God is indeed all-powerful and as good as you claim He is, then why would He allow your Satan to exist? It only makes sense if you suppose that Satan is doing exactly what God wants him to do. The very idea that an angel could rebel against God is preposterous if you believe that angels were created to be entirely good. Turn to the left here, please. We are drawing close."

They leave behind the gurgling stream. Dandelions and nettles grow in the soft soil. Otto picks one that has gone to seed, blows on it to scatter the fluff. Frieda told him you may make a wish if you manage to scatter them all in a single breath. In the three years of their marriage, he has never been able to.

"You are not giving me any choice now," Otto says. "You made me kill my brothers in arms, and..." His breath—though he doesn't need to breathe, he still has to draw in air and expel it if he wants to talk—catches in his throat.

Don't think of it don't think of it don't think of it...

He clenches his fist around the dandelion stem, focuses on the crunch of it. Some seeds still cling to the heart of the dandelion. He makes himself count them until he is calm again.

The necromancer patiently waits for Otto to come back to himself, then giggles and says, "Well, I am not the Almighty, now am I? Besides, you were given many chances in life to turn away from sin and do good, yet how have you used them? Let's keep walking as we talk; there's a dear."

"Who are you to judge? You sold your soul to Satan."

"That I did," the necromancer admits, smiling. Bemused.

"Why?"

"When God would not listen to my prayers, I turned to Satan instead." He kicks a pebble toward Otto, whose feet kick it back to him without him meaning to.

"What could be so important that you had to beg Satan for it?" Otto asks.

"Enough about me. I believe we were talking about your life, and all the chances you were given to do good and chose to do nothing instead, or worse: evil. We need only look at that sad farm where I found you. You didn't have to torture that farmhand before you threw him down the well. Why, you needn't have killed him at all!" He deftly manages to lift the pebble into the air with a twist of his foot, bounces it twice on his shoe, then kicks it to Otto as if it is a pigskin ball.

Otto passes it back to him. "He attacked us."

"Perhaps," the necromancer says and smiles in that strange, sly way of his, eyes flashing golden in the light, "but you can't say the same of the farmer's daughter."

Her whining sobs echo in Otto's head. He puts the dandelion stem in his mouth, chews on it. The sound it makes is loud enough to banish that phantom weeping. "I didn't rape her," he says sullenly.

"And thus you presume yourself free of sin? You stood by and did nothing whilst your soldier friends had her time and time again." Again he bounces the pebble on the top of his foot; again he passes it to Otto.

"What do you expect of me, man?" Otto grumbles and kicks that blasted pebble hard enough that it disappears into the underbrush. "That's what happens to girls and women, both when it's war and when it's not. She's not the only one, and she won't be the last."

The necromancer shrugs, then fishes three bones out his pouch. He juggles them for a few seconds, then throws them high and catches them on the back of his left hand. "Do you really think that just because something is common, it is therefore without fault?"

"Of course not, but it is the way of the world. It isn't as if I could've stopped Gottfried, Wolf, and Fergus, either, even if I had wanted to."

"Which you didn't. Say you are right, and nothing you could have done could have kept your friends from raping her; that still doesn't leave you blameless. Or do you suppose that hitting her in the mouth with your fist so you needn't be bothered by her weeping was a Christian thing to do? You could have tried to soothe her suffering. Instead, you added to it."

"Then let me die properly, so that I may be punished in Hell for what I did," Otto snaps.

Again, the necromancer giggles. "Who says you aren't in Hell already? Or do you like being a rotting corpse who must bow to my every will?" He pinches a bit of skin on Otto's arm, which tears with a soft squelching sound.

"Don't do that!" Otto exclaims and bats away the necromancer's hand. "It hurts, and you know it won't grow back!"

After the farm—*don't think about it don't think about it don't think about it*—the necromancer drained Otto of his remaining blood, then filled his veins with a concoction of vinegar, alcohol, and herbs to slow down the process of putrefaction, but that doesn't mean Otto isn't rotting a little already.

The necromancer unceremoniously drops the bit of flesh he has torn from Otto's arm. "Don't whine. I can always try to put you in a different body."

Otto shudders. He can't help it. The thought of inhabiting another body is grotesque, but even worse is that in this way, he can live on indefinitely. Suffering is infinitely more bearable when you know that it'll end. "I'm attached to this one, thank you very much," he says with a lightness he doesn't feel.

The necromancer stops walking and tilts his head back, his nostrils flaring and his mouth half-open as he drinks in the air in greedy gulps. "Say, do you smell smoke and meat cooking?"

Otto does. Despite being dead and thus requiring no food, the scent makes him salivate.

It doesn't take long for them to reach the root of that smell. In a clearing, two dirty men are crouched around a fire. They are skinny and filthy, their eyes large and wild. Otto has seen that look before in men whose minds have never left behind the battlefield. These men certainly look like soldiers to Otto. Instinctively, he places his hands on the pommel of his sword, ready to pull it out. Then, his eyes fall on what the men have been cooking, and his stomach twists, and the bit of dandelion he ate tries to climb its way up his throat. He gags, spits it out. It hasn't been digested at all.

Knowing that people who are starving sometimes turn to eating the dead is one thing; to see it, actually see it, the cut-up body and the yellow bone and the meat marbled with fat on which flies crawl, well, that's something else entirely.

Next to him, the necromancer begins to laugh. Soon, he's shaking with it. In his black clothes, he looks like a twitching beetle. "Pretty perverse, this," he says when he finally has breath to speak with.

One of the men lowers his eyes, ashamed. The other picks up a rusty knife, the whites of his eyes showing like a shying animal. "What do you want?" he asks.

"Otto, would you kindly dispose of these men?" the necromancer commands, because for all that it is wrapped up to look like a question, it is an order that Otto can't refuse. Despair and hatred surge inside of him. It would be easier to bear this servitude if only the necromancer wouldn't act as if it is voluntary. The sooner they find this skull, and he can wish for his life and freedom back, the better.

Don't think, he tells himself as he wields his sword, cutting neatly through skin and fat and arteries, for just as he knows how to keep a man alive for days as he tortures every drop of information out of him, so does he know how to kill quickly.

Don't think don't think don't think whatever you do don't think...

Thinking only gets you killed.

Though he's dead already, so what does it matter?

When it is done, and Otto has wiped his sword and hands clean on clumps of grass, he finds that the necromancer has gathered some body parts of the unfortunate wretch whom the two men were cooking and is arranging them on the ground. Together, they fail to make a whole body, and the necromancer clicks his tongue in annoyance.

"What are you doing?" Otto asks, his nose and mouth pressed to the inside of his arm. The body parts are ripe with rot. The two men he just killed must have been absolutely desperate to even consider eating it, let alone going so far as to actually cook it. Perhaps it was a mercy that the necromancer ordered them killed. Their death by the sword was quick and thus much kinder than the slow violence of food poisoning.

"I think this may be the peasant who won my skull from your dear friend Gottfried," the necromancer says. "That begs the question: Who has my skull now? I'd like to know who we are pursuing and must ultimately face if we are to get it back, though how am I to do that if I have a corpse that lacks the parts it needs to talk?"

For a moment, Otto fears that he must fish bones out of the boiling pot, or worse, cut open the men he has just killed and root around their guts for whatever bits of flesh, bone, and gristle they haven't digested yet.

The necromancer glances at him from the corner of his eye and chuckles. "No need, dear Otto. Go find the peasant's head for me, please. The bones tell me it has rolled that way."

As Otto goes to look for the head, he tries to extinguish his thoughts the way he would a candle, completely and all at once. But trying not to think is only possible if he focuses on his senses instead, and that's hardly preferable.

You do not see, he thinks as he bends over the head, which is lying between some weeds at the edge of the clearing. It is dented with rot, the skin a greenish gray. The eyes are gone, as is part of the tongue. Eaten, most likely, but by man or beast?

You do not feel how slimy it is, Otto thinks as he picks it up, careful to hold it far from his clothes. Some black fluid dribbles out of its mouth.

You do not smell the stink of that fluid, so strong you can taste it, which you do not. You do not hear the way it crunches and squelches as you carry it.

But he does.

Of course he does.

He places it at the necromancer's feet, then plucks some grass. There's a way to whistle with a blade of grass; Frieda knows the trick of it. He sets to braiding it instead, anything to distract himself.

The necromancer frowns as he scrapes a bit of mold off the head's temple with his dagger. "Oh, but I do hate it when they're all cut up and decayed like this. What spirit wants to be called back to a body as rotted as that?"

It's not as if the farmhand had any trouble with that, Otto thinks and shivers.

The necromancer looks at him with an expression halfway between offense and hurt. "There's a big difference between simply puppeteering a corpse and calling back its soul."

Can he see into my mind? Otto wonders. He must, surely, or else how could he know Otto's full name? And why not? Why shouldn't a witch who can puppeteer corpses and soldiers around also be able to see into the hearts and heads of people he has enslaved?

"This dead peasant might not be of any use to you if he was already dead when the skull was taken," Otto says. His hands are trembling, and he keeps dropping the pieces of grass he has gathered. He balls his hands into fists, crushing the grass, releasing its good clean scent.

"You're wrong there. Once the dead have been called back to this mortal plain, they have certain powers."

"What sort of powers?"

"Knowledge, the power to spin illusions, manipulation of the will through dreams. You might try your hand at those yourself one of these days, Otto. The longer you are undead, the more powerful you grow. It'll be something to look forward to, I'm sure."

Otto can't feel queasy anymore, not exactly, not without a working stomach, but he feels something close to it. Maybe the necromancer is right. Maybe this is Hell.

Meanwhile, the necromancer is still talking. "This peasant might know where the skull is, though I don't see how he can tell us anything without a tongue and lungs." The necromancer prods the dead man's throat, and it takes all of Otto's willpower to focus on the grass bleeding sap into his palm rather than on the squelching.

"The larynx has been crushed. What a pity," the necromancer sighs. He saunters over to one of the men Otto has killed, crouches next to him, peers into his mouth. "This one still has a functional larynx. Are you any good with a needle and thread, Otto?"

He is, though soon, he really wishes he wasn't.

10

URSULA

ALL IS NOT WELL WITH Elsebeth.

Ever since they kissed, now almost a week ago, she has been waspish, her mood so foul Sister Ursula is sometimes sure she can almost see it.

Though perhaps it's not the kiss that is to blame for this, but Sister Ursula's knee. It's all black and blue and swollen. Putting weight on it hurts abominably.

The best thing would have been for Sister Ursula and Elsebeth to remain where they were and allow her knee time to heal. Except for the *Nachzehrer*, the village had much to recommend it: food, beer, and a hearth with enough wood to keep a fire going for days.

Only Elsebeth insisted that they keep moving. "We found this village. That means others could, too. Soldiers, or worse," she said.

"Worse? What could be worse than soldiers?" Sister Ursula asked.

"You know what I mean!" Elsebeth snapped. "I have stayed

alive for as long as I have because I kept moving. I shan't change that now."

Sister Ursula can walk, but only for short stretches at a time, after which she has to rest. She manages a little farther every day as her knee slowly heals, but all the same, their progress on the road has been exasperatingly slow.

When Sister Ursula has to sit down, Elsebeth scavenges for food, or she mends her dress with fabric she found in the house they stayed at the night of the *Nachzehrer*'s attack. She also found a pair of shoes that fit her there, so at least it wasn't all bad. Sometimes, she sits staring without seeing, her eyes like two dull shards of stone in her face. At other times, she cries soundlessly. Sister Ursula will look up from her hands folded in prayer or from the cattails she is cutting up or some other small task, and see that suddenly Elsebeth's cheeks are awash with tears. Yet whenever Elsebeth catches the other woman looking at her, she scowls and turns her face away.

Sister Ursula wishes only for things to be right between them. Multiple times a day, she prays for this, clutching her rosary so hard that it leaves a string of little indents in her palms; Elsebeth gave it back to her the day they left the village, with no explanation as to where and when she found it. The string is still broken, but the girl did clean it; there was not a speck of blood or dust on it.

That evening, they find an abandoned farm, which is a lucky thing. These past few nights, they were forced to sleep out in the open. They had to make a fire or risk perishing of cold, but neither of them slept well, afraid the smoke would draw unwanted attention.

After they eat a meal of cheese and cured meat from the *Nachzehrer* village supplemented by some beer and pickles from the farm, Sister Ursula decides to polish the glass of the reliquary. It is futile—as soon as they pick up the box, their fingers will inevitably smudge the glass again—but surely the saint will see the care she takes to keep her little home clean and appreciate the effort? She certainly looks quite content, grinning with her yellow teeth. She's missing one next to the incisor. If they follow the route Elsebeth has decided upon using the saint's map, they will come quite close to Sister Ursula's convent, so perhaps they can take a detour, stay there for a bit, and find a replacement tooth for her there?

"Say that the saint wouldn't give you one wish, but as many as you'd like, no matter how silly. What would you wish for then?" Sister Ursula asks.

"Saints don't exist, and neither do wishes," Elsebeth says sullenly. She's making a poultice for Sister Ursula's knee from wild herbs.

Sister Ursula laughs uncomfortably. "Come now, you doubting Thomas. You won't know that for sure until we have reunited the saint's skull with her body."

Elsebeth grunts. Her mouth is a tight line, her brow as creased as a roughly handled broadsheet. Sister Ursula can feel the anger and hurt waft off her like the stench of something left to rot in the summer sun.

"Please just indulge me," Sister Ursula begs as she bends closer over the box. Her face, reflected in the glass, becomes superimposed on that of the skull. It's a strange sight. She quickly straightens her spine, changing her reflection.

Elsebeth shreds some herbs with her fingers. "I don't know what 'indulge' means."

"It means that you'll do it for my sake. Please? I'll go first. If I could wish for anything in the world, even silly small things, I'd wish for teeth that never rotted and never pained me." A year ago, one of her molars went bad, swelling her cheek until it was round and red as an apple. When Sister Junius grabbed the tooth with pliers to extract it, the pain was such that Sister Ursula almost fainted. Every now and again, she pokes the hole left behind with her tongue; the silky-smooth feel of her gums is strangely delightful.

"That's not silly; that's just common sense. Not many things are worse than an ache in the tooth or ear. My little brother Friedrich's ears would often become inflamed, and he would weep so sorely with the pain of it, it would break your heart. Had he lived, those constant infections would probably have left him deaf." She stops suddenly and turns her face to the window, looking so lost and helpless that Sister Ursula has to sit on her hands to keep from reaching for her; she fears her touch will not be welcome now.

"You're right. My example was bad. Let me try again," she says, hurrying to keep whatever emotion threatens to overwhelm Elsebeth from pulling her under. "If I could wish for anything at all, I would wish for a cup that would always fill with milk whenever I was thirsty."

Elsebeth drags the needle out, the thread rasping softly against the fabric. "How is that silly? You are no good at this game at all."

"What silly thing would you wish for then?"

"I can't think of anything silly. After everything I've suffered, I think all my wishes are sound."

"The Lord sends no more than you can bear," Sister Ursula says without thinking; it is what her sisters and she tell each other whenever something bad happens.

Elsebeth's face darkens. "That's a lie!" she spits. "I don't claim to know why the Lord made what happened to my sister happen, but I do know it's more than I can bear, and definitely more than she could, for she died lying in the dirt where the soldiers dropped her when they were done with her, as if she were no more than a soiled bit of cloth."

"Elsebeth, I never meant—"

"No! I want no more of your religious prattle. It sickens me!" she shouts and dashes outside, leaving Sister Ursula stricken and feeling ill.

"Oh, Ursula, you absolute fool," she whispers and knuckles her eyes so hard, she sees spots, like little pools of spilled blood darkening the sand.

That night as they lie in bed and try to sleep, Sister Ursula can bear their discord no longer.

"Elsebeth, are you asleep?" she whispers. The girl is lying with her back to her and has been sleeping so for the past few nights. No more kisses, no more stories, no more tearstained confessions of the horrors she has witnessed.

She doesn't reply, but her breathing isn't deep and even enough for her to be asleep.

Sister Ursula swallows, then continues. "I am sorry for what I said earlier. I spoke without thinking, and I fear I was both callous and cruel. Please know that I am deeply sorry for it. If I could take those words back, I would."

For a while, it seems that Elsebeth won't respond. When she does, her voice is small. "It's not your fault any of that happened."

Sister Ursula waits to see if she will elaborate, but no more words come. She licks her dry lips. "Well, I am sorry all the same. I wish I could help you. Won't you let me?"

"I am beyond help."

"No one is beyond help." Sister Ursula hesitates, then gently touches the girl's back. She tenses; her spine stands out like a line of pebbles. Sister Ursula must use her wish to save Sister Hildegard's soul from purgatory and to ensure the safety of her sisters still living, but if she had one more wish, she'd use it to wish Elsebeth well again, both in mind and body. She'd undo everything that has scarred her, drag out those memories like a faulty thread.

Sister Ursula folds her into her arms, presses her nose to the back of her neck. The hair there is soft and fine. She inhales the smell that's all Elsebeth's own and that has come to mean safety these past few days, no matter that Elsebeth has been so plagued by melancholy and anger. "Won't you let me help you?" she murmurs.

Elsebeth is crying again. "I know not how," she whispers. "My head is so full of memories and thoughts that there's no room for anything else. Mayhap my mind is broken. It's not normal to relive all these memories of awful things that happened to me, that I did to survive… At times, I wonder if I ever even left the farm at all. Mayhap those soldiers got to me after they were done with Margarethe, and I am dead, and this is Hell."

"If this were Hell, then nothing good would happen to you," she tries. "Yet good things have happened."

"Mayhap that's part of my eternal punishment. It's mighty cruel to give someone something good and then snatch it away from them."

This is no good. If she is to help Elsebeth at all, she must distract her from all the horrors festering inside her mind. A wound can't heal if you keep picking at it.

"Tell me: What is the Latin name for a daisy?" she asks.

"Daisy?" Elsebeth asks. In her surprise, she turns to Sister Ursula.

A lock of hair lies plastered against her cheek. Sister Ursula takes it, tucks it behind her ear. "Yes. Do you remember?"

"*Bellis perennis.*"

"And the common dandelion?"

"*Taraxacum officinale.*"

"If there's still room for Latin in your head, that means your mind isn't broken." She wipes at Elsebeth's wet cheeks with a corner of her blanket, then kisses her temple where the veins lie so close to the surface she can feel the blood throb through them. "Won't you tell me a story?" she asks.

"I can't think of any," Elsebeth sniffs.

"Please?"

It takes a while, but eventually, Elsebeth begins to talk. "There was once a girl who wanted a husband who would always be true to her," Elsebeth begins, the sentence broken into three strange pieces as her breathing, still affected by her crying, hitches. "But only Jesus Christ is always true, and so she was still not married when she was well into her twenties, even though she had a pair of quick, deft hands, was fair of face, and had hair that looked like spun gold, so long it dragged behind her in the dust if she did not sew it to her head in long braids.

"The day before she turned eight and twenty, she had had enough. She went to a local wise woman who had made a living out of blessing the cattle of the local peasants. This woman was said to know many things, and so the girl asked her where she could find a man who would always be true to her."

Sister Ursula dabs at Elsebeth's eyes with a wet handkerchief to soothe them. She whimpers at the touch of the cold fabric, at the relief it brings to the puffy flesh.

"What did the woman tell her?" Sister Ursula prompts her.

"The woman made cruel sport of the girl, first sending her to a nunnery to gaze upon a papist carving of Christ, for He will always be true, then sending her to the graveyard, for dead men will not alter and thus will remain always true also. When the girl came back a third time, the woman understood she meant business.

"'If you give me your hair, I shall tell you where to find a husband who will always be true to you, and how to catch him,' the woman said. The girl loved her hair, but wanted a husband more, so she cut it all off. The woman then told her where to go and what to do. After she was done, the girl raised her eyebrows, for what she had been told was strange. 'If you are making mischief, I shall come back and strangle you with my braids,' she told the old woman, for she may have been fair of face, but she was also terrible of tongue.

"Yet she did what the old woman had told her to, and wandered to the river, where she found a filthy vagabond. He was dressed only in a pair of torn trousers and a shirt. His hair and beard were long and matted, and he stank. He was also possessed, for this was a long time ago, when such things still happened. In his eyes, the girl could see many things looking back at her, all of them quite evil.

"'What an ugly old maid you are, with your hair all hacked off,' the vagabond said, for one of the demons that possessed him was proud and haughty and delighted in hurting others.

"The girl huffed at this. 'I'm not,' she said. The vagabond smiled and said, 'Then prove it, and take off your dress.' The girl had been prepared for this by the old woman and had gone home before wandering to the river. Over her own dress, she wore her grandmother's dress, her mother's dress, and sister's dress also.

"She took off her grandmother's dress, and underneath the possessed vagabond found not milky skin to defile, but another dress.

"'My turn. Take off your shirt,' the maid said, and though the vagabond grumbled and spat, for the demons inside of him were both proud and wrathful, he had no choice but to do as she said.

"'Take off your dress,' he said, and she took off her mother's dress.

"'Take off your breeches,' she said. He gnashed his teeth and said many lewd things, for all demons are lechers, but the girl would not be moved, and so he had to do as she bade him.

"'Take off your dress,' he said, and she took off her sister's dress.

"'Take off your skin,' she said, for the vagabond had no more layers betwixt the air and his skin. At this, he turned pale, fell to his knees, and begged her to take back her words. She might have, for a man weeping and groveling is a pitiful sight indeed, but she had only the one dress left, and so she told him firmly to take off his skin.

"Having no other choice, the vagabond had to take off his skin. She took it to the river and scrubbed away all the filth and all the demons clinging to it using fistfuls of sand and mud, then beat his skin with sticks until it was all clean; she may have had a terrible tongue, but she was not shy of work. When she was done washing it, she strung it from a tree to dry. Then, she took it back to the trembling vagabond and dressed him, and behold: Now that he was no longer demon ridden, he had turned into a rich merchant's son, handsome and kind. To thank her for banishing the demons that had driven him mad many years ago, he married her and stayed true to her forever, and if they didn't die, they're still living on today."

Sister Ursula wipes at a crumb of salt stuck at the corner of Elsebeth's eye. "What a wonderful story! Thank you for telling, *mein Liebchen.*"

Elsebeth flushes fiercely at being called "my little love"; Sister Ursula can feel the heat beat off her cheeks. "It's only a silly story that my grandmother told me," she murmurs, but she's smiling all the same.

"I don't think it's silly."

"No, me neither," Elsebeth confesses. "In truth, methinks it would be nice to have someone take off my skin and wash and beat it clean of all the filth that has come to cling to it." She hesitates, then traces Sister Ursula's eyebrow with a fingertip, smoothing down the dark hair. "Why are you so kind to me?" she whispers.

Again, Sister Ursula finds that the words she has at her disposal do not suffice to explain properly all she feels and thinks. "Kindness is godly," is what she settles on.

Elsebeth's hand has traveled down her face, cradles her cheek. It's a peasant's hand, all rough and red from work. If Sister Ursula had a third wish, she would wish for an easy life for Elsebeth so that her hands might grow soft. "Are we friends again?" she whispers.

Elsebeth strokes her cheek with a calloused thumb. "We never stopped being friends."

Sister Ursula's heart soars. That night, for the first time in months, perhaps years, she sleeps easily.

11

ELSEBETH

I AM KISSING URSULA'S BREASTS, and it is sweet. We are naked as babes on a bed of velvet and down. The feel of her skin against mine has me trembling all over, or mayhap it's the way the blade of her hip presses against my cunny.

"Ursula," I moan, placing a trail of kisses from her nipple to her throat, which is pale, veined, and hot as sunstruck stone. "Oh, Ursula, how sweet you taste and feel!" I close my eyes and run my hands through her hair. Unlike my own hair, which is wispy and fine, hers is thick and a little coarse.

"Cease thy writhing and moaning, thou little harlot, and heed me, for I've a need of thee," a voice whispers in my ear.

"But you feel so good," I whisper back, my fingers tangling in her locks.

And then I realize.

It's not Ursula's voice.

I go cold all over. When I lift up my head and open my eyes, it's not Ursula's face I see, but the saint's skull.

I know then that I am dreaming.

I flush from sole to crown, so violently that the tears spring into my eyes. I push Ursula's body (but is it still Ursula's body if it has the saint's skull as a head?) away from me and cover her with a sheet to preserve her modesty. I wrap a sheet around myself also, though shame has me running hot. "Why are you here?" I snap.

The skull grins, but then she has no lips to purse and so must always grin. "How sorely I have vexed thee! Didst thou not mean to kiss me? Didst thou think 'twas not I, but the nun, mayhap?"

"Stop it!" I snap.

"Thou art welcome to kiss me some more, if it pleases thee. It has been a while since I've had a body, even in dreams. Alas, most people think of me only as a skull, and so a skull I must be." She runs her hands all over her body, shuddering in delight. "Oh, but it feels good to have skin again!"

I grab her wrists so as to still those wandering hands. "That's not your body. Don't touch it so. It isn't right."

She looks at me all sly. "Methinks thou only sayest so because thou art ashamed. Dost thou think it sin, to long for another's body? If that were true, then it seems to me I came to thee at the right time, or thou wouldst have sinned most grievously."

I did not think it possible to burn hotter than I already am, but I do, so ashamed am I. "This is only a dream," I retort.

"It would be sin still, no?"

"It wouldn't be. I dream all manner of things, some of them very vile. It does not mean I want those things to truly happen. And why are you rooting around in my mind? Why do you peep and lurk? My dreams should be my own, and are not for you to see! Now tell me what need you have of me, then leave me to my dreams." Though now that I know I am dreaming, I can't keep kissing dream Ursula; it was innocent only when I knew not what I was doing, and what good is kissing her if she doesn't have her head?

"Very well," the skull says in that reedy voice of hers. "The nun and thou must hurry. The necromancer and his servant are gaining ground. They will soon sorely hound us. The time has come for thee to leave behind thy slothful, gluttonous ways and continue on thy quest to return me to my body, which I miss more than I can say."

Her words are unjust, and anger rises in me as sap does in trees. "Ursula can't walk any farther or faster than she does because of her knee!"

"Pah!" the skull says, and if she could, I am sure she would spit. "If thou keepest moving at this slow pace, she shall soon no longer need to worry about her knee at all!"

I let go of her wrists and draw the sheet tighter around me. "If there even is a necromancer pursuing us. Mayhap this is no more than a silly dream." Sullenly, for I am still ashamed the skull has seen this dream and aggrieved that she has spoiled it for me, I add, "If you want us to move faster, you should heal Ursula's knee. I thought saints had the power to make the blind see again, the deaf hear, the dumb speak, and the crippled walk."

She swoops at me like a bird of prey. I shriek and raise my

hands to my face, but too late. She has caught my left lobe between her sharp little teeth. As soon as she lets go, I draw back and clap my hand over my stinging ear.

"You bit me!" I exclaim.

"And how right that serves thee, thou little saucebox!" the skull snaps, her arms folded in front of her chest. She gnashes her teeth in a way that makes me wince.

A little blood runs down my neck. I rub at it. "That's not very saintly of you," I say. Her bite does not pain me overly much, but the shock of it has loosened my tongue.

"'Tis thine own fault for believing me some meek, martyred maid. Now heed me, you wretched wench: On the morrow, the nun and thou must make haste, unless thou wouldst like to face the necromancer."

She hesitates, then takes hold of my hands and asks in a soft, uncertain voice, "Before thou wakest, wouldst thou hold me in thine arms? 'Tis been a while since I had skin. I forgot how it hungers."

I open my mouth to say something, I know not what, but I have come awake, and once more the skull is nothing more but bone shut away in a box.

When morning comes, Ursula wakes me. "Look, Elsebeth, your poultice worked a miracle. My knee is much better!" she says, and indeed it is. It's still yellow and green, but the swelling has gone.

Her dear face creases with worry and she touches my ear. "You hurt yourself," she says.

I feel my earlobe, which is sore and sticky with half-dried blood. I remember my dream, and my heart leaps like a hare inside my chest. Has the saint's skull…?

But no, such things are not possible. It's much more likely that I scratched myself in sleep, and my brain took the pain and stitched it into my dream. It has done so before. When my monthly bleeding begins in the night, I dream I am being stabbed, and two winters ago, when there was nothing to eat, and Margarethe and I did nothing but lie near the hearth for warmth, I often dreamt the same dream, of something dark and hungry living inside of my belly gnawing on my insides.

We leave as soon as it is light. As we walk, I am not exactly happy, but I feel awake and full of life, and that's much better than I have felt in a long while. Mayhap it's because Ursula can walk so much better now; mayhap it's because the sun is warm and the air is full of the scent of rising sap and green things growing.

I think it's mainly because of Ursula's hand in mine, though.

I can't stop myself from toying with it. I map the lines on her palm with my fingertips, move her fingers this way and that, stroke the dips and crags of her knuckles. It's such a common thing, a friendly hand to hold is, but I didn't have one for so long that I grow almost drunk on it now.

The skull has reason to be glad also. In the abandoned farm, we found a satchel for her. I carry her now, strapped carefully to my chest so she won't bounce around and break her brittle teeth, though I think secretly to myself that a few broken teeth might make her less mean.

I have not yet told Ursula of my skull dreams. There are many things that I think about against my will, but this one thing I can push out of my mind very well, for most dreams are nonsense. My grandmother said they are only worth heeding when you have had the same dream thrice, because only then is there any truth to them, for three is the number of the Lord.

Soon, we have entered the woods again. Although Ursula's knee is much better, we still stop often, so she can rest and I can forage. April is a cruel month, lean and full of hunger, this year more so than others. The winter we had was bitterly cold, and it clings to the land still, leaving the earth hard as a crust of burnt bread and the trees loath to bloom. They are full of buds clenched closed as tightly as a miser's fist around a coin.

"Dandelion," Ursula says. She has to call out, for I have strayed a little way from her in my gathering.

"*Taraxacum officinale*," I reply.

"Crocus?"

I kneel down to pluck a dandelion. "That's an easy one. *Crocus*."

Ursula laughs. It's a surprisingly deep sound, and dear to me. "Sometimes, life is easy like that. Nettle?"

I do not reply, for what I see has knocked all the Latin straight out of my head.

Hidden in the undergrowth lies a boy.

Had I not knelt down to pluck that dandelion, I would not have seen him. So close is he, I can brush his dirty hair from his forehead if I reach out.

But I don't reach out, and I don't brush his dirty hair from his forehead, for he is a dead boy. He is so thin, his bones look as if they are trying to burst through his skin, which hangs loose like fabric in some places but is pulled taut as a drum in others. He has no eyes, just two meaty caverns in his face. His eyelids have been torn to shreds, likely by the very same birds who have eaten his eyes, and they hang in front of those empty sockets like tattered curtains.

No living boy, this.

Yet for all that he is dead and for all that he has no eyes, I know he is looking at me. When I lower my hand with the dandelion, his head moves also.

A revenant, then, but what kind? It's hard to see with him hidden in the undergrowth, all dappled by shade and sun.

I daren't move. I am so afraid, my limbs are shaking, and I feel as the cows must after a long winter shut away in their stables: ready to bolt and aggrieved that I can't, for if I run, he will come after me. In this, revenants are like wolves, bears, and other meat-eating things; if you run, you make yourself the prey and tell them that the hunt has begun.

If only he would just leave us be! We want nothing to do with him, for he is a vile thing.

Unclean.

Unnatural.

Ungodly.

So stuck am I in thought that I do not hear Ursula draw near until she lays a hand on my shoulder. The touch is light, yet it strikes me like lightning. I whip around, my heart racing.

The moment I turn my back on the dead boy, he slithers out from the hollow where he has been hiding. Quick as a snake, he strikes. With his little hands, the nails long and filthy, he climbs up my legs until he's on my back. There, he clamps his legs, skinny as two sticks, around my ribs and wraps his arms around my neck.

He does not weigh much because he's no more than skin and bone, but he stinks, and the pain in my throat where his arm presses hard against it is terrible. "Home," he whispers in a voice that sounds ancient, not like a little boy at all.

I know then what he is.

An *Aufhocker*.

One who jumps on the backs of unsuspecting travelers and kills them unless they find him his grave.

12

OTTO

OTTO'S STRATEGIES TO STOP HIMSELF from thinking don't always work. Take, for instance, what happened when the necromancer brought that peasant they found in the woods back to life. For all that Otto has done his best to banish the memory of that wretch telling them about the two women whom he gave the skull to, he fears that it will haunt him for as long as the necromancer sees it fit for him to walk this earth.

Yet sometimes, in moments that must be blessed by the Almighty, proving that Otto is not forsaken entirely, his mind will simply stop working of its own accord. Afterward, he will remember only snippets. Their time in a deserted little town the necromancer's bones have led them to is such a moment.

The snippets Otto remembers are thus:

Standing in the graveyard littered with the dead, going from body to body to find a fresh one to resurrect so they can ask whether the women with the skull came through.

Settling on a dead child ripe with rot, though luckily not so rotted that he must pull body parts from other corpses and sew them together to create something capable of speech.

Her screams, not high-pitched as you'd expect from a child, but low and guttural, and the necromancer frowning and saying, "I hate it when they do that."

A walking corpse interrupting them, babbling things that almost make sense but never quite, though perhaps they might, if only Otto can keep listening for a little while longer...

When it unhooks its lower jaw and Otto sees inside its gray mouth full of teeth, he is shocked into alertness.

"A *Nachzehrer*!" the necromancer says and claps his long pale hands together in delight. "Oh, but it's been a while since I have seen one of those. No wonder our skull thieves have fled from here. Go and kill it, Otto; there's a dear. You remember how to do that, don't you? From the farmhand?"

Otto does. He draws his *Katzbalger* and circles the revenant, whose milky eyes follow his every move.

"In the name of our Lord and Savior Jesus Christ, I beg of you: Please stop whatever you are doing and let me go," it babbles, the words all slurred because its lower jaw is dangling like a piece of meat from a butcher's hook, but Otto has never shown mercy before, and even if he was inclined to do so now, the necromancer's command forbids it.

The *Nachzehrer* lunges, its rotting tongue lolling. Otto easily sidesteps, then cuts off one of the monster's hands. It flops to the ground. Black blood oozes from the stump.

Again, the *Nachzehrer* tries to grab Otto; again, he lops off a hand.

"I am growing bored," the necromancer says, his spidery fingers toying with the little bones he uses for tracking. "Finish this, please."

The next time the *Nachzehrer* charges, Otto shears through its neck with his sword. The head lands with a thud, the lower jaw still unjointed, the flesh around it folded and draped. The *Nachzehrer* stumbles around for a few more heartbeats before it collapses and falls still.

Next, the necromancer makes Otto gather all the bodies on a great heap to burn them. He drenches them with lamp oil, then tucks bits of paper and wood chips into their mouths and pockets, anything that will burn, really, though once a body has caught fire, the fat will make it burn well and long. In that way, human bodies are like candles.

The smell when Otto sets them on fire is familiar to him: half rot, half sweet meat cooking. There is no comfort in this familiarity.

The necromancer's yellow goat eyes glow as bright as the flames in the dark. They are such a horror to look at. Otto thought he might get used to them as time wore on, but they still sicken and frighten him just as much as when he saw them for the first time. How wonderful it would be to work his thumbs into the necromancer's sockets and pop out those unnatural eyes like grapes! Or he could puncture them with a needle, the same he was forced to use to sew that dead peasant back together, and watch in grim satisfaction as yellowish fluid drips down the necromancer's cheek like yolk. Alternatively, he could burn out the necromancer's eyes, leaving nothing but shriveled tissue behind.

Tearing, stabbing, burning; there are many ways to blind a man.

Only Otto can't carry out any of them, of course, because he cannot hurt this witch, and even if he could, it would be unwise; the necromancer may have killed him, but he is now also Otto's only hope of getting his life back. He'll never find the saint's skull on his own.

Still, he can't help but think that, if only it wasn't for the necromancer, he could have spent this night making love to his sweet Frieda, and afterward eat the bread she bakes for him and admire the look of the golden necklace he stole for her around her throat instead of torching a pile of corpses. Though if that's what it takes for him to be able to go back to her, he'll do it, just as he spent the past years marching for days in the pissing rain, cleaning muskets, digging trenches, and suffering all the other drudgery of life as a lowly soldier in order to pay for her upkeep.

Otto stares at his gore-smeared hands. His skin has torn along the folds of his palms, and the seven nails that remain have turned this disgusting brown color. These hands are fit for nothing but killing, and soon not even that. It's as if all the murdering and maiming he has done no longer merely stain his soul but can now be read on his skin, too. It makes him feel used and unclean.

"That's how that farmer's daughter felt, you know. Sore and soiled, used and abused," the necromancer says without looking away from the heap of burning corpses.

If that's true, it's not to be wondered at that she cried so. But instead of drying her tears and telling her that all things, both good and bad, will pass, Otto had no compassion for her, no kindness, only annoyance and anger.

Violence upon violence upon violence.

And for the first time in twenty years, Otto is fiercely tired of it. Softly, he begins to weep, yet all that drips from his eyes is a single tear, dark and foul.

13

URSULA

ONE MOMENT, SISTER URSULA IS basking in the spring sunshine and laughing with Elsebeth as she teaches her the Latin names of flowers. The next, some creature is attacking the girl she has come to feel so protective over.

For once, fear lags behind, and so she has not frozen yet and can pull the little knife she always carries with her from her pocket. Where to strike? Her eyes dart over Elsebeth's attacker, looking for a soft spot to sink her knife into. She sees the side of its torso, so thin all the ribs can clearly be counted, the spine standing out like a string of marbles, the joints all swollen and much thicker than the limbs that connect to them, and all of it small.

It's merely a child, she thinks, and that makes her falter.

She blinks, looks closer.

It *is* a child, but there is something very wrong with it, even outside of its thinness. Its skin is grayish and mottled, and its eyes…

It's dead, she realizes.

In that instant, fear hits her as hard as a fist to the face. She sways, the hand holding the knife turning slick with sweat so that she could never strike at this walking corpse for fear the weapon will slip from her grip and slice up her palm, or worse, plunge into Elsebeth.

All the color drains from the world. Black spots dance in her vision, and sound becomes oddly muffled. Time stretches and contracts in strange spurts, like a curl of hair that lengthens when being pulled. Then, time rushes back, and with it color, scent, and sound. As if to compensate for that moment of near blindness and deafness, her senses are blown wide-open. She notices all sorts of little things: the way the birds have quieted and the only sound is of the wind rattling the bare branches; the fineness of the boy's hair as the wind lifts it, each strand pale and thin as spider's silk; the smell of him, which is not the powerful, ripe stench of decay but something more gentle, as if he is moldering rather than rotting.

There is something quite dreadful about his face. It's not even the lack of eyes, though that disturbs her very much; it's more the expression it wears. The face of the *Nachzehrer* that almost killed her was blank as a death mask. This boy's is anything but. It is equal parts grim determination and despair.

She feels that funny sensation at the back of her skull again, where it is joined to her spine.

You are such a coward, she thinks bitterly as she has to look away for fear she might faint otherwise. As she does so, her eyes snag on Elsebeth's face. The girl's cheeks have gone livid; even her lips have been drained from all color so that she looks almost corpse-like in her terror.

She is even more afraid than I am, Sister Ursula thinks, and that somehow snaps her out of her frozen state. She takes a step closer.

"Don't!" Elsebeth says.

The boy bares his teeth and snarls. His gums are gray, as if he has been drinking ink. He tightens his hold on Elsebeth, choking her.

Sister Ursula backs away, and the boy loosens his hold a little. Elsebeth begins to cough. The sound is horrible, all raspy. She bends over, gagging. When she straightens, the blood has rushed to her face, and she looks more like herself again.

Sister Ursula wipes her free hand on her dress, then transfers the knife to that hand. "Another revenant," she notes.

"An *Aufhocker*, to be exact, wanting to be returned to his grave," Elsebeth says. Suddenly, she whimpers, and it breaks Sister Ursula's heart to see her scared and in pain, but she daren't come close. In her pocket, she feels for her broken rosary. The familiar feel of the wood all warm from resting against her thigh gives her some strength.

She asks, "If he likes his grave so much, why did he leave in the first place?"

Elsebeth makes to shrug, but the boy tightens his grip around her throat again. Wincing, she aborts the movement. "My grandmother never told me the reason. Mayhap he wandered in his sleep, or mayhap someone dug him up and moved him elsewhere, or mayhap there's some other ground for it that you and I can never know whilst we still live. Does it matter? He won't let go of me till we have brought him where he wants to be."

"But we can't!" she exclaims. Every moment they dawdle is a moment Sister Hildegard has to spend in purgatory, her soul scraped and sanded a little closer to cleanliness, and that's all Sister Ursula's fault; the choir mistress would not have to suffer as long if she had seen a priest before death, might even have gone straight to Heaven.

Tears warp her vision, making Elsebeth and the boy blend together until Elsebeth looks humpbacked. She rubs them away with trembling fingers. "We can't," she repeats, quieter now. "The saint's skull—"

"Will have to wait till we have gotten rid of this dead boy. If we don't take him where he wants to go, he'll strangle me." Elsebeth attempts to smile bravely, revealing her strong white teeth, the incisors sharp. "Don't fret, Ursula. Aren't saints supposed to be quite forgiving? It's not as if we tarry on purpose."

"But how are we to know where his grave is?"

Elsebeth's smile turns pained. "Fret not. He'll lead us there."

Despite Elsebeth's assurance that the *Aufhocker* would show them the way, he does nothing but cling to Elsebeth at first. It's not until the day has mostly gone that he suddenly digs his knees into her ribs to stir her to the left.

Elsebeth snaps, "I'm not a horse. If you want me to go somewhere, you can tell me in words, or if you have forgotten those, then point."

The boy sticks out his tongue, making Sister Ursula gasp.

"What? What is it? What did he do?" Elsebeth demands to know, craning her head to see.

"He stuck out his tongue at you."

"Oh, so you're not merely a dead boy, but a rude one, too?" She stops walking. "Go ahead, then. Strangle me. I don't care. I am not going to take you back to your grave if you're going to behave like that, you ungrateful little wretch."

The boy hisses and tightens his grip around Elsebeth's throat, but she stands unmoving, although her face soon turns red and then blue.

"Stop!" Sister Ursula cries out. "If you strangle her, then I…I won't allow you to climb on my back. I'll run like the devil himself is after me, and you won't catch me, because my legs are a lot longer than yours, and also I'm not dead. You'll have to wait for someone else to come along then, and I think you'll be waiting a very long time, because all this time we have been in the woods, we've not met a single soul. You'll fall apart before that happens."

The boy relents, slumping against Elsebeth's back with a deep sigh.

"That's what I thought," Elsebeth gasps, rubbing at her throat.

They walk until dark. Then, they find a clearing and make a fire to stay warm. They cook. Still the dead boy clings to Elsebeth. He grows restless when they sit down to eat, muttering and keening.

"You want some, too?" Elsebeth asks, offering him a bit of jerky. The boy hesitates, then takes it and starts gnawing on it. "Don't drool on my dress, and careful of your teeth. They are probably none too tight in your gums."

When they make to sleep, the boy mewls with discontent. Elsebeth ignores this. She has to lie on her stomach. He pinches her as soon as she closes her eyes.

"Do that again, and I'll box your ears till they fall off your head; see if I don't!" Elsebeth snaps.

"*Home*," he whines.

"You'll have to wait," Sister Ursula tells him, trying to sound stern. "Elsebeth is tired. She needs to sleep. We'll continue tomorrow." She curls up next to them so that they may share each other's warmth. She has no desire to touch the dead child any more than she has to, but Elsebeth matters more, and so she conquers her fear and revulsion.

"There," she says. "That's nice, isn't it?"

The boy mutters something. He keeps twitching and readjusting his grip on Elsebeth, making it impossible to sleep.

"Maybe you should tell him a bedtime story," Sister Ursula tries, and so Elsebeth recounts the story of the man who ate the snake and could talk to animals. The boy falls asleep before she reaches the ending.

"He's just like my little brothers," Elsebeth whispers. "They never wanted to go to bed, either, and then I would tell them a story, and they'd be asleep before I could say, 'And if they didn't die, they're living on today.'"

"If I could take him from you, I would," Sister Ursula says.

"I know," Elsebeth responds. She takes Sister Ursula's hand and squeezes it.

Despite everything, they sleep. Once, the boy whimpers, waking Sister Ursula. Do the dead dream? Elsebeth said he might have wandered from his grave as he slept, so Sister Ursula supposes they must, though she hopes he doesn't, for doesn't dreaming imply a certain level of consciousness? It would be a horrifying thing indeed to know that you are dead and rotting, yet to wander the world still. Better to be nothing but a puppet for Satan to move through, like that *Nachzehrer*.

The boy mewls something that is almost a word. She hesitates, then brushes the hair from his forehead to soothe him. It's a pale blond, the sort that will turn white as thistledown in summer for a few years more before it darkens to ash as the boy becomes a man.

Only this boy will never grow up, and though that is a common tragedy made more common still these past two decades filled with war and hunger and disease, it makes Sister Ursula's throat constrict and her eyes burn. Despair and sadness lie heavily on her chest, almost as if she has her own *Aufhocker* clinging to her.

Sometimes, in her weakest moments, she wonders if there even is a God, for how can He be all-knowing and good, yet still allow such horrors to exist? It's not to be wondered at that Elsebeth struggles in a similar manner with her faith.

Sister Ursula fishes into her pocket for her rosary as she pushes the thought away. Despair only serves the devil. Better to cling to love, hope, and kindness, all these good things that energize her to help.

Dear God, she prays as she holds the broken strand of beads, *please look after this little boy, for like all children, he is blameless. Make that he can lie down and shed all his burdens, that he may find the rest that so far has eluded him.*

Please also take care of my sisters, flung far and wide by the hand of war. Give Reverend Mother Regina the strength to lead us, and dear Sister Junius the means to heal my sisters who decided to stay behind and protect Your house. I also beseech You to have mercy on Sister Hildegard, whose death is my most grievous sin, and my parents, who must have offended You greatly with their fornicating ways.

And please, beloved Husband, show Elsebeth that she is loved, and give her the strength to bear all that You have seen it fit to burden her with, that she may find happiness again in this world.

Amen.

Come morning, Sister Ursula's knee is tender from all that walking. She has probably overdone it, but what else could she have done? She wants to liberate Elsebeth from this dead child as soon as possible, because her knee is nothing compared to Elsebeth's whole body. The girl is all sore and stiff from having slept on her belly and moves like someone thrice her age. Sister Ursula gives her some willow bark to chew on and tries to loosen the girl's muscles with her fingers, only the dead boy clings so fiercely to her that Sister Ursula can't reach the painful knots in her neck and shoulders. Once, he even growls at Sister Ursula, showing her his mismatched teeth, all crowded and crooked like the gravestones in an overused cemetery.

"Oh, hush you," Elsebeth snaps. "She won't try to pry you away from me, though I wish she could, for you have made me mighty sore."

"Home," the boy whines in his gravelly voice.

"Yes, yes, home. Have some patience, won't you? From the look, feel, and smell of you, you've been dead for some months. Methinks you can wait some hours yet."

In the end, the boy doesn't have to wait more than three. The closer they get, the more fretful he grows, mewling and digging his bony knees into Elsebeth's ribs, and his long nails into her shoulders and scalp.

Elsebeth bears it all in silence, though with a fierce scowl on her face.

Always a fighter, she, Sister Ursula thinks as they come upon a cottage at the edge of the woods.

A woman is sitting propped up against the door, her long red hair wrapped around herself like a shawl. She is so thin, she looks simultaneously ancient and very young, her eyes huge in her shrunken face. In contrast, her belly is distended, as if she is in the final weeks of pregnancy. Her lips are stained green.

As they approach, Sister Ursula a little ahead of Elsebeth, who is weary from carrying the boy whilst being pinched and scratched at, the woman smiles in a strange way, like one drunk or sleepwalking. There's a blade of grass stuck to her teeth.

"Are you an angel come to fetch me?" she asks Sister Ursula.

Sister Ursula swallows against the lump of emotion in her throat. If only she could be! How much more bearable life would be if she were made free of sin.

Before she can say anything, the woman's eyes fall on Elsebeth and the dead boy riding on her back, and her face turns as still as a puddle of water on a windless day. At the same time, the boy says, in that awful croaking voice of his, not at all like the voice of a child but of something much older and no longer quite human, "*Mutti*!"

Sister Ursula whips around to look at Elsebeth. "Did he just call her his mother?"

"He did."

"I thought he would take us to his grave, not his home?" Then it strikes her: If this poor boy has died of hunger, as his mother seems to be on the brink of doing, his family might not have had the strength to take him to the nearest graveyard, which must be several miles from here. They might, instead, have buried him somewhere near.

She kneels down next to the poor woman, gently takes her hand, which feels like the hand of a corpse, and explains to her why they have come. At first, she isn't sure whether the woman has heard her, because her face remains so still, but once she is finished, the woman sighs and says, "I suppose you better come in then."

14

ELSEBETH

HERE'S A RIDDLE: WHAT IS worse than hunger?

Some might say pain, but that's not always true. Pain is not accompanied by hunger, but hunger has a friend in pain, pain in the belly, the joints, and the head, until everything aches, and you feel weak and faint.

Others might say losing a loved one. Though I agree that there's little more dreadful—and I should know, for I have lost my grandmother, my mother, my father, my big sister, Margarethe, and my little brothers, Friedrich and Johannes—I still think hunger is worse, for it makes us care not for such loss and in that manner sullies our love.

The priests and other godly men might say sin, for it stains our souls and displeases the Lord, whom we must strive to please and love above all other things. That is true for papists and Protestants alike, but then I ask you: Is hunger not at the root of many sins, if not all of them? People hunger for pleasure and power, but even hunger for bread can twist us into liars and thieves.

(And sometimes even fornicators, like it did me.)

And so my answer to this riddle is simple: Very little is worse than hunger, mayhap even naught.

The *Aufhocker*'s mother is so starved, she can't walk anymore, only crouch and crawl as she takes us inside her house. It's a humble home: a hearth, a table with some chairs, a bed. The woman drags herself to the bed like a lizard, then sits down against it, likely lacking the strength to crawl in. For a while, she is beyond speech, just sits panting. Her face has gone slack and strange again, making her look like one already dead, which no doubt she soon shall be. I have seen people like her lying at the side of the road, too weak to stand, too weak to crawl, too weak to defend themselves against those rifling through their pockets or tugging at the boots on their feet.

I would like to sit down on one of the chairs, for my back is sore from having to carry the *Aufhocker* all this time, but he still won't let go of me, there's not enough room for the two of us, and I fear I won't get up if I lie down again, so I keep standing.

"Where is your husband?" ask I.

"Dead," the woman croaks.

Ursula, always so generous with her love and attention, sits down next to the woman and pushes a strand of hair out of her face. "Did you bury him next to your son?" she asks.

The woman looks at her hands. They are thin, the nails brittle and broken. They're stained green on account of her ripping out all that grass to eat. "No. The ground was too hard, and I lack the strength. He's in the shed outside. Couldn't keep him laid out in here once he began to stink." Her voice is as dead as her eyes.

Ursula gives her a bit of our water to drink. "I see," she says. "I'm very sorry for your loss, and I am sorry to trouble you at such a difficult time, but please will you tell us where your little boy's grave is? He won't let go of my companion until we have taken him there."

"I don't know."

Ursula takes the woman's hands in hers, blows on them to warm them. "What do you mean, you don't know?" she asks, her voice gentle.

I lay my hand on Ursula's arm, for I have the truth of it between my teeth now, and it is bitter, and it is vile. "Ursula," I say softly, "this *Aufhocker* has no grave."

She frowns. "But you said that an *Aufhocker* always wants to be brought back to his grave. You said—"

"The boy told me he wanted to go home, and so I thought that must mean his grave, for what home does a corpse have if not his grave? Mayhap that was the truth in the old days, when people were properly buried in churchyards, but it's not true for this one."

"But then how…?" Sister Ursula asks.

I am still not looking at her, only at this wretched woman. It's as if her face is a splinter that my eyes have snagged on. "Your boy has no grave, for he wasn't buried at all, but left to lie where he died, which was someplace in the woods, wasn't it? Methinks he must have crawled into the undergrowth because he couldn't walk anymore. He was too tired, too hungry, and too weak to keep wandering, and so there he died and there he lay until I happened upon him."

My hand is still resting on Ursula's arm. When she finally understands, I feel all the muscles draw taut inside of it till it's hard as a piece of wood. "You took him to the woods and then left him there to die," she whispers. "But why? How could you do such a thing?"

The *Aufhocker*'s mother sobs, but only once. "Look around you, woman," she says tiredly. There are odd pauses in her speech, as if she's forgotten how to speak or finds that this takes too much strength. "We are poor. When winter came, there wasn't enough food for the three of us to last until spring, but if it were only two of us, we might just manage. We thought that, God willing, the harvest might be plentiful this year, and then I'd crop again and birth another child. My husband said I might forget this one then..."

"And did you?" Ursula asks, her voice trembling.

Something like scorn passes over the woman's face. "Of course not. I can tell you have no children of your own. It's a wonder, to have a babe grow inside of you for three seasons, to feel him flick around inside you like a fish..."

I shudder at her description. I cannot help it. The idea of a babe growing inside my belly has always horrified me. I saw how the women in my village went into marriage young, healthy, and smiling, but as they dropped child after child, losing teeth and hair with each one, they grew gaunt, sick, and old before their time, until they died of a fever or something else, their bodies all used up.

Finally, my eyes unsnag from the woman's face. I look at Ursula, whose chin has puckered like a prune as she tries not to weep. "If he has no grave, we must make one for him," say I, "else I know not how I am ever to get rid of him. He won't let go till I am dead or he falls apart, whichever comes first."

While Ursula tends to the *Aufhocker*'s mother, I stumble to the back of the cottage. It's good land that lies behind it, though untilled and choked with weeds. Likely the woman doesn't know she can eat those, too, or she wouldn't be stuffing her mouth full of grass. I know well how grass only pains the belly.

In the shed, I find her husband's body, as she said I would. His face, hands, feet are looking quite well for someone who has been dead some months now, likely on account of the frost, but other parts of his body have rotted to the bone.

No, not rotted, I think as I look at the clean edges at his wrists. I have to press my mouth to the inside of my arm to stifle a retch, it's so awful. An edge that clean can only be made by a knife.

"*Vati*," the *Aufhocker* croons.

"Yes, yes, that's your father," I say, "or what is left of him after your mother made a meal out of him. Now let's see if we can find something to wrap him in and then a shovel so that we may bury the two of you."

Using one of the blankets on the bed—the woman says I may, for soon she won't have much use for it anymore—I wrap the corpse quickly, cutting away the fabric around his mouth, grunting with the effort. I swear this boy grows heavier and heavier with each passing hour. He reminds me a little of my brothers, who would cling to my and Margarethe's skirts after my mother had been struck down by the plague, always crying or clamoring for something. When they died, first Friedrich and then Johannes some days later, a part of me died also. I want more than anything to have them back, want it so much so that I have thrown in my lot with a papist even though I don't believe in any of that stuff, because a small stubborn part of me can't stop asking *what if, what if, what if.* All the same, I'd be lying if I said I missed my little brothers' constant neediness. I pray I shan't ever have any babes of my own.

Though mayhap your prayers have been answered already and you are barren. If not, you'd have a mewling babe at your breast already, wouldn't you? The thought wells up from the pit deep inside of me where I bury all the horrors, and it takes me a moment to push it down again, which is a vast improvement; last time all that filth bubbled up to the surface, it took me days, and poor Ursula suffered because of it.

Focusing on the dead man in front of me and the task at hand helps. I don't want Ursula to see him and realize that his wife has been eating pieces of him. If she does, I'll lie and tell her wild pigs did it. It's better that way, for her and that wretched woman both.

When I am done wrapping him, I grab a shovel and mark out a spot in the garden. The ground is tough. I am used to hard work, for there was nothing but on the farm, but this past year, I've grown soft, though not as soft as Ursula, who has come out to help me dig.

A good grave should be so deep a grown man can stand up in it and his head not reach the lip. If it's not as deep as that, the stink of the corpse will attract wild dogs and pigs, who will dig it up and eat of it.

Or his wife, I think and shudder.

To dig such a grave can take days even if it's done by two strong gravediggers. Ursula and I aren't that. We pant and sweat before we have even dug a foot. Soon, poor Ursula's hands are blistering something frightful.

"Why don't you go sit with the *Aufhocker*'s mother and talk to her, one papist to another?" I suggest as she stands waving her hands in the hope that the cool wind will blow away some of the hurt. I'd hate for her beautiful hands to grow as red, tough, and ugly as mine.

Ursula looks away. "After what she did to her little boy, I don't know if I can."

"Don't talk nonsense. You are a nun, and a selfless one at that, and methinks she has a stronger need of you than I do. Besides, what use are you to me if your hands are all wounded? It's bad enough your knee pains you so already."

"I could clean and tidy, and maybe see if I can cook something for her," Ursula muses.

I don't much like sharing our food, seeing as it is likely wasted, this woman being at death's door already. I tell Ursula as much.

Ursula's eyes find mine again. "Might it not be a kindness to give her some food and let her die knowing that there are still decent people out there?"

I shrug. "Mayhap, but since she will die no matter what we do, methinks it's better if we save that food for ourselves. We need it more than she does."

Once she has left, I dig, and I dig, and I dig. There's not much more to say of it other than that, though of course that doesn't really tell you what it is like: the same thing over and over again, yet full of pain. At some point, I get blisters despite my calluses, and I have to wrap my hands in bits of cloth.

When it's done, I am sore all over. My hands are raw and sting without pause, and my knees pain me something fierce. If this is what my grandmother felt daily, it's not to be wondered at that she complained so often about her wretched knees.

My back hurts more than anything, though. It's as if my spine is made of wood, all stiff and unyielding, and someone has pushed a knife into the lower part of it and twists it every few breaths, sending shoots of pain up and down, burning so hotly that I can feel it even in my thighs. Oh, but what a trial it is to have a body!

By now, Ursula has come back out to help me. Together, we carry the dead man and lower him into his grave.

I turn my head to the boy still clinging to me like a barnacle to the hull of a ship, and I say, not quite gentle for I am in too much pain for that, but not harshly either for he can't help what he is and was made to be, "Get off, you. I've dug you a grave. It even has your father inside, so you won't be alone. More I cannot do for you."

Finally, he lets go of me and crawls into the hole we have dug, where he curls up next to his father and grows still. It's such a relief to no longer have to carry him that I close my eyes and just bask in the bliss of it for a minute. When I open them again, I find myself shying like a whipped horse from the task at hand. It's no small thing to bury the boy. He no longer lives, yet he is not quite dead either, and so it feels wrong to throw dirt on his face.

I swear that Ursula can read my thoughts as if they were written on my forehead, for she comes to me and lays her hand sweetly on my arm and says, "Would you rather I do it?"

For a moment, I am weak and almost tell her yes. Then, I find some strength, and I shake my head instead. "You will say it was God's will for this child to cling to me. Mayhap it was. Mayhap it was merely chance. No matter what it is, fact is that he found me and trusted me to take him home. I must see it through to the end now."

She lays her hand on my cheek and strokes a line with her thumb, and it's as if she has branded me. "You truly are a good, virtuous woman, Elsebeth, no matter what you may say or think," she says.

She goes inside to fetch the *Aufhocker*'s mother so she can see us bury her husband and son. The two of them watch as I shovel the dirt back into the hole. I try not to look, not to think or feel.

When it's done, Ursula makes the sign of the cross over the grave and says a prayer, and I too bow my head and fold my hands and say, "Amen" when she's done.

The woman crawls back into the house when the prayer has finished, groaning and sobbing softly.

Ursula comes to stand behind me and squeezes the muscles running from my shoulders to my neck. I moan. I can't help it; her touch is half pleasure, half pain. I let my head fall back so it rests against her breasts.

"It's all over now," she whispers and drops a kiss on my head.

My throat is all tight, as if I still carry the boy on my back and he has his arm wrapped around it, softly strangling me. "Do you think that, if it's all true and there is a wish at the end of all of this, mayhap the saint will take away these horrible memories once we have given her her head back?" I ask.

"Is that what you will use your wish on?"

I laugh a little. "God, no. I want to wish for my family to be returned to me. I hope she will heal my hands, your knee, and our minds out of the goodness of her heart, an extra reward for all our hard work."

She rests her chin on the top of my head. "I hope so."

15

ELSEBETH

IT'S TOO LATE TO GO elsewhere, and so Ursula and I must sleep inside the cottage with the woman. We eat a watery soup Ursula has cooked for us out of some weeds from the garden; we daren't give the woman anything stronger for fear it will kill her outright, and daren't let her know we have any other food on us for fear she will kill us. She may look half dead, but even someone as weak as she can kill another if given the chance.

When we are done eating, Ursula helps the *Aufhocker*'s mother back into bed, then prays together with her. The woman falls asleep soon. Her breathing is labored. Once you grow as thin and hungry as she, even drawing in air is weary work.

I sneak a bit of food from my pack then, for I am mighty hungry still. I think then that I am not much better than that *Aufhocker*'s mother; had I been in her shoes, I might have taken a few bites out of my dead husband, too. In this, she and I are not alone, only I know not whether that's a comfort. A woman from a village near where I lived ate her dead husband and then dug up two bodies and ate those, too. I also heard that a woman from a different village ate five of her children.

It had kept me up at night, that story had. Did the mother kill them to eat them, or had they been dead already? Surely they were dead, for what mother would kill her child to eat them, even if she were a reluctant mother?

(Such as I would have been, had that soldier saddled me with a babe.)

I suppose all the horror deep inside of me is rising to the surface again, because next I think about a story I heard from a neighbor, of yet another woman who ground bones from the dead to dust and used that dust to bake bread. It must have been a beautifully white loaf of bread if she used only bones, though probably not a good one, probably very crumbly and tasting only of ash and grit. But when you are hungry enough, you will eat anything and think it sweet, if only because it stops the horrible pain in your belly.

I know, because I have eaten all manner of strange things so as not to become like one of those poor wretches at the edge of the road, some of them very unclean and unwholesome, like rats and grass and my father's leather belt and sheets of paper and bark from a tree and once a pebble, though that was an accident. I only meant to suck on it. Margarethe had told me that sucking on a pebble would help with the hunger.

Only it was not true.

Nothing helps with the hunger, only eating, and sometimes not even that. Sometimes, that just makes the hunger worse. It grows and grows and grows until it has pushed everything else inside you to the side, even the thought of God, until you're no better than the beasts in the field.

No, until you are worse than the beasts in the field, for everyone knows animals are free from sin; they have no souls that can be tainted.

As I sit thinking about all of this, Ursula takes the skull out of her glass box to check her hair for vermin. When she is done, she kisses the skull's brow, and I can't help but wish she would kiss me, too. That might stop all these horrible stories from swirling around my head, at least for a little while.

We undress for bed, but neither of us can sleep, even though we are weary to our very bones. Too much has happened.

"Can you check my head for lice?" I ask, for when I was a child, nothing could make me fall asleep faster than my mother or sister touching my head. I sit in front of the hearth as Ursula combs out sections of my hair, her face close to my head so she can see the little insects and their eggs better. Every breath ghosts deliciously over my scalp.

For a while, we don't talk, but I am selfish and can never be close to her and not wish to draw her attention to me, and so I say in a soft voice so as not to wake the *Aufhocker*'s mother, "I used to delouse my brothers after my mother and grandmother were taken by the plague. They'd never sit still, and I'd grow vexed with them. I wish I hadn't. They couldn't help it. They were only little."

"Soon, you'll be able to make amends," Ursula promises. She pulls a little scab from my scalp and tosses it into the fire. It smells strange as it burns. I am reminded then of those three witches, how the air was thick with the smell of burning flesh, hair, and cloth, and I shudder, tear my eyes away from the flames, and look at the skull instead. With her eternal grin, she seems satisfied, almost merry. Then again, she has much to be pleased about, all snug on her purple pillow, which Ursula has plumped for her.

I can hardly believe that this bit of bone with her glass eyes and dusty hair will return my family to me, and yet I can't stop hoping that it will, either.

Ursula gently tilts my head so she can check behind my left ear for nits. Some hair slithers across my forehead, making my brow tickle. I rub at it. Margarethe's clog left a scar, and that gladdens me, for it's only right that those we love mark us as their own.

"Do you remember you asked me what I'd wish for, if I had a second wish to waste on something silly? I think I finally have an answer for you," I say.

She plucks an insect from my hair, and into the fire it goes. "What would you wish for?"

"I would like to mark my skin in some way with little pictures of everyone I love. That way, I could carry them wherever I go, and it would not matter how far away they are from me, because I could still look at them."

"That is a sweet idea," she says as she combs my hair back into place. "Where would you want them?"

"My arms and hands, I think, so I can easily look at them. Though maybe my grandmother should be on my cheek so she can whisper more stories in my ear." I stand and roll my head from left to right to get a crick out of my neck. When I turn around, Ursula is fiddling with the comb, rubbing the teeth with her thumb. Her cheeks are flushed, though mayhap that's just because of the heat of the fire.

"And I? Would you have a little picture of me, too?" she asks, looking up at me with a boldness in her eyes that instantly makes my belly squirm.

"Of course," I breathe.

"Where would you have me? Here?" she asks as she places her fingertips on the back of my hand. "Or here?" She moves her hand up, to the inside of my wrist, and I shiver in delight.

"Here," I whisper, and I take her hand and press it against my chest, over the place where my heart beats. It is racing now, the blood rushing through me.

Ursula's face lights up with a smile. It makes her eyes crinkle, and she looks so sweet that I want nothing more but to shed every stitch of clothing still on my body and press myself against her so she touches as much of me as she possibly can.

I love you, I think.

I open my mouth to say it thrice, for three is the Lord's number and will make it true, and speaking such things out loud gives words their own power also, but I've not the chance.

Satan has found us.

16

URSULA

FOR A MOMENT, SISTER URSULA has no idea what just happened. All she knows is that there is a bang as sudden and loud as thunder that makes her tear her hand out of Elsebeth's grip so fast, she has no memory of it later.

Another bang interspersed with the crunch of wood splintering.

At the third bang, the door gives way.

For a moment, there is nothing, just a rectangle of darkness so complete, her mind struggles to make sense of it.

Through it come two men.

No, not men, she thinks. From his goat's eyes glowing in the darkness like the twin flames of candles, his dark curls, his long fingers tipped with sharp nails, she knows the one on the left instantly for what he is: the devil himself, come to drag her sorry soul straight to Hell for what she did to Sister Hildegard.

The woman on the bed must have recognized him too, for she begins to wail. The devil looks at her with his head cocked. The light of the fire carves strange shadows on his cheeks, so that Sister Ursula for a moment believes it is no face at all, just a skull with two burning coals for eyes.

Beside her, Elsebeth roots frantically through their belongings for her knife, but what use is that, or any weapon, really, against such evil?

To the *Aufhocker*'s mother, the devil says softly, "You are a sorry sight indeed, Sophie Valentina Bauer. You weigh as little as your soul is heavy." He turns to the man he has brought with him. Sister Ursula immediately recognizes him as a soldier from his stance and sword.

"Do us all a favor, and take her out of her misery, Otto darling," the devil says.

The soldier moves toward the woman. She scrambles to get away from him, gibbering, pleading, but she's too thin, too weak.

"I'm sorry," the soldier whispers.

The snap of her neck as it breaks makes hot urine run down Sister Ursula's thigh, plastering her shift to her skin. The stench of ammonia is thick in the air, burning in her nose.

The devil sighs, then turns his flaming eyes on Sister Ursula. They flick down to the little puddle in which she stands, now rapidly cooling, and again he giggles, a high-pitched sound that sounds so wrong, so unnatural that it would have made her wet herself again if there was any fluid left in her bladder. As it is, she can only stand and stare, once again frozen by fright.

"Please don't hurt us," she whispers.

"I'd rather not, but I will if you force me. So you see, my dear

Sister, this is entirely up to you. Now I'd like to make this visit brief, so why don't you step aside so that Otto here can grab the reliquary behind you?"

The soldier takes a step forward, his sword gleaming in the dying light of the fire in the hearth. The sweet, cloying smell of rot hits Sister Ursula all at once. It's so potent she can taste it. It makes her stomach twist. She gags. Tears cloud her vision.

Elsebeth grabs Sister Ursula and pulls her behind her. Her other hand is wrapped firmly around her little knife. "Take another step, and you'll regret it; see if you don't," she says, and though her hand holding the knife isn't steady, her voice is.

The soldier's eyes widen in surprise. "You," he breathes.

The devil looks from the soldier to Elsebeth and back again, frowning a little as if teasing out a willful thread. Then, his face, pale as a fish's belly, smooths. He claps his hands together like a child and lets out that horrible giggle again, making Sister Ursula's flesh crawl. She has often imagined what Satan might look like—red or black hair, cloven feet, horned—but she somehow never thought of what he would *act* like. Though even if she had, she supposes it would not be like this, so gleeful, so utterly delighted.

"Oh, but how fun!" he laughs. "The world is a small place indeed!" He wipes at his eyes with a long white finger.

"Give us the skull," the soldier pleads.

Elsebeth bares her teeth at him. "No."

"Please. You don't want me to come and get it; you really don't."

Sister Ursula's heart is beating so fast, and her breath comes in such speedy bursts, she feels faint and sick. She feels her throat for her rosary to steady herself, only her rosary is in her dress pockets. Still she can't stop searching for it, her icy fingertips raising goose-flesh at her throat and chest.

Elsebeth still stands her ground, her whole body taut and ready. "I'd like to see you try," she says to the soldier.

"You don't, if not for your own sake, then at least for your friend's," the soldier says. Up close, Sister Ursula can see there's something off about him. His skin has a gray hue to it, and his face is strangely slack in places, like the skin has been draped over his skull and might slide off at any moment. His hands, too, are clearly human and yet not quite, the fingertips all blackened, the nails gone, exposing the flesh underneath. It's not wet and pink, but brown and dried up.

He's dead, she realizes, *he's dead he's dead he's a walking corpse like the* Nachzehrer *he's dead he's dead as Elsebeth and I soon will be too all dead dead dead DEAD...*

"Please," the soldier pleads, "you don't know what he is capable of."

"He's quite right, you know. I love to laugh, but when my patience runs out, I'm afraid it shall be at your expense and that of the nun here," the devil says. He's leaning against the door with such nonchalance, you'd think he was at a party that bored him, rather than in a poor woman's shack full of death. Though if you are the devil, such harrowing sights are probably so common as to be boring.

"Touch her, and I'll gut you, and gladly so. You wouldn't be the first pig I killed," Elsebeth snarls, and despite her overwhelming fear, Sister Ursula feels a wave of pride and affection sweep through her.

She is braver in this single moment than I shall be in my entire life, she thinks. She feels the cool, wet patch in her shift and is battered by shame so strong, she'd weep with it if only she wasn't so scared.

The dead soldier glances at the devil from the corner of his eye, which makes him look like a scared animal. "Elsebeth," he says softly, "do as he says, and give us that skull, or you'll rue it in ways you can't yet imagine. I should know."

Elsebeth glances at Ursula, then back to the soldier. "No!" she says, her voice cracking.

Satan sighs. "You leave me no choice then, dear girl," he says, and to Sister Ursula's surprise, he does look sorry. He turns to the soldier. "Get that skull, and use whatever force you must."

"Please don't make me," the soldier moans.

The devil tuts. "Come now. You've never had much trouble with rape, torture, and murder before. Off you go, dear Otto. Go get me my box."

The soldier keeps pleading even as he advances, his sword swishing through the air as he adjusts his grip on it. For a dead man, his movements are still surprisingly supple.

So this is how it ends, Sister Ursula thinks, *at the hands of a revenant, in a shack in the middle of the Bavarian Forest.*

All those miles traveled, all those horrors faced and overcome, all this love that has steadily grown between her and Elsebeth, and it will have meant nothing.

The saint won't be reunited with her body.

Sister Hildegard will continue to languish in purgatory.

Her fellow sisters flung far and wide by the war won't be blessed and saved.

Elsebeth's poor sister, Margarethe, and all her other relatives will remain dead.

Elsebeth, her brave, fiery Elsebeth, will die in pain and fear, her heart still full of doubt about God, about love.

And Sister Ursula herself? She will join Sister Hildegard in purgatory, because she will die without having received the last sacraments. That is, if this monster doesn't drag her straight to Hell, from which there is no escape.

"No!" Sister Ursula cries out. She stumbles back, grabs the rosewood box with the skull inside. Her hands are so deadened by fear, she has to clutch it tightly to her chest to keep it from tumbling out of her grip. A sharp corner presses a bruise into her solar plexus. "There's no need for violence. You can have it. You can have everything, but please don't hurt us!"

"Ursula!" Elsebeth hisses.

"I'm sorry, I really am, but I don't want us to die!" she says.

"But your sisters, and my family, and—"

"I know, I know! But if we don't give up the skull and we die here tonight, they will still be lost and dead, won't they? At least this way, you survive."

"Wonderful!" the devil says, folding his hands together. "Otto, if you please?"

The soldier takes the box from Ursula. This close, he reeks so badly that she can taste it, even as she tries not to breathe. He looks at the skull, which is no more than a pale shape in the poor light. A shudder ripples through him.

"My dear ladies, now that this bit of business has been satisfactorily concluded, Otto and I shall take our leave of you," the devil says and bows. On the threshold, he whips around, cape flying around him like dark wings, and says, "Oh, and please don't bother coming after us. It would be quite useless, I assure you. As I said, I'd rather not hurt you, but I will if you force my hand."

As soon as they are gone, Elsebeth drops her knife. It clatters to the floor, then lies there, the flames of the fire making the blade wink. "Oh, Ursula," she whispers, "what are we to do now?"

Sister Ursula falls to her knees. She presses the heels of her hands to her eyes and sobs, but only once. "I don't know."

You pathetic coward, the little voice inside her head sneers. *Purgatory would be too kind for what you have done. You have betrayed everyone.*

PART III

"Long is the way and hard, that out of Hell leads up to light."

—John Milton, *Paradise Lost*

17

URSULA

SHAME AND GUILT AND SELF-HATRED batter Sister Ursula, wave after sickening wave. She wishes the Lord would smite her, for how can He allow her to live after what she has done? She should have defended that skull with everything she had. Her death would have been that of a martyr then, worthy of admiration and respect. Instead, she will have to live a coward's life.

Whilst Sister Ursula wrestles with these personal demons, Elsebeth moves to the *Aufhocker*'s mother. She closes the woman's eyes, binds her jaw, folds her hands.

"Poor thing," she says. "At least the grave I dug for her husband and child is still fresh, meaning the earth will be loose. That'll make it much easier to dig it all up this time around. She's such a slight slip of a thing, I'm sure she'll fit right in. Mayhap the *Aufhocker* will be grateful for it, too. It'll be like sleeping between his parents then, all safe and snug."

Sister Ursula is still so mired in shame, she stays silent for fear she will begin to cry if she doesn't. Her eyes are sore with unshed tears. She can smell herself, this mixture of piss and fear sweat, and it revolts her.

"It's all right, Ursula," Elsebeth says softly. She comes to her and lays her hand on her shoulder to comfort her. Sister Ursula shrugs it away, not because she does not want it, but because she doesn't deserve it.

"You go dig that grave," she manages to say. "I'll take care of this mess."

Elsebeth hesitates, seems to chew on some words, but rather than spit them out, she swallows them down.

As soon as she is gone, Sister Ursula takes off her shift, cleans herself up, then puts on her dress. The fabric is rough and unpleasant against her bare skin, but she deserves that, too.

When she feels inside her dress pockets for her rosary, she finds the skull's map as well. It's useless now. Perhaps she should throw it away. Instead, she thrusts it back into her pocket. Let it serve as a reminder of her cowardice and failure.

With her shift, she mops up her puddle of urine. That done, she scrubs at the floorboards with a rough-bristled brush. There's no soap to be found—maybe the woman ate it, since soap is made out of animal fat and wood ash, and is thus kind of edible—so she uses a fistful of sand instead.

Coward, coward, coward. Selfish, selfish, selfish. You can try and erase this stain all you want, but Elsebeth has seen, and she'll remember, and so will you, and so will the Lord, who sees all, she thinks as she scrubs at the stain. Shame lies on her chest as heavy as a millstone.

Still, what else is there to do but try and clean what she has fouled?

When the floor is as clean as she can get it, she crushes some flowers against the wood in the hope that their bruised stems will release their strong, fresh scent and overpower the stink of her shame.

Next, she takes her filthy shift to the little stream that runs close to the house. The sun has risen by now, allowing her to see what she's doing as she kneels down on the bank and sets to cleaning her shift in the burbling water, which is bitterly cold, the sand scraping her skin painfully.

As she scrubs, beats, and wrings, she is reminded of that fairy story Elsebeth told her, about the woman who took a man's skin to the river and washed it so thoroughly that all the demons who possessed him were drowned in the water. Prayer and confession are what washes a soul clean, but it would certainly be nice sometimes if that process were as tangible as a bit of skin you could scrub and beat, then hold up to the light to see if you'd done a good job. If sin, shame, and all the other things she'd rather be rid of would stain her skin like wine, then this stream would run red if she were to plunge her skin into it, like Moses turning the river Nile to blood, and…

Elsebeth interrupts her train of thought as she crouches down next to her. Her hands are filthy from all her digging.

Sister Ursula throws her shift over the branch of a nearby tree, then sets to unwind the bandages wrapped around Elsebeth's hands, wincing in sympathy as she reveals the raw, blistered skin underneath. "Oh, you poor thing," she says.

Elsebeth puts her hands into the streaming water, hisses at the cold. She doesn't look at Sister Ursula, who is grateful for this; it's easier to bear all these feelings when she doesn't have to see the disappointment in her beloved's face. Instead, they look at the water as rays of the rising sun turn it these beautiful shades of blue and purple, almost like wine. There is something quite lovely, quite peaceful, about just sitting here, listening to the water as it runs over the stones and the sand.

When Sister Ursula finally finds her voice, it comes out thin and reedy; her throat is sore from trying to keep from crying. "What are we to do now that we have lost the skull?"

Elsebeth thinks for a while, then says, "I don't know. Mayhap you should go back to your convent, and I should go to my aunt, the way we meant to, before we found each other."

Of course she wants to leave you now that she has seen what a coward you are.

Sister Ursula tilts her head back, as if the tears burning in her eyes will roll back into her skull and she can keep from shedding them that way. "Is that what you want?" she asks, trying to keep her voice light.

"No, but what else is there to do?"

"You could come with me to my convent. We always need farmers to work the convent's lands. I am sure one of the families might take you in. Or you might help us in other ways. You might work in our gardens, or do laundry, or any number of tasks." She realizes she is pleading, but what does it matter? Pride is a sin, and even if it wasn't, she'd gladly grovel to keep Elsebeth with her.

But Elsebeth, always pragmatic, asks, "What nunnery would let a Calvinist like me stay with them? And I won't convert, Ursula, not even for you. That would be a lie, and that I cannot abide."

"I would never ask that of you. I just want... Without you, I can't..." She makes a soft choking sound, feels for her rosary, presses the beads hard against her fingertips to ground herself. She takes a deep breath and says in a voice a little less tear choked, a little more reasonable, "There is still time to think about it; we will be traveling together for some days more even if you decide to go to your aunt. And you can stay at the convent for a while, too, if you wish, before you decide. Unless, of course, you can't bear the sight of me anymore."

Elsebeth looks at her, a frown thick between her brows as if carved there with a knife. "Why would I not be able to bear the sight of you? Because you wet yourself? Those things happen. You aren't the first, and you won't be the last."

"No, not because of that." She takes another deep breath, feels it hitch in her chest as it gets caught on all those feelings tangled there. "I gave him that skull, Elsebeth!" she bursts out. "I didn't resist; I just gave it to him. I should've fought, I should've done something, anything but bend so easily to his will, and now all is lost, and I..."

Elsebeth picks at one of her blisters. "Methinks it was a clever thing that you did, not a cowardly one. You may call my big mouth bravery all you want, but if I'd had my way, we would have gotten killed and much worse besides, and for what? That necromancer would still have gotten the skull then. Sometimes, fear is a good thing. It keeps you alive."

Sister Ursula shakes her head wildly. "No, no! We *need* that skull, Elsebeth! How else will you wish for your family back? How else will I end poor dead Sister Hildegard's suffering in purgatory and finally rid myself of all this guilt and shame? How will I ensure my living sisters will be well?" Her tears fall into the water, which streams too fast for the surface to be much disturbed by it.

"Ursula—" Elsebeth begins, but Sister Ursula won't let her go on.

"A poor Ursula I am! When the Huns besieged Cologne, a prince fell in love with sweet Saint Ursula. This Hun promised her she would be spared if only she'd marry him, but rather than submit to such heathen lust, she defied him and was martyred. She was less than half my age. But what do I do when things get frightening? I freeze, and I buckle, and I piss myself like an infant!" She thrusts her hands into the wet sand and balls them into fists; the feel of the grains scraping against her skin helps to ground her a little.

"And what did Saint Ursula get for her trouble? Her head got cut off, that's what."

"Actually, she was pierced through with an arrow. The manner of her death matters little, though. What matters is that she became a saint and thus an example for us all. I dishonor her name. No matter that it was Satan himself who came to call on us; I should have stood up to him *precisely* because he was the devil. There are stories all over of common peasants who trick him, who outsmart him, who stand up to him, but I, a bride of Christ—"

Elsebeth says, "That wasn't Satan, Ursula, but a necromancer aided by a mercenary."

Sister Ursula turns to her in surprise. "A necromancer?"

"A sort of sorcerer who raises the dead."

"I know what a necromancer is, Elsebeth, but why do you believe that creature who took the skull from us is one? Surely Satan can make the dead rise and, in that way, mock the miracle of resurrection?"

"So can some witches and sorcerers, or else the Bible wouldn't tell us that talking to the dead is displeasing to the Lord," Elsebeth says. She hugs her knees to her chest and rests her chin on top of her knees. Her short hair, pale, fine, and thin as silk, whereas Sister Ursula's is dark, thick, and coarse, falls forward and obscures her face.

"But how are you so certain it was a simple witch we saw, and not the devil himself?" Sister Ursula presses.

"The skull told me he was a necromancer and not Satan in my dreams," she whispers.

"The saint came to you in your dreams?" Hope and wonder shift the stone of shame on Sister Ursula's chest, making her feel much lighter. She shakes her hands into the water to wash away the sand, then wipes them on her dress and takes hold of Elsebeth's left hand, carefully avoiding the broken skin of her palms. A hundred questions crowd inside her mind, words inside her mouth. "What did she look like? What did she say or show you? Oh, but this is a miracle!"

But why did she not come to me? she thinks but drowns that question immediately; Elsebeth, so lost within her Protestant dogma and all the horror she has suffered, is in much bigger need of a miracle than she herself is.

"The first time, she was just a skull bobbing around like an apple in a barrel," Elsebeth says, her voice soft and hesitant. "She told me the necromancer and a mercenary whom he bewitched were looking for her, and that I should wake up, for you were in grave danger. That was the night you had wandered out and the *Nachzehrer* had gotten you."

"And the second time?"

With her free hand, Elsebeth brushes the hair from her face. Her color is up, though that might just be the cold. "Some days after we left that *Nachzehrer* town. She was mean to me then, calling me all sorts of names, saying we had to hurry lest the necromancer catch up to us." She smiles wryly. "I suppose she was right to be so rude after all."

"Why did you not tell me?" Sister Ursula asks, doing her best to keep any hurt from bleeding into the words.

"I thought that they might just be strange stories my mind spun as I slept. You know I don't believe in saints, and dreams can be so mighty strange that only a fool would think they mean anything. Then, I thought that, if the skull really crept into my dreams and sent me signs from God, she'd do so thrice, for three is the number of the Lord. Until then, I thought it better not to tell you. I did not want to worry you. Not that it matters anymore, now that the necromancer and Otto have stolen her from us."

"You speak of him as if you know him." She remembers the stricken look on that soldier's rotting face and adds, "And he seemed to know you."

Elsebeth is quiet for a long time. When she speaks, she won't look at Sister Ursula, only at the water flowing so beautifully, a little miracle that doesn't stop being miraculous just because it is so ordinary. "I'm loath to tell you, for you will look at me with different eyes once I have."

Sister Ursula shakes her head wildly. "I won't, I won't! How could I ever think anything but well of you?"

"You won't think well of me after I've told you this."

Sister Ursula says, "By God, I won't think poorly of you. I won't, I won't, I won't." She punctuates every sentence with a kiss, one on Elsebeth's knuckles and two on the inside of her wrist, where the skin remains smooth no matter how hard the work. "There. I've sworn it three times by the Lord, and so by your own admission, it must be true. Now won't you tell me?"

"You are silly," she says. She sighs, then straightens her spine, her shoulders tensing. "Remember how I told you my sister made me run when the soldiers came, and I did? Well, once my panic had run its course, I went back for her."

Sister Ursula sits very still, even though that phantom ache has begun in her stomach again, that sense of a spreading something, not quite pain but not quite pleasant, either. Whatever Elsebeth tells her now, she mustn't interrupt, or the girl will gather all those memories back to herself and keep them inside, where they will forever fester.

"I couldn't find her at first, and I thought that mayhap those soldiers had taken her back with them. They sometimes do that if they take a liking to a girl, or if they think her family has money. They won't give her back then until you've paid whatever they ask of you, and the longer it takes, the worse they treat her. But they hadn't taken her. When I found her…I… She…" Elsebeth stammers.

"You don't have to describe it to me if it hurts too much," Sister Ursula says.

Elsebeth briefly closes her eyes. "It was the worst thing I have ever seen, Ursula. I don't think I can put it into words, not even if it didn't pain me, and that it does, horribly so. So bad it was, it struck me mad for a while, and thank God for that. It was a great kindness, that madness of mine. Had I not lost my wits, I think I may have… God forgive me, but I think I may have done myself an injury.

"I ran mad," Elsebeth continues, "and in my madness, I fell in with the baggage train of the imperial army. I had nowhere else to go. Everyone else in my village was dead or had fled. A soldier took a liking to me. His name was Gottfried. He was a mercenary, just like that man Otto. The two of them were friends. That's how he recognized me: I often spent time with his wife, helping her bake bread. She was a baker's daughter before she wedded, and Otto was a miller's son once, before he turned his hand to war making.

"But it's not Otto who matters here, but Gottfried. He brought me trinkets and fed me bits of bread dipped in milk and slices of apple he cut for me himself, and in that way won my trust. Soon, he began to use me in the way a man should only ever use his wife. And God forgive me, for all that I hated him for it, my body would at times draw pleasure from the things he did to me, no matter that I did not want it to…"

Elsebeth buries her face against her knees in shame and sobs.

Sister Ursula sits stunned for a moment, not knowing what to do. Then, she hugs Elsebeth from behind. The way she's sitting, she's all taut muscle and hard bone, and it's uncomfortable, but then so many things in life are; why should this be pleasant?

"I often begged him not to," Elsebeth says, the words muffled, "for it was not right or proper for him to use me so, but he just slapped me and said that I shouldn't whine, for did he not feed me? Did he not keep me warm? Did he not protect me from the other soldiers? It was more than many a farm girl could say. Besides, he said, none of this was his fault. It was war, and war makes beasts out of men."

She raises her head, wipes at her cheeks with the hem of her dress, sniffs. Her gray eyes are sharp as flint underneath the tears, her mouth an angry slash. "Mayhap it's true that men can't help acting like beasts. My grandmother told me some fairy stories in which men are turned into beasts, and beasts they must remain until a woman comes along to tame them and turn them into men again. But life is no story, else it would make more sense than it does, and even if it were, I didn't want to tame Gottfried, for even if he were a prince, I could never forget how he had used me."

Wordlessly, Sister Ursula hands Elsebeth her handkerchief. She wipes her nose with it, sniffs again. "I may be a silly farm girl who knows very little on account of not being able to read and write, but I am not entirely stupid. I know some things are right and some things are wrong, and what he did to me was wrong. As soon as there was a break in the winter's cold, I ran from him. From then on, I lived on the road, too scared to trust anyone. Until I found you."

"And I am gladder than I can possibly say that you did," Sister Ursula says.

Elsebeth roughly rubs her eyes, then goes on as if she hasn't heard. "That's why I was so cruel to you after you kissed me. It was not your fault, but when you and I kissed, and you let your hands travel up and down my body, I felt that same lustful pull in the pit of my belly that I had felt at times when he was rutting with me, and I was so ashamed I hoped God would strike me down. Sometimes… sometimes, I wish I were dead already, that my suffering may cease."

"Elsebeth—" Sister Ursula begins.

"I would never kill myself. You don't have to be afraid of that. A man in my village hanged himself. He was always melancholy, I know not why. They wouldn't let his family bury his body, but they threw it on the trash heap to rot out in the open as a warning to all, because suicide is displeasing to the Lord." She smiles, and it is both sad and a little mad. "Though I suppose it doesn't matter anymore now, does it? All those people dying left and right, and no one to bury them properly. But fret not, Ursula. I know you and I don't believe the same things, but I believe in Satan, and I believe he has a claim to my soul. I have no desire to meet him any sooner than I have to."

"I don't believe Satan has a claim to your soul," Sister Ursula says, "and if he does, well, then he shall have my soul, too."

Elsebeth's hand forms a trembling fist around Sister Ursula's handkerchief. "Don't mock me. You don't believe that."

"I believe that if you are damned, then so am I, because I have sinned more than you. You see, when I told you about Sister

Hildegard, I wasn't entirely honest. I let you believe I left her at the side of the road, but that's not true. I didn't even think of that. All I thought was that we had to hide, but for that to work, we couldn't make any noise, only Sister Hildegard kept screaming, so I…I placed my hands…" She has to take a shuddering breath to steady herself. "I placed my hands over her mouth. She struggled mightily at first but then grew slack. I thought her strength had merely spent itself, but when those men had finally passed us by and I looked at her, I saw she was dead."

"That doesn't count. You didn't mean for that to happen."

"Neither did you mean for Gottfried to use you, and yet it happened, didn't it? If you are damned, then so am I."

"That's no consolation to me," Elsebeth hisses.

Sister Ursula takes the handkerchief from her, dips it into the stream, then raises it to Elsebeth's face to wipe her cheeks and eyes and brow, only the girl flinches away from her. "You aren't damned, Elsebeth," Sister Ursula says calmly. "Being raped is not a sin."

"But it was! It was," Elsebeth cries out, "because sometimes, I enjoyed it!"

"You didn't. You said you hated Gottfried for what he did to you. Your body may be a traitor, but your soul is pure."

Elsebeth shakes her head wildly, her hair slapping her cheeks. "No, no! I am damned, Ursula, damned, damned, damned!" She pounds her fists against her forehead.

Sister Ursula draws her onto her lap.

At first, Elsebeth fights her, screaming and kicking, but Sister Ursula won't let go of her. She holds the girl, rocks her from side to side, drops kisses on her tear-smeared face. She tries to think of something to say, but once again, words fail her. Perhaps it's for the best. What words could possibly soothe Elsebeth's troubled soul? She has often found that, for her, the Bible can be a balm, but it is as Elsebeth just said: Her way of worship is not Elsebeth's, and as such holds no comfort for the girl.

As Sister Ursula holds her tight, she catches her nightdress fluttering in the breeze from the corner of her eye, all clean now, like that merchant's son in Elsebeth's fairy story once the woman had washed his skin. It's an old motif. In the Bible, there is plenty of washing, both in the symbolic and the literal sense: Christ washes the feet of His disciples, and before that, Mary Magdalene washes Christ's feet, dries them with her hair, then anoints them with perfume, showing love, devotion, and humility.

An idea comes to her then, so simple that it might just work.

She is no fairy-tale maid, and no Mary Magdalene, either, just a coward, but if her life as a nun and now this strange quest with the saint's skull has taught her one thing, it is that divinity may be found in the humblest and unlikeliest of places.

She bends over Elsebeth's softly sobbing form and whispers, "Come to your feet, *mein Liebchen*, for I know how to make you well again, and free of sin."

18

ELSEBETH

URSULA DRAWS ME UP AND makes me look into her eyes. They are brown, like many good things are: rich earth, and bread, and the rabbits I often spy when the sun sets, playing in the fields like children do, fast, fierce, and full of joy.

"Do you trust me, *mein Liebchen*?" she asks.

How could I not when she calls me her little darling?

I nod; I can't speak yet, for a pain has risen from my heart and locked my throat as tightly as my father's chest of tools.

She touches my cheek, and it's so tender that I feel like I might cry again, likely would, had I not spent all my tears just now. They have made my head pound, and my eyes and throat ache, though I feel a little lighter for having shed them.

Ursula undoes the buttons of my dress, and my breath comes quick and fast, and doesn't seem to travel far into my chest at all. I stand very still. One by one the buttons yield to her touch. She takes her time, and I know not if she does that because she enjoys this, or she fears I shall buck and shy in the way a horse does when it has been ill-used, as I have been by Gottfried.

The dress is too big on me now, but starvation can't alter the shape of our bones, and I am broad hipped, so she still has to tug on the fabric to get it to come down.

She places her hands—so hot, so beautiful, so soft—on my shoulders, the fingers questing underneath the straps of my shift and touching my skin, and it's so sweet I shiver. There's that pull low in my hips again, which I have only ever felt with that soldier before and then not always, and I wonder, is this the devil tugging at me, gathering me to him, impatient for a soul he knows he's owed?

I moan, this sad, frightened sound.

Ursula freezes, but only for a moment. I swear she can read my thoughts again as if they're pictures painted on my forehead, for she cups my cheek and says softly, "If something is done to make you well again, it's not a sin."

And I want to believe that, I really do, but I don't know if I can.

She must sense this doubt in me, for she says quickly, "Trust me, *mein Liebchen*. Trust me, and let me make you well."

Why not trust her? She is sweet and knows many things that I do not, bookish things, not like the farm things I know, like how to pluck a chicken, how to know if there's rot upon a plant, and how much vinegar to add to a jar to pickle the Lord's bounty so we may last the winter.

And have I not trusted her so far already? I trusted her enough to come with her, no matter that this journey seemed a foolish papist quest to me from the start. To doubt her now when I know her much better, well, that strikes me as silly.

"I trust you," I say.

She smiles, and it's like a bank of clouds breaking so that golden sunlight can fall on the earth, and I think to myself that life may not be so bad after all if I had her to smile at me like that every day.

My shift follows the way of my dress. Ursula holds my hand to steady me as I step out of the pool of fabric at my feet. My legs are like reeds, all hollow. I stumble. She steadies me, and we are flush against each other now. I think again of rabbits. I caught one once and felt its little heart pound like a war drum in a chest so small, I could have crushed it with my hand. My heart races as quickly as that rabbit's heart, and I feel just as vulnerable.

Ursula takes a shuddering breath, then steps away. Whilst I fold my clothes neatly, Ursula unbuttons her own dress, but when the time comes to take it off, she falters.

"What is it?" I ask.

"At the convent, we always keep our shifts on, even when we wash. For chastity, you see. There's a trick to soaping up your body whilst still clothed. It has been such a long time since I've seen my own body naked..."

That only proves to me that nunneries are queer places indeed. I have often seen my grandmother, my mother, and my big sister, Margarethe, naked, and my little brothers, Friedrich and Johannes, as well. My father, too, when I was still a child.

"Are you afraid?" I ask.

"I don't know that I am."

"You said there's no sin in it if it is done to make me well," I say.

She laughs. "I can't argue myself out of that one. How right you are."

I am broad hipped and strong, a farm girl through and through. If these times weren't so lean, I'd likely go to fat, and gladly so. Ursula is shaped differently, tall and thin, though not strong. It's a marvel to me that they say God has shaped us in His own image, yet our bodies differ so; if He exists, mayhap God has more than one shape?

When we are done drinking the other in, she takes my hand and leads me into the water of the river. I hiss, it's so cold, but I don't resist, for I trust her even if I don't know quite what she means to do with me.

She kneels, and I want to tell her not to do that; she might cut her knees on the sharp stones hiding in the riverbed, and her knee must still be tender from when she bruised it when that soldier attacked her, but again there is a moment in which my thoughts seem to leap out of my head and into hers, for she looks up at me and smiles sweetly and says, "Don't fret, *mein Liebchen*. I am used to kneeling, and the riverbed is quite soft. Feel for yourself."

I kneel down also and groan as the water streams over my thighs, my rear, my cunny. It's really awfully cold.

In the moments that follow, Ursula washes me with handfuls of water and sand. She doesn't rush, even though it's cold. She even scrubs carefully between my toes. When she has arrived at my face, she draws me to her, eases me onto her lap so that my head rests in the crook of her elbow, as if I am her babe.

She looks at me with those big brown eyes of hers, cow eyes really, just as beautifully fringed and mournful. This unearths a memory, something I had forgotten until now, of our cow, whom Margarethe had called Kamille, and how I used to stroke her warm hide as she stood cropping the grass with her blunt teeth. My father said she had no soul, but my grandmother told me sometimes cows could speak, and if I was kind to her, and kept her fed and clean, perhaps Kamille might one day tell me one of her cow secrets. When this war is over and I can live somewhere without the fear of soldiers—*but with Ursula*—I hope to have another cow like Kamille.

Ursula touches my eyebrows, my nose, even traces the whorls of my ears with her wet fingers, burying the memory of Kamille. I wonder briefly if she's anointing me or means to baptize me into her faith, but no, she'd not shame my trust like that.

She gently lowers me into the water. It rushes into my ears and nose. When she pulls me out, I gasp and splutter. She smooths my wet hair out of my face, tucks it behind my ears. I want to tell her then that it used to be very long and thick, and Gottfried used to marvel at it, wind his hands into it, and tug on it, and so I cut it all off when I fled from him, for he had soiled it with all that grasping, but I say nothing.

Sometimes, to speak is to sully.

I am scrubbed clean now. We get out of the river. With my shift, we dry ourselves. I make to put my dress on, but Ursula shakes her head at me. "I'm not done yet," she says. She goes to the tree where her shift is drying and breaks off some twigs, and I know then what she means to do.

My throat locks again. It's so like her, so sweet and innocent, to think that a bit of scrubbing and a beating can cure me of what I did and was done to me. It does not work like that.

But I promised to trust her, and to go back on a promise is a kind of lying, so I let her lead me to the tree, and I wrap my arms around its trunk.

I shiver. It's not from the cold this time; I know that much.

The first touch of the twigs against my skin makes me flinch, though only because it startles me. Ursula beats me all over, doing it very gently, not enough to hurt but just hard enough to redden my skin and get the blood to flow.

It vexes me, this gentleness. She keeps treating me with a kindness I know in my heart of hearts I do not deserve, no matter that I crave it.

I look at her over my shoulder. "Harder," say I.

"I don't want to break the skin and draw blood. I don't—"

"Harder," I command, for wickedness cannot be driven out by a soft hand.

The next slap of the twigs lands on my rear with a meaty thwack. It stings my skin, makes it burn. I can't help but gasp.

Such strength!

Such fervor!

Such viciousness!

I never thought her capable of it, and it is both startling and delightful. I close my eyes. "Yes," I say, and I laugh a little, "like that."

Soon, the blows are falling down on me like rain upon the land.

Ursula seemed so sweet and frail to me. I never expected such passion from her.

As Ursula beats me, I flinch, writhe, and shy away; I cry out, laugh, and moan. For a moment, I act like my mother when she was overcome with love of the Lord and fell to the ground grimacing and gibbering, only it's not a godly love that I feel. This beating does what no amount of hard work or prayer ever did before: It turns my mind upside down and lets everything pour out, all thoughts of sin and shame, and all memories of Gottfried and my poor sister, Margarethe, and many other foul things besides.

Out, out, out they tumble.

And then
my mind is empty
I need not
think
and it is
sweet
it is
bliss
it is
heaven
heaven
heaven...

When Ursula finally stops, I slide to the ground, feeling spent and empty, but pleasingly so. I rest my cheek against the smooth bark of the tree and try to catch my breath.

Ursula kneels next to me. She is flushed and heaving, the twigs broken and bloodied in her hands. Her eyes glitter something fierce.

"There," she says. Then, she shudders and drops the twigs to the ground, wipes her hands on the grass. I take them and bring them to my mouth. I suck on her fingers one by one. They taste of metal and of salt, and faintly bitter. When they are all clean, I rub my cheeks against them like our cat used to do.

"Thank you," I whisper.

She swallows. Something clicks in her throat. "Whatever sin you think clung to you, whatever has you feeling so ashamed, sad, and angry, I have scrubbed it away and beaten it out of you now."

My mind rights itself, and my thoughts come running back, eager to climb back into my skull. "Oh, Ursula, that's not how it works. Certain kinds of suffering stain forever, and—"

Ursula grabs my upper arms, then digs her nails into them with such force, I gasp then hush. She brings her face close to mine and hisses, "You once told me you had your belly full of God and that you didn't want my papist prattle. Well, I have my belly full of your ungodly prattle now, and I shall have none of it anymore. Mark me, and mark me well. Whatever sin that soldier may have committed as he used you, it is his to bear now, and his alone. You are free of it, and of all other horrible things you may have done to survive. I have cleansed and claimed your soul for God, whether you believe in Him or not."

This strict Ursula stirs something inside of me. There's this pull in my belly, this tug, as if she has wound string around me and is gathering it up. I look her boldly in the eye. "What about my body?"

"What about it?" she breathes. There's less than a handspan between us; if I were to lean forward a little, I could kiss her.

Which I want to, very much so.

I do.

I do.

I do.

Say I, "Gottfried claimed that for his own when he used me."

She swallows; again, her throat clicks. "We can't have that, now can we?" she says. She lets go of my arm. The skin burns as if branded. She takes my hand instead, brings it to her mouth. Our gazes are snagged on each other as she kisses the palm of my hand. It's a chaste kiss at first, cool and dry. She keeps kissing that same spot, and soon, her mouth grows warm and wet, and I feel, softly, the press of her teeth as her lips part.

The beating she gave me was unexpectedly hard, savage almost. To have her kiss me now with such calm and such tenderness breaks something inside of me.

When she lets go of my hand, I touch it with the other, rub the spot she kissed and sucked, as if I can spread the feeling of it.

"That bit of skin is mine now," she says.

"Is that all you want of me?" I ask.

She doesn't smile. Her eyes burn hot. "No," she says.

In the hours that follow, she claims every last bit of me.

19

URSULA

OH, SISTER URSULA THINKS, *ELSEBETH was right: The saint's skull really does bob around like an apple in a barrel.*

She's back in her convent, at the altar where she and her sisters worship. When the Protestant troops sacked their convent, they took the golden candlesticks, ripped and soiled the embroidered altar cloth, and toppled the statues of saints from their sockets and smashed them up with hammers. As for Christ on the cross: the less said about what they did to Him, the better.

But here, the wooden image of her Heavenly Husband still hangs on the wall, the saints stand tall and unbroken, the altar cloth lies clean and uncreased, and the candles burn.

A dream then, this.

The skull is floating a little above Sister Ursula, looking down on her with its glass eyes. It has a halo, though the light isn't that warm honey-like light that so many artists try to reproduce by using gold leaf. It is cool instead, and it pulses brightly one moment, then very softly the next, as if they are underwater.

"Ursula," the saint says, and though Sister Ursula sees the jaws move, the voice doesn't spill from between the pearly teeth, slightly blue in their opacity. She hears it in her head instead. "Be not afraid, thou bride of Christ. I come to thee in this dream with a task for thee."

I am experiencing a miracle, Sister Ursula thinks.

One of the most beautiful things Sister Ursula has ever felt is the profound and unending love of God for her and all of His creations. It is no easy thing to put that experience into words, but if pressed, she'd describe it as submersing herself into a hot bath and floating in the warm water, feeling as safe and loved as a babe in its mother's belly, for His love is both a feeling and a place.

Yet the feeling that smites her now, that cleaves into her breast and makes her gasp, is no gentle bath. It is sudden and violent, a riptide pulling her under.

When it is done battering her and spits her out again, she realizes that she has fallen to her knees, that her hands are clasped in prayer. The saint's skull is moving from side to side in front of her face, no longer gently bobbing like something waterlogged, but fast and sharp, like a bee moved to anger, like a hand waving impatiently to draw attention.

"Finally," it says once Sister Ursula blinks and sits up straight, "thou hast returned to me. I feared thou wouldst wake first, or that thou might tumble into a different dream and I would have to chase after thee like a hound after a rabbit."

When Sister Ursula hears her own voice inside her head, it has only one volume at which it can speak to her; the saint's voice, though, is very loud and not quite pleasant.

Sister Ursula doesn't know whether to cry or to laugh. "Forgive me, sweet saint, I beg of you. I meant no offense. If it pleases you, tell me how I may serve you, and I shall serve you till the last bit of air has left my lungs, my heart has contracted for the last time, and the last drop of blood in my veins cools and congeals."

The skull tilts to the side in the manner of one cocking their head, then chuckles. It is a strange, dark sound. "How prettily thou speakest! Silver-tongued thou art. No wonder that peasant wench followed thee, even though she believes not in saints."

Sister Ursula flushes with such force, her cheeks and throat feel scalded. That feeling of absolute awe that battered her has left her feeling raw.

"Very well," the skull goes on, "I shall tell thee how thou may serve me. Through thy fault, I have fallen into the hands of a sorcerer of Satan. This witchy wretch means to use me to grow his dark powers, which he shall then use to spread sin and misery wherever he goeth."

Sister Ursula bows her head in shame. She feels sick and full of hate for herself. No amount of confessing and repenting—*or washing and beating*—shall wash her clean of this sin.

Mea culpa, mea culpa, mea maxima culpa—

"Dost thou heed me?" the skull shrieks.

Sister Ursula snaps her head back up. "Yes. Forgive me, sweet and merciful one. I am a weak woman, a coward, a—"

"Did I ask thee to list all thy many faults, woman? This is no time to tarry. Pah!" the skull interrupts, and Sister Ursula has the strange feeling that it would spit like Elsebeth sometimes does, if only it still could. Saints are strange and unknowable.

Sister Ursula opens her mouth to apologize once more but manages to swallow those words. Instead, she asks, "How may I make amends for my sins against you?"

"Thou must steal me back from the sorcerer and return me to my body," the saint says lightly, as if this is a small matter, simple to complete.

Sister Ursula feels her stomach sink. "Steal you back? But I am only a silly woman, ignorant and afraid, whilst that sorcerer has all the dark arts of Satan at his disposal, and—"

"And thou the power of the Lord, so what fearest thou? Or dost thou mayhap think that the Almighty is not, in fact almighty, and no match for the serpent dwelling in Hell?"

"No, of course not, that would be heresy, but I don't know how Elsebeth and I can—"

The skull swoops close to Sister Ursula, who prostrates herself on the ground. "Dost thou dare question the way and will of the Lord?" the skull hisses.

"No," Sister Ursula whimpers, her eyes trained on the cool flagstones, "I just don't understand why He chose me when there are much worthier vessels for a quest as holy as this."

"Spare me thy modesty. I find it tiresome. Better to rejoice that thou hast been chosen, no? 'Tis a prayer answered, methinks, or didst thou never dream of carrying out grand deeds that will make thee a little more worthy of being the wife of Christ? Bask in that feeling, and question not, but let the Lord move through thee."

"Yes," Sister Ursula whispers. She can repress all questions and critical thoughts; she has been taught to do so ever since she entered the convent, because such perfect obedience is what God demands of them. She sits up straight, clears her throat, and says, "I shall make you proud, saint... What may I call you?"

The skull thinks for a moment. It is disconcerting to look at a face that always grins and never blinks. "Names matter not to the Lord, who knows all His children."

"But I am not the Lord and would like to know what saint I have the pleasure of serving," Sister Ursula says gently.

"Very well," the skull grumbles, "If thou must call me something, then let it be by the name of Columba."

Sister Ursula frowns. There is only one Saint Columba she knows of, a martyr whose patronage focuses mainly on witches and wizards. The skull can't be her, though; both the French and Spanish claimed to have her holy body, but the French one was destroyed by Huguenots some decades ago, and the Spanish one lies in a church many miles from here. There are, of course, many saints, too many to know them all, but how odd that there is another Saint Columba only a few days' travel from her convent, yet she hasn't heard of her. As a rule, churches aren't secretive about their reliquaries, because they draw pilgrims and, in that way, money.

"Thou art doing it again!" the skull shrieks. "Questioning, questioning, questioning! They should have called thee Thomas for how much doubt thou holdst in thine heart!"

Sister Ursula makes to apologize, but she doesn't get the chance. The burning candles extinguish, the Christ on the cross warps, the altar cloth turns into a smear of color.

The dream dissolves.

She wakes.

20

OTTO

DON'T THINK, OTTO TELLS HIMSELF as he follows in his necromancer's wake, *don't think, not even a single thought, no, don't think at all.*

But though he tries to focus on the wet grass flicking against his legs, the cold little smells of the stream burbling close to them, and the necromancer's giggles, he can't get the image of Elsebeth out of his head. Her face all pale from fear, her hand shaking as she held the knife, her mouth set so grimly…

Some pictures sear themselves into the brain and won't be scrubbed away, but it's strange that this should be one of them. Otto didn't hurt the girl, after all, only had to threaten a bit of violence before the nun gave him the skull.

But still his mind fixes itself upon Elsebeth's face. Is it only the shock of finding someone he knows? Though 'knows' is too big a word. Unlike Frieda, who spent hours with the girl as they did laundry, baked bread, and performed other household chores,

Otto had never had much to do with her. Why would he? She was just Gottfried's little whore.

No, not whore, Otto reprimands himself. *His little toy more like, to do with as he pleased whenever he pleased, and what she wanted and felt didn't matter, because she was just a thing to him, as I am to my necromancer.*

They have stopped walking by now. The necromancer sits down, heedless of the wet ground, and takes the skull out of her box. In the pale light of the moon, the bone seems almost to glow. A slight breeze keeps ruffling the hair, as if an unseen hand is picking up a lock before dropping it again.

Otto imagines slapping the skull out of the necromancer's spidery hands, imagines it tumbling to the ground and breaking into clean white shards held together only by the fine silk wrapped around it. He imagines grabbing a fistful of that hair, lifting the sordid thing into the air, and then throwing it into the stream so the water may carry it far away from here. Water can cleanse. Water can destroy. Though maybe it's better to set the whole thing on fire first, then trample the blackened fragments of bone until nothing but ash remains.

Otto does not lunge at the skull, though his hands itch. Instead, he turns to the necromancer, who sits gloating at it. "Will you release me now?" he asks.

The necromancer doesn't tear his enraptured gaze away from the skull. The skin of his hands is so sallow, the color is barely distinguishable from the pale bone. "No," he says.

Otto represses the urge to throw his hands into the air. The more he moves, the bigger the chance he will damage his joints and limbs beyond repair. Already his body pains him, though not as much as it should. "Why not? You have your skull now, don't you?"

The necromancer chuckles. "My dear Otto, do you believe I brought you along only to obtain this skull? Think a little harder, please."

"Then why?" Otto asks, despair roughening his voice. "Why did you bring me if not to help you? Am I just a thing to you, something to play with? Or are you my own personal demon, come to show me all I have done wrong in my life? For I have done many wrong things. I know that now. You've shown me."

"Such as?" the necromancer asks, looking up from the skull. The two of them have matching grins.

Otto swallows thickly, looks at the ground. He feels like a schoolboy being chastened. Normally, that would enrage him, but he feels too tired for anything as hot and potent as fear now. "I shouldn't have tortured that farmhand before I threw him down the well. I shouldn't have smacked that farmer's daughter in the face and broken her teeth, no matter how she wept and moaned and groaned. I should have tried to keep her safe from my fellow soldiers."

"Go on."

"What are you, a priest? Must I confess all my sins to you?"

"Why not?" the necromancer says, and he isn't smiling now. "Why don't you tell me everything you have done that you knew to be wrong but did anyway?"

Little flickers of fear make the blood in Otto's hands and feet run cold. His mouth opens of its own accord, and the words spill out like vomit. He is powerless to stop them. "I shouldn't have stood by and done nothing when my fellow soldiers raped that servant girl in Magdeburg," he says and marvels that this is the first thing that comes to mind, for it's been almost four years now since that city fell to the imperial troops and almost everyone inside was slaughtered.

"I shouldn't have laughed at her as she cried. When we found her master cowering in his study, I shouldn't have tied him to his chair and burned his feet till they were all black and cracked to get him to tell us where he kept his money. I shouldn't have cut off his fingers to get his rings. When the others went deeper into the house, into the nursery, where the baby lay, I shouldn't have let them grab it and dash it against the wall until the brains ran down the wood. I shouldn't have..."

It turns out there are a lot of things Otto shouldn't have done.

21

ELSEBETH

WHEN I WAKE SOMETIME IN the afternoon, the sun hot on my skin, for we never made it back to the shack after we made love in the sweet long grass, I feel sore all over. It's not to be wondered at, bruised and bloodied as I am, but it's not unpleasant. Though some sand sticks to my skin, I am slick with drying sweat, and my cunny is all wet, I feel quite clean. I feel light also, as light as a dandelion seed that the wind blows this way and that.

I study Ursula. She's still asleep, her dress pulled over her like a blanket. I look at her pretty long fingers, which brought me to such bliss only a short while ago. I remember how they felt inside of me, her hand twisting sweetly just underneath my womb, and I flush and smile. My eyes travel up that pretty white hand of hers to the slender wrist, the swell of her arm, the way it curves into her shoulder, and I feel love, tenderness, and many other things surge inside of me.

Mayhap it's unholy, this love for her that has taken root inside my breast, but I am weak and can't rip it out. I fear it has grown too strong for that anyway, and to pull it out now would wound me terribly.

Not that I want to rip it out. I want to nurse it like a bit of coal so it can keep me warm. For so long, I have survived on small sips of beauty, but now that I've drunk deeply of it, I'd rather die than go without.

Mayhap it's not so bad to be damned if I get to be with Ursula, I think.

Before I met her, that thought would have terrified me and filled my head with fear, doubt, and guilt. Now, it still frightens me, but only a little. I sit with that feeling for a moment, then push it out of my head; I want to be filled with thoughts of other things now.

I wriggle underneath Ursula's dress until I'm between her legs. The fabric is thin and lets the sunlight through, and so I can see very well. I stroke her thighs, so white and warm, the hair that covers them like dark down. She shifts, and for a moment, I think she comes awake, but she only sighs and grows still again.

With my fingertips, I follow the green veins that marble her flesh and through which the blood, sleep sluggish, streams gently. A few hours ago, it pounded as wildly as a storm-fretted sea. Remembering that, my own blood sets to running, and lust makes my belly ache.

No, I think, *not lust. Ursula told me it's only love, and love is no sin.* I rub my cheek against the inside of her thigh, inhale her scent, and I am content, happy, and many more things besides.

When I have mapped her thighs well enough in my mind

that I can think of them whenever the world grows ugly and cruel again, and I can be comforted by their beauty, I move my eyes and fingers higher. The hair on her mound is much darker and coarser, and beautifully curled, almost like a sheep's pelt. In places, it's long enough to braid. How beautiful she would look with pink ribbons tied in neat bows! I wind a curl around my finger and delight in the feel of it. Again she sighs and shifts, but this time, she wakes. I can feel it in the way the muscles in her thighs tighten a little, and in the way her breathing changes.

When I am done running my hands through her hair, I gently nudge Ursula's legs aside. Between the fur lie beautiful folds of flesh, all snug like a rosebud.

"Indeed, you are like a rose," I whisper, "for like a rose, you are pink and fragrant, and when loved, you bloom." I touch her with the tip of my finger and find she is slick. My belly clenches and spit runs into my mouth as it does when I think of something delicious.

"Oh!" she sighs, and the sound is precious to me.

Gently, I part her folds. No rosebud after all; she is open and sweet for me.

I touch her with the tip of my tongue, and then I am lost. I lick, lap, and suck, and I moan and close my eyes as I do so, for she is delicious. She tastes like biscuits, like meat, like brine, like fish, all these wholesome things.

She begins to flow, and soon, so do I. I feel it on my thighs, sticky and cool. A corner of my dress has caught between my legs, and I moan and thrust so that the rough fabric rubs me just right.

As I pleasure her, she winds her hands in my hair to keep my mouth on her. She tries not to scratch, tries not to pull, for she is a sweet thing, all gentleness and compassion.

But I don't want her meek.

I want to ravish and raze her as she did me. It's not long before she goes wild, tugging on my hair. For a moment I freeze, for it brings back the memory of Gottfried, but I remind myself it's not his hands on me, and I grow calm again.

Ursula is gasping and moaning. The blood is marching through her veins now, fluttering as frantically as a moth caught behind a curtain. Her thighs clench around my head as she spends, and then I am spending also.

When we have both been battered by bliss and grown calm again once more, I wipe my mouth and chin with my hands and nestle next to her.

"*Mein Liebchen*, how sweet you are," Ursula says. Her color is up, and her eyes are dreamy.

We should get up, see if our shifts have dried, mayhap wash our dresses in the stream—at least those bits that have our spending on them—but it's heaven to lie here, and so we are full of sloth and do none of those things.

Until she suddenly sits up, her body all taut.

"What is it?" ask I.

"I just remembered my dream. Oh, Elsebeth!" She puts her hands to her mouth and laughs.

"That must've been quite the dream, to make you laugh so," say I.

"It was, oh it was!"

As we lie side by side, she tells me all of it. With every detail—the old-fashioned way in which the skull speaks, how ill-tempered she is, how she moves around as if she's underwater—I feel something come alive inside of my chest, this little flickering flame of hope that fills me with warmth, for how could Ursula and I dream her in the same manner when I barely told Ursula anything about her?

I cannot dwell on this miracle for too long, though, because what use is it to us when we have lost her? "It's all very nice that the saint commands you to come fetch her," I say to Ursula, "but how are we to do that?"

I expect her to slump a little and admit that she doesn't know. Instead, her eyes stray to the side, and I feel her mind pull away from me as she thinks. When she speaks, it's in a slow, almost dreamy voice. "When I gave Saint Columba's skull to that soldier, I didn't give him the map. I didn't think of it, and he didn't ask for it, but, well…"

"I don't think he needs it. He's a witch. He used dark arts to find us. No doubt he'll use his dark arts to find his way to the saint's body, too."

"No doubt," she agrees with me, "but what I meant to say is this: We may not have the skull anymore, but we know who does, and we know where they are going."

"So?" ask I.

"So we can intercept them."

"The necromancer will strike us dead, then defile our corpses by using them as puppets for all his evil deeds," I say, but I have sat up very straight, for her words are fanning the fight lust in me.

When I was firm in my belief in God, I used to feel like this, too: strong and eager.

She sits up as well and clasps my hands. "*If* he sees us, yes, but that he won't, not if we are quiet and sly. Think about it, *mein Liebchen*: A proud and evil man such as he is not used to being defied. He won't expect two weak women such as you and me to come after him to take back what he stole."

Ursula speaks sense. The blood races through my veins. I feel all restless. I pull one of my hands free from her clasp and use it to tear out bits of grass. There's something pleasing in feeling the blades resist being pulled in twain, in the way the roots cling to the soil, in the smell of rich earth being turned and sap being spilled. "He may not expect us, but that doesn't mean we can just take the skull and not expect him to find out, if not straightaway, then soon after," I say.

"If we swap Saint Columba's skull for a different skull, he won't. He might not even realize it's gone until he reaches the spot where her body is buried, and then it shall be too late, because we will have reunited her skull and body already and claimed our wish. Oh, *mein Liebchen*!" Her face is all flushed and her eyes shiny as if with fever.

I twist some grass around my finger, watching the tip go all pink. "He has mastered many dark arts. Won't he feel the skull is gone without looking at it?"

"Maybe, but I am sure the saint's powers exceed his, and she shall prevent that from happening."

I don't know about that, but all the same, this idea pleases me. But I cannot allow myself to trust it, not yet, not when it's not complete. Plans can so easily go awry. "Where are we to get a skull?" I ask.

"That's probably the easiest part of the plan. The graveyards are overflowing with the dead. Why, we might even take the skull of that poor *Aufhocker*'s mother, or at the very least her hair; it has the right color, if not quite the right texture."

I can scarcely believe that this woman, who wouldn't let me bury a dead man face down to keep him from becoming a *Nachzehrer* because that would be ungodly, and who often blanches at gruesome tales and sights till she looks ready to faint, is now proposing we defile a body by chopping off its head.

Ursula chuckles a little, as if she can scarcely believe it herself. "It's awful, I know, but what are our choices here? We can walk away from this, wash our hands of the whole affair…"

"But then I shall never see my grandmother, my father, my mother, and my big sister, Margarethe, and my little brothers, Friedrich and Johannes, again, and you shall be haunted by your Sister Hildegard," I whisper.

Ursula nods, her face grim. "I know. And some may say that's the way of things, that the Good Lord wouldn't have called them to Him if He didn't mean to, and they may be right or they may be wrong, but there is also this to consider: If we give up now, we will allow the necromancer to claim a wish from the saint. He shall use that to aid the devil himself."

I shudder. I can't help it. For many years, Bavaria and other parts of Germany have been the devil's playground already. If his servants grow in power…

"Don't you see, Elsebeth?" Ursula says. She cups my face and makes me look at her. "God has chosen you and me as His instruments to stop the necromancer and the foul lord he serves. All we need to do is cut off that poor woman's head and travel hard and fast."

"A sin is still a sin," I say, for though I want my wish very badly and I have done many a vile thing in my life, the idea of cutting off a dead woman's head sickens me.

"Sometimes, we must sin in order to do good. God will forgive us, I'm sure, or He wouldn't have asked this of us at all." She wets her lips with her tongue, and I am suddenly seized by the need to kiss, lick, and suck them till they're all swollen.

I blush and look at my hand, which is ruffling the long grass. If I were to bring it to my nose, I am sure I'd still smell Ursula underneath that good grass smell. "How prettily you speak," I murmur.

"Do you not think I speak true?"

I look up at her big brown eyes. They are all aglitter now. "That I did not say. It's just...our parson said we humans hanker after sin like a hound after a bowl of water when the hunt is done, only I don't think that's true, or at least not always. Some sins truly are awful. If we are to take that woman's head, I want us to be sure of our plan. Let's say we boil it till the flesh falls off. What then? It won't look like the saint's skull."

"My convent is on the way to where the saint's body is buried. We can get some gauze there to wrap it in. We can sew the hair to the gauze and embroider it whilst we travel. It needn't be done very well, just enough to fool at first glance. I doubt the necromancer takes the skull out of its box much; he's in thrall to Satan and, as such, must naturally feel a certain kind of revulsion for something as good and holy as a saint's bones."

I rip out another blade of grass. By now, I have a small pile of it, and my fingers are tinged green. "What about the glass eyes? Has your convent a pair of those, too?"

She shakes her head. "No. But not to worry. God will provide them in one way or another, I'm sure. Now come, *mein Liebchen*. We have much to do and very little time to do it. The longer we sit around talking, the farther the skull moves away from us."

I put my hands to my face and groan. "All that hard work to put that poor wretch in the ground, and now I shall have to dig her up again."

She bends close to kiss me. "I know, I know, but I shall be there to help you."

She stands, but before she can move to put her dress on, I take her hand. "If we are to do this, you must promise me one thing," I say.

"Anything for you, *mein Liebchen*."

"After coming up with such a bold plan, you may never call yourself a coward again."

She laughs. "Never," she promises me and laughs, then kisses me again, and I think with only a little shame in my heart that I'd do much worse than cut into a corpse if it makes Ursula kiss me like that.

22

URSULA

OVER THE PAST FEW YEARS, Sister Ursula has experienced a great many horrors: the siege of the castle of Eichstätt, where she thought she would surely die; the plundering of her convent; her and her sisters' flight; the death of Sister Hildegard; the attack on the road where she would have been raped and murdered were it not for Elsebeth; the *Nachzehrer*, the *Aufhocker*.

As she and Elsebeth cut off the head of the *Aufhocker*'s mother, skin it as well as they're able, then drop it into a simmering pot to get rid of the remaining strips of flesh and tendon, Sister Ursula wonders if there's perhaps a limit to what the human mind can take before it either cracks or grows callous. If horrors happen to you all the time, do they stop being horrors and simply become ordinary life? That would explain why soldiers can murder and maim with such ease.

But Sister Ursula's mind is not like theirs, or it simply hasn't reached its limit yet, because although the work isn't as horrific as some of the other things she has gone through, it still frightens and revolts her.

Halfway through, that funny feeling in her head that always blooms when she sees anything disturbing overpowers her, and she wakes some minutes later with Elsebeth cradling her head in her lap, crying softly.

"I thought for a moment the Lord had struck you down and you were *dead*," the girl sobs. She has a bloody smear on her forehead where she has brushed away the hair with a gore-smeared hand.

"I fainted, I think."

Elsebeth drops kisses on her face. "Please don't ever frighten me like that again. Now you stay here and rest for a bit. I'll see if the flesh has softened enough to peel off."

But Sister Ursula shakes her head. As a nun, she believes firmly that anything worth getting is worth suffering for, and that she mustn't let anyone suffer on her behalf if she can help it; Jesus has already suffered enough for her.

Everything for Jesus.

"It'll be faster if we both peel," she says.

It is.

For the next three days, they travel hard in order to reach Sister Ursula's convent, where they will gather the fine silk they can wrap the skull in and stitch the dead woman's hair to.

The closer they get, the more nervous and excited Sister Ursula becomes. For weeks, she has worried about the sisters who stayed behind. Apart from Sister Junius, the others are all old or frail, sometimes both. It really shouldn't be wondered at if one of them has passed, like Sister Valentina with her necklace of cankers. That should not be an occasion of mourning but of rejoicing, for that sister will have joined her Husband in Heaven. All the same, not knowing whether they are dead or alive drives Sister Ursula to distraction.

She talks incessantly about her sisters and the ways of the convent to Elsebeth, partly so that the girl knows what to expect, partly because the words just keep tumbling out of her mouth.

Elsebeth, by contrast, grows more and more quiet the closer they get.

"What's wrong, *mein Liebchen*? Are you afraid my sisters won't like you?" Sister Ursula asks her as they are walking the final mile toward the convent. They have already spied the building, large and beautiful, and Sister Ursula's heart is beating so fast with excitement, she feels slightly sick.

Elsebeth shrugs. "Papists usually have no love for Protestants. They may not like me for that, or for my rough peasant ways."

"Not at all! My sisters will see your generous, brave heart, and they'll have no choice but to love you deeply and dearly. That's how it was for me, anyway. I think I may have loved you from the moment you took my hand." And she flushes deeply, laughs, and takes Elsebeth's work-roughened hand and kisses the meat at the base of her thumb.

Elsebeth flushes as well, a deep purplish color that is reminiscent of a wine stain on white linen. "You are too sweet for your own good."

"Would you rather we not tell them you are Protestant?"

"No, for that would be lying, though mayhap it's better if we don't tell them about the saint's skull. It would be mighty complicated to tell them all, and they might not agree with what we are doing, might try to keep you here as they think it all over, but we can't spare the time for that. What say you?"

But Sister Ursula doesn't respond. She has stopped walking. What she has seen makes fear flare inside of her chest, suffusing her limbs until she must stand stiff and still once more, like a wooden puppet waiting for another to move her.

"What's wrong?" Elsebeth asks, but terror has stoppered Sister Ursula's throat, and so she cannot speak, only stand and stare, her heart battering her chest.

Their order is a cloistered one. To allow their minds to focus completely on God, they try to separate themselves as completely from the world as possible. The sisters are only allowed to leave the convent grounds if circumstances leave them no other choice. To keep them inside and the world outside, all the doors should be firmly closed and locked at all times.

But the front door is neither locked nor closed. It gapes open, the cool hallway beyond shrouded in shadows, and so something must be horribly wrong.

"Ursula? Speak to me, please," Elsebeth says. She moves in front of Sister Ursula, touches her cheek. Sister Ursula's face has gone numb; she feels the calloused fingers only faintly, as if she's stuck in that limbo between waking and dreaming where everything is muffled.

Elsebeth takes hold of Sister Ursula's chin, makes her tilt her head down. This breaks the spell, at least a little; when Sister Ursula manages to speak, her tongue feels like a slug, and the words come out sounding strange and oddly graceless, like dead things. "Something is wrong. Something bad has happened here."

Elsebeth frowns. Two lines appear between her brows, so stark and deep that it seems impossible that they'll disappear when her face relaxes, and yet they do, they will, at least for now. Not so many years to go anymore until such creases become permanent. Sister Ursula might have some wrinkles already. She doesn't know; she hasn't seen her face in a long time, because the convent has no mirrors, which are only baubles that encourage vanity, and whatever glimpses she has caught in the reflection of a pane of glass or puddle she has done her best to forget, to…

She realizes she has gotten lost in her own head again. She blinks, makes herself focus on Elsebeth's pale eyes. "What did you say?"

"I said, 'How do you know something bad has happened?'"

"The door," she whispers. She swallows thickly. "It should always be closed, but it isn't. That means that something has happened to my sisters, something big and terrible that has prevented them from living by our order's sacred rules."

"Mayhap they decided to leave after all and forgot to lock the door, and it's nothing as sinister as you fear. Come, let us go inside and see." Elsebeth turns around, begins to move toward the door, which still gapes so darkly, so horribly, like the maw of an animal intent on eating her alive.

Sister Ursula says, "I daren't go inside." As soon as the words have left her mouth, she knows them to be true. "God curse me for a coward, but I daren't go inside. I can't, I can't, I can't, please don't make me, because I can't..." She realizes she's babbling, but she can't help herself. When Elsebeth comes close to her, she backs away, raising her arms as if to fend off a blow, and still she pleads and begs.

"Peace," Elsebeth says. She places her hands against Sister Ursula's cheeks and makes her look at her again. "Peace, Ursula. I won't force you to come with me if you daren't. I understand. You needn't explain to me. But someone has to go inside, if only because we need that gauze so that our fake saint's skull looks real. Now tell me: How many of your sisters will I find inside if they haven't left already?"

"Seven."

"Seven," Elsebeth repeats. Her mouth and eyes are all grim determination. "You wait here now till I am back. If anything happens, scream for me, and I will come running."

Don't leave me alone! Something inside of Sister Ursula wails, but she presses it deep down, and what comes out of her mouth is simply, "I don't want you to go inside, *mein Liebchen*. I don't want you to get hurt."

Elsebeth gives her a crooked grin, though her eyes remain cool with fear. "I think I can take some old maids in a fight if I have to."

Sister Ursula doesn't laugh.

Elsebeth's smile fades. "Be comforted, my love. All shall be well."

Sister Ursula watches Elsebeth go inside, and the day is so bright and the hallway so dark that it looks as if the convent swallows her in one big bite.

Sister Ursula kneels in the dust of the road and takes her rosary out of her pocket. She prays as she waits, but there is no gathering of the senses, no turning inward, no sweet sense of love to salve her troubled soul. It is merely something to make the time pass as she waits for Elsebeth to come back and tell her what horror she has found.

Not horror per se, she thinks. *My sisters may have fled after all, as Elsebeth said. They may be alive and well. They...*

Elsebeth staggers outside, whey-faced, breathing fast and hard, and Sister Ursula knows then that the worst has happened.

Her sisters are dead.

With this realization, her fear shifts and changes.

Before, she wanted to stay ignorant.

Now, she wants to know.

No, not "wants"; she *needs* to know. She needs to see, smell, and experience what has happened to her poor sisters, who are not of her blood but are her family all the same. Whatever she will find in these cool and lofty rooms will scar her mind and heart, of this she has no doubt, but it also beckons her.

Sister Ursula strides to the door, feeling nothing but the fear roaring inside of her veins and the siren's call of the horror inside of the convent.

Elsebeth grabs her wrist, and the shock of it is enormous.

"Don't," the girl says. She's pale and sweating like a piece of cheese left out on a hot day. "Don't go inside, Ursula, please. Your poor sisters are terrible to look at." She swallows thickly. "I wish I hadn't seen."

"I must, I must, I simply must..."

"You don't. There's naught you can do for them now. If you go inside, you'll regret it. It's better not to know sometimes. Please let me carry this for you."

But how can Sister Ursula do that when the burden Elsebeth carries is so heavy already? Better to share the load. Anything else would be selfishness and cowardice.

Elsebeth's grip around Sister Ursula's wrist tightens. "It's not cowardice," she hisses, as if she has read Sister Ursula's thoughts. "Fear isn't a bad thing. Bravery is a virtue only when there's fear, for how else can it be bravery? It's better if you don't go in, believe you me, for they... Ursula, no!"

Sister Ursula has already ripped her hand free and is running, running, running.

23

ELSEBETH

AS I WATCH URSULA RUN into the convent, I do something decidedly sinful.

I curse.

I was taught that God knows better than I what is good for me, for all humans are ignorant and sinful. No matter how bad the things are that God sends our way, they're for our betterment, even if we cannot see that, so we must try and submit with gratitude and grace.

But I am neither grateful nor graceful, so I curse, and I spit, for I have always found anger easier to bear than despair.

When I am done, I follow Ursula inside.

I find her on the threshold of what I think must be the infirmary, hands at her mouth as if to keep in a scream.

Inside are the bodies of her sisters.

Someone has laid them out; their hands are folded around their rosaries, and their jaws have been bound to keep them from gaping open. They are all dried up and wizened like the apples my family and I would put on the windowsill to preserve them so we could eat them during the barren winter months. On their faces and at their throats, they have black marks as large as eggs, and just as round and bulging.

There's only one sickness I know that drapes a necklace of big black beads around its victims' necks.

The plague.

I am not afeared to sicken with it, for I had it as a child and survived, but I know not whether Ursula has, so I move a little in front of her, ready to grab her if she should move closer to them. Once she is calmer, and I can leave her alone again without fear, I shall catch a frog for her, kill it, and rub it on one of those plague spots, and then I shall put it on a bit of string and make her wear it around her neck so that it rests between her breasts. It's what the gravedigger in our village swore by, and he didn't catch the plague when it sickened me, nor when it burned through Bavaria some years later and took my mother and grandmother.

For now, it's best I stay close to her. Grief is its own kind of madness, and there's no saying what we do when we catch it.

Ursula has dropped her hands, though what comes out of her mouth is no scream, but a whisper. I lean in close to catch the words. "One, two, three, four, five, six. One, two, three, four, five, six. One, two, three..." she mutters, almost as if she's compelled to it, like *Nachzehrer* are when you spill seeds, needles, or other small things at their feet.

I ask, "What are you counting?"

"The bodies. There are six of them, but there should be seven. We left seven sisters behind. That means one of them is still alive," she gasps.

I feel as if I have gulped down a glass of ice water, all cold and sick. I say with as much kindness as I can, "Just because we're missing one body doesn't mean she's still living. Please, Ursula, my little love, you mustn't hope." It feels awfully cruel to speak to her so, but it's better that she expects nothing, for hope can kill as surely as a sword.

But it's too late already. Hope has possessed her, drawing the blood to her cheeks, making her eyes glitter all hard and brittle like glass. "One of my sisters is still alive. I can feel it, like an ache, in here," she says and presses her hand to her breast.

I feel an ache there, too, but it's for a different reason. "If she was alive, why didn't she call out to us?" ask I.

"Maybe she's sick. Maybe she hasn't heard us. Maybe she's frightened and is hiding. She doesn't know you, and I am dressed as a laywoman. Or maybe she has left this place and is traveling to join Reverend Mother Regina."

I want to tell Ursula that I don't think that her fellow nun has gone away, for I don't think any Christian, be they Calvinist, Lutheran, or papist, would leave someone to rot in the open air if they could help it, just like we didn't do that with the *Aufhocker* and his family, but I can already sense that Ursula won't believe me. We'll just end up talking in circles, so I say, "Let us look for her then."

We decide to split up. It's faster that way; if there's one thing we never have enough of, it's time.

Finding the first six nuns was easy. All I had to do was follow the open doors and then my nose; there's a gentle stink to them, though mayhap it's more their nightgowns and bedclothes that reek, having soaked up the sweat, piss, and other fluids that flow freely in both sickness and death.

I decide to go to the graveyard first. If there's a fresh grave, we will know where the seventh sister has gone. If not, then we must look for her in every room, of which there are many.

The convent frightens me. I suppose it's partly because I know it's a den of papists, and that childhood fear is hard to shake, but there's something else also, something in the air, something still and heavy.

Mayhap this place is haunted.

Ursula spent most of her life behind these walls of cool stone. Was she often scared here, I wonder? Mayhap it's different when there are nuns everywhere and you can be comforted by the sound of their slippers, the swish of their habits, and their soft breathing. Indeed, as a girl, I sometimes thought secretly how nice it must be to become a nun, much better than marrying and having babies until you die or dry up, only Calvinists don't have nunneries.

All those women together once. Not anymore, not now. They've been scattered across the land like a handful of seeds thrown carelessly, some of them claimed by the earth.

Somehow, the graveyard frightens me less than the convent, even though it's fearful in its symmetry: all these dark crosses in neat rows. The markers are all the same. If you want to visit a certain grave, I suppose you must count to find it.

I walk between the rows looking for fresh graves, of which there are none. I turn back to the convent, so large and looming, and take myself back inside. I've not gone far when I hear Ursula scream.

We shouldn't have separated, I think as I begin to run, my hand seeking out the little knife at my belt and clasping it tightly.

I run down the dark hallways, my heart wild as a bucking rabbit, that minnow of fear swimming up and down my spine again. "Where are you?" I scream, for the convent does strange things to sound, strengthening it so that my feet hitting the floor are loud as gunfire, or swallowing it and spitting it out elsewhere, making it sound as if I am not alone.

Ursula doesn't answer me.

I turn down another hallway, find there's only a door at the end of it, firmly closed against me. I growl in frustration, turn on my heel, blindly dash down some other way. "Ursula!" I scream again, but she doesn't heed me or, more likely, hasn't heard me over her own screaming, so awful, the sound of something inside of her breaking.

This building is a labyrinth, and I know not what way to go.

I find the bell tower only by accident, when I stop my running and lean against a door to catch my breath, and it swings inward so that I tumble inside and almost fall onto my own knife. Ursula's screaming is very loud here, and it seems to go on and on without pause, because the walls don't absorb it but throw it back so that it bounces this way and that.

I run up, up, up the stairs of the bell tower, my legs burning and sweat making my shift stick to my back. When I reach the top, I find Ursula on her knees and her hands clasped as if she's praying.

But what she's praying to is no plaster saint, no golden crucifix studded with gems, no wooden Christ painted with bold colors as if he's an actor on the stage.

It's the corpse of the seventh nun.

She has hanged herself, but she has made a poor job of it. Looking at her hands, which are all bloody, I think she must've choked to death slowly. Her face is all black. The tongue is swollen, as are her lips. Her eyes have gone cloudy and are bulging something fierce, as if they're ready to burst out of the sockets. A fly crawls over the right eyeball.

She twitches.

My heart leaps up my throat, and though my wild dash through this labyrinth of a convent has made me run hot, I feel all chilled now. *She's alive*, I think, *she's alive she's alive how can she be alive she's alive…*

But no. There's a draft in here, and it makes the body swing slightly.

Ursula screams again, a shattering sound full of pain and rage. I clap my hands over my ears, but I hear it still, and I wish I hadn't come after her, that I hadn't heard. The scream goes on for a long time, until her lungs are all empty. She's quiet for a moment as she draws breath, then screams some more.

I put my arms around her. If I could draw out some of this hurt and feel it for her, I would. She's all taut, so that it is like holding on to a tree. I hold her, I kiss her, I rock her, all these things she has done to me before to calm me, but still she sits hard and cold. At some point, she ceases screaming. I think she has gone deep inside herself. Her eyes have that look to them.

It's a danger, this retreating into oneself. The mind can be deep and dark enough to drown in.

"Please," I say, "wherever you are wandering now, don't go any further. Listen to my voice, and come back to me."

Three times I have to beg. Then, Ursula blinks, and her eyes lose that hard, dull look as they focus on the body of the dead nun.

"Her name was Sister Junius," Ursula whispers. Her voice is all hoarse. I heard of a man who screamed and screamed and screamed when he heard his wife had died in childbirth. He went on until something in his throat broke, and then he could never scream again.

"How can you tell it's her?" I ask, for her face is so bloated and misshapen, I wonder if I would've recognized it, even if it had belonged to someone I grew up seeing every day.

Ursula points to the sandaled feet that dangle above the ground. The nails have a strange blue color to them, and the toes are all black. On the left foot, the two little ones are missing. "A dog did that when she was a child," Ursula explains. "The wound festered, and she sickened so terribly that everyone thought she'd die. Her parents prayed and prayed, and promised to God they would give her up to Him if only He spared her life, so when she lived, she was sent here. She was our infirmarian, and she was training me to replace her, should she..." Her breath hitches. She puts her face in her hands and moans, and that's somehow worse than her screaming.

"You loved her, didn't you?" I ask.

She doesn't speak, and for a moment, I think she hasn't heard my question, that she may be wandering again in her mind, but then she whispers, "Yes, I did. Of all my sisters, I loved her the most. I wasn't supposed to. Nuns must strive to love everyone equally, but we are only human, and so I loved her more than the others. What she has done is unforgivable, and she shall suffer for it."

When Ursula looks up at me, her eyes are wet and round. "Why? Why did she do this?"

"Mayhap her mind was addled by the death of her sisters. God knows mine was when Margarethe died." There are whole days I don't remember, all these holes in my memory that I daren't look into too hard for fear they're not empty and whatever hides there will eat me alive. That's why I mustn't let Ursula turn inward entirely.

Ursula takes a shaking breath, and I think she might finally cry, that she might finally let the wet fall from her eyes and let the sobs tear her apart till she feels a little better, but instead her face contorts in hatred. She screams again, a harsh, awful sound, then jumps up and runs this way and that, smacking her hands against the walls, the floorboards, the door.

I make myself small, for there's no telling what Ursula might do now that madness has gripped her.

Only it's not madness after all, I realize as I sit all huddled in a corner trying not to cry, for this vale has had enough of my tears already. Ursula is chasing after the flies that have gotten into the bell tower, drawn in no doubt by the stink of Sister Junius. "I hate flies," she hisses as her eyes dart around wildly looking for them. "I hate them, I hate them, *I hate them*! I can't understand why God made them. What purpose do they serve other than to aggravate, to sully?"

I've never heard the word "aggravate" before, but I can guess its meaning. "Mayhap the fly had a different purpose when in Eden," say I. "Mayhap the devil recruited it, like he did with the snake."

She hunts them some more, but it doesn't take long for her rage to spend itself. At last, grief takes over. When I draw her to me, she is no longer hard and distant as a piece of carven wood, but soft and pliant, and I think of the story my grandmother told me of an artist who couldn't find a woman who pleased him, so he made his own out of wood, or mayhap it was stone. The material doesn't matter. Whatever she was made of, he loved her so well that she came alive one day, and he wedded her, and they lived together in married bliss till the end of their days. Margarethe liked this story, but I never did. I didn't mislike it because it's idolatrous to love a statue so, but because I thought a man who could find not a single woman he liked must never marry, for he must be bitter, vile, and small of mind, with a special kind of hatred in his heart. The wife of such a man is marked for harm and hurt.

Ursula weeps for a long time. My leg goes to sleep where she leans on it, but I don't move, for this pain is only very little compared to hers.

At last, her sobs peter out. Her face is hot, wet, and much swollen. I fear her head must feel bruised and her eyelids cut; I know mine do after I have cried so fiercely. I blow on her eyes to soothe them, trying not to ruffle the lashes, for the feel of an eyelash out of place is vexing at the best of times, which this is not.

Ursula blinks fast against my breath on her eyes, and some more tears slip out. The ones from her right eye are tinged pink; I think she has burst a vessel. I brush her tears away with my thumb. She puts her hand over my mouth to stop my blowing and locks eyes with me. "We must get that skull back, Elsebeth, now more than ever," she says.

I rest our heads together. "Yes," I say, though my heart is chilled. "Yes, we must."

24

OTTO

THE SUN RISES, AND SETS, and rises again. Although Otto's voice cracks, his throat feels as if he has swallowed shards, and he weeps till his head feels too tight and his eyes are sore; even though his tear ducts produce nothing but the occasional reeking black tear, the necromancer takes no pity on him, and so Otto must continue to confess to his sins. Only when the necromancer grows bored does he break Otto's enchantment.

"Enough for now," he declares and yawns hugely. "We shall eat and drink, we shall sleep, and then we shall be on our way."

Otto sinks down, too wrung out even to sob.

The necromancer bends over him and pats him on the head. "There, there," he says, "I bet it must have been quite a relief to purge yourself of all that filth, you naughty boy. We shall continue some other time."

Otto wishes he were well and truly dead.

Over the next few days, as the necromancer uses his little bones to find their way to the saint's body, Otto retreats into himself. He prepares meals for the necromancer, he walks, he sets up camp, and he remembers none of it.

The only times he is snapped out of this state is when the necromancer takes the skull out of her box, which happens once or twice a day. He fingers her red hair, traces the line of her jaw, once even presses a kiss to her teeth, which makes Otto's stomach roil, dead though it may be.

There is something about that skull that is revolting, though Otto is hard-pressed to say what. He isn't usually affected by human remains, not anymore, only his own body, which is rotting quite severely now, his skin discolored and ruptured in places, his belly distended, his eyes feeling dry and scratchy. Maybe it's because the skull belongs to a saint, and Otto is a sinner bound to a witch. Her presence naturally makes him uncomfortable because it reminds him of the filthy state of his soul, which is especially tender now that the necromancer has made him recount his sins. The worst of it is that there are so many more Otto hasn't yet spoken of, like that time he cut off a farmer's fingers joint by joint so that it took a long time until only the palms were left, all because the man had refused to hand over his horse when Otto's general asked; he had said he wouldn't be able to plow his fields without it, and then what would the army eat next year?

Now, he looks at his own fingers, all black with rot, the nails gone, the flesh hardened to leather in some places and strangely slimy in others. The tips of his index finger and thumb of his dominant hand have fallen off, revealing the bone underneath. It looks oddly yellow in the light of the fire he has made to cook the necromancer's supper. He imagines the farmer's fear, his despair, the sickening pain, and he shudders.

"How horrified you look, dear Otto," the necromancer says, glancing up from the skull in his lap. "Would you like to tell me about it?"

Immediately Otto hides his ruined hands behind his back, as if he's a little boy trying to hide some small infraction from his father. "No, no, please. No more of that, I beg of you. I don't want to talk about all this filth anymore. I am so tired of raping and maiming and killing," he groans. His voice still hasn't recovered from his outpouring of sin, and is all rough and low. Likely it will never recover. Until the necromancer finds him a new body, he'll be stuck with this raw whisper, like that fellow soldier who took a butt of a sword to the throat during battle and spoke in this high-pitched whine until a farmer gored him to death.

"You wish to retire?" the necromancer mocks him as he combs through the skull's hair with his fingers. "Live in a little cottage with your beloved Frieda rather than in a leaky tent, wake to the smell of her baking rather than unwashed bodies and horse dung, see your cows frolic around rather than some soldiers fighting over a game of dice, a stolen cup, a whore?"

"Yes, I wish that very much," Otto answers. He fears that his time with the necromancer has made him unfit to be a soldier. If that creepy skull gives him a wish as well as that necromancer once they return it to its body, he'll spend it wisely on a life for him and Frieda far away from the horrors of war.

The necromancer smiles again. Otto has been so focused on his goat eyes that he only now realizes the man has more teeth than most. They all crowd together like epileptics at a public beheading; it is believed that drinking the blood of someone healthy and recently dead can cure all manner of ailments, including the falling sickness, and so those poor wretches afflicted with it stand close to the scaffold with cups in hand, hoping to catch the blood as it spouts from the neck of the executed. "Who says you get a wish?"

Otto feels as if a cold finger brushes past his spine. He represses a shudder. "If I am bound to you still and must follow you until you've returned the skull to its body, then why wouldn't I get a wish as well as you? They say God's love is endless and He loves a sinner, don't they?"

"You misunderstand me, dear Otto. What I mean is this: Why do you think there is a wish at the end of this journey?"

Otto blinks in confusion. "Because that's what Gottfried told me, and he heard it from that Swede who had the skull before him."

The necromancer stops combing the skull's hair. "What, exactly, did Gottfried tell you?"

"That this is the skull of a saint, and if you return it to the saint's body, she'll give you a wish. That's why you are doing all of this, isn't it? Because you want to use that wish for something?"

The necromancer's dark eyes widen. Then, he laughs. He laughs so hard, he shakes with it, and it's like watching someone having a fit. Between his long lean fingers, the skull shakes as well, as if she, too, is laughing.

It takes a long time until his laughter ceases. By then, the necromancer's sallow face has gone red in ugly patches and is wet from both tears and sweat. He wipes it on his sleeve, then looks at the skull, and that sets him off again.

"What's so funny?" The necromancer's hysterical laughter and that disgusting skull have made all the hairs on Otto's body rise. Some primal part tells him to flee, to run as fast as he can if he wants to live, but his legs are still bewitched and won't listen to his brain.

Still the necromancer laughs.

"What? What is it?" Otto screams, and his throat is on fire, and it's somehow the worst pain he has ever felt, even worse than that bullet that went through his arm a little while after Magdeburg, though maybe that's because the body remembers pain so poorly once it has passed, but even though his throat feels cut and peeled, he grabs the necromancer by the shirt, shakes him roughly, and hisses, "What is so fucking funny, you fucker?"

"God, you reek. We should find you a new body soon, don't you think? This one won't last much longer."

Otto refuses to take the bait. "Tell me!"

The necromancer smiles, and it's awful. "This skull belongs to my wife."

PART IV

“How can I live without thee, how forego
Thy sweet converse, and love so dearly joined,
To live again in these wild woods forlorn?
Should God create another Eve, and I
Another rib afford, yet loss of thee
Would never from my heart; no, no, I feel
The link of nature draw me: flesh of flesh,
Bone of my bone thou art, and from thy state
Mine never shall be parted, bliss or woe.”

—John Milton, *Paradise Lost*

“And Ruth said, Intreat me not to leave thee, or to return from following after thee: for whither thou goest, I will go; and where thou lodgest, I will lodge: thy people shall be my people, and thy God my God:

Where thou diest, will I die, and there will I be buried: the Lord do so to me, and more also, if ought but death part thee and me.”

—Ruth 1:16–17

25

ELSEBETH

ONCE AGAIN, URSULA AND I spend the night in a house belonging to death. It's the third time since we met, so it must mean something, three being the number of the Lord and all that, but all I can think that it means is that there's a lot of death in this world.

Before nightfall, though, there's much to do.

We don't bury the bodies. There's no time to dig seven holes, not if we want to be on our way again tomorrow to hunt down the necromancer. It's not right to just leave them as they are, though, so Ursula sets to washing them and dressing them in unsoiled clothes. I want to do it myself at first, afeared that Ursula will sicken with whatever killed them, but she tells me in her voice all hoarse from screaming that it's all right, she had the plague before and is safe from it now.

"You must make sure no fabric touches their mouths, or they'll become *Nachzehrer*," I tell her, "and you must place something on their eyes to keep them closed, for it is bad luck to look the dead in the eye. My grandmother said that their stare might stun you, and if they turn into restless corpses, anyone who has looked them in the eye when they were dead shall be bound to them."

Ursula doesn't respond. Mayhap she hasn't heard, yet when I make to repeat myself, she takes my hand and squeezes it, and I hush.

We cut Sister Junius down. Ursula doesn't want anyone to know the manner of her death. I wonder if that's a sort of lie, but it's done out of kindness, and if Ursula uses her wish to save Sister Junius, I suppose it may not matter.

It's an awful thing, to cut her down, for she is much rotted. I don't want to touch her, but I steel myself, and as I wrap my arms around her waist, I go deep inside of myself and hold the image of Ursula's face all flushed after I've loved her well into my mind, and that helps, but only a little.

When Ursula has cut the rope and Sister Junius comes down, her upper body snaps forward. Black and foul liquid sprays from her mouth. I have to let go of the image of Ursula then, for I don't want to link dead Sister Junius and black corpse juice to Ursula in my mind.

Once we have eased her down on the floor and I have managed not to vomit, I offer to help wash the body and lay it out, for those who die by their own hand are more likely than anyone else to be damned and wander restlessly until rot has claimed them completely, but Ursula shakes her head.

"This I must do alone," she says.

Mayhap it's better like that, for I have no love for this woman whom I know not, but Ursula brims with it, and it seems to me that the dead deserve at least a little bit of love.

I decide to make myself useful in another way. I look for food. The cloister gardens are a mess, all torn up, likely by soldiers, though mayhap also by some of the peasants who work for the convent, because even if the fear of God burns strong in your heart, in the end, the hunger burns stronger. I gather what I can and what I know to be edible. Next, I go find the kitchen and the pantry. There's not much left. The nuns may have hidden some food in strange places where plundering soldiers are not likely to look, but I don't want to go poke around any more than I have to. Besides, there's no time. I prepare what I have found.

After I've cooked, eaten, and kept some for Ursula—even if grief strangles her hunger, I shall make her eat, for I need her healthy and strong—I go look for some of the fine mesh silk similar to what the saint's skull was wrapped in. When I finally find some, I set to cutting it to size for our fake skull. I can't sew it up just yet, for we still lack the glass eyes, and I know not how else we might add those later on if the skull is covered already, but I can attach the red hair. It's delicate work and hard to do without daylight, but there likely won't be any time for this later.

It's rather a gruesome job, sewing all those strands of hair we took from a dead woman to the silk, but in some strange way it reminds me of home. In the evenings or on long winter days when there was no plowing, planting, or harvesting to be done, we'd all sit together near the hearth. My father would repair his tools or whittle something out of wood, and my mother, Margarethe, and I would sew. We'd sing as we worked, hymns, mostly, or we'd tell each other stories from the Bible. Every now and then, my grandmother would tell us one of her fairy stories. My mother disapproved, for she felt these stories were ungodly, but my dad was a little milder, and because he was head of our household, and because a wife should heed her husband and children their father, it was he who determined what we could and could not tell.

I try to sing as I sew. My voice falters before I've finished my song, for it feels wrong to raise my voice here, not only because this is a house of death and mourning, but also because everything around me is so quiet. I feel like there is something lurking in the convent's dark corners, and if I make a lot of noise, it shall know that I am here, it shall know where to find me.

Something that has had a good long look at Sister Junius as she hung there slowly rotting and will wear her face as a mask to fool us, I think, and I shudder and prick my finger. As I suck on it, I look at the dead woman's hair piled in my lap. Hunger ate up the shine, leaving it all muted and brittle, but the candlelight paints it all these different shades, and so it's almost beautiful.

"There you are," Ursula says.

I shriek and jump to my feet. I manage to catch the skull, but the hair that is not yet sewn to the silk flies everywhere.

"I'm sorry. I didn't mean to startle you," Ursula whispers as she and I gather the strands, raking them with our fingers to get the dust and the tangles out.

"Why are you whispering?" I whisper back.

"I shouldn't talk at all. It's the Great Silence. I haven't been observing it very well lately, since Sister Hildegard died and I was alone. It feels wrong to speak here, but I didn't want to frighten you, make you think I had gone mad..."

"That's kind of you. Have you eaten yet?"

She shakes her head. I make her take a few bites of the dinner I cooked. When she is done, she motions for me to come with her. I gather up the skull, the mesh, and the hair and follow her deeper into the convent, inside what I suppose must be her cell.

"Every cell is sacred," she whispers. "No nun may enter another's cell without permission. This place is for her and Christ alone. It's both a bridal chamber full of love and bliss, and a crucible in which we fight our darkest demons. I am letting you in here, Elsebeth, because you are very dear to me, and I...I want you to see this, I want you to..."

I put my fingers against her lips. "Hush, my love," I say. "You said you mustn't speak till morning, so please don't speak, not for me."

She nods gratefully, then opens the door and lets me inside.

For a bridal chamber and crucible, this room seems awfully bare. It has a bed, a stool, and one shelf, no more. The shelf holds a pitcher, a bowl, three books. The bed is hard and small. We barely fit here, but that doesn't bother me. We have slept in worse places. I hold Ursula tight to me, listen to her breathing. I wish I could kiss her and love her, and in that way make her forget all the horrors, but I don't know if she'll like it now, in here.

If I were to come live here with her once her still-living sisters return, would she let me creep into her room at night, to hold her as I am holding her now? Or would she not want me here, afraid of what might be done to us if we were caught? Ursula told me they are not supposed to love one person more than the others and that touch here is as rare as a miser spending a coin, for the sisters seek the death of all flesh so that their minds may turn to God, their Heavenly Husband, completely. I know not how a nun might be punished for having a special friend. Mayhap they'll beat her, or starve her, or make her kneel on shards of glass. I have heard that papists can do all manner of sinful things, like witchcraft, fornication, and other deeds Satan would delight in and be proud to call his own.

Though if I am quite honest, now that I have been with Ursula for a while, I no longer think it's all true what I have heard. Mayhap some of the most gruesome things I was told are just stories meant to frighten us away from popery. All the same, I don't think Ursula and I can live here together, at least not in the way I'd like, and...

My thoughts are interrupted by Ursula. She sobs in her sleep, this sad, frightened sound, and I make to wake her, but she has hushed already, so I kiss her head instead and hope the feel of it somehow travels into her dreams and makes them less horrible.

"Don't you fret," I whisper into her hair. "We shall steal back the saint's skull from the necromancer, and you shall have your wish, and all you have seen and smelled and heard here shall be undone, and I shall wish for..."

I have a dark thought then.

I might use my wish for Ursula and me to stay together.

But no, I mustn't be selfish. I must use my wish for the good of my family. I should ask to have them brought back to life.

Only what if it's greedy to ask for so much? In His life, Christ made only three people come back from death. What if the saint makes me choose between my grandmother, my mother, my father, Margarethe, and my little brothers, Johannes and Friedrich?

Then she won't resurrect all of Ursula's sisters, either, and the two of us shall have to wish for something else. Mayhap it's good to have another wish up my sleeve, just in case.

And that wish shall be for me and Ursula to be together, for she is mine to protect, mine to cherish, mine to love, I think.

But only if my family can't be brought back to life.

I want more than anything to have them back.

Don't I?

26

URSULA

DURING THE NIGHT, SISTER URSULA has many disturbing dreams that fade upon waking. All she remembers is Sister Junius's blackened face. If she could draw, she'd sketch out her face as it was before death in an effort to get rid of the horrible sight of her all rotted. It has stamped itself upon her mind, and she fears that it will stay there no matter how much time passes.

You shouldn't have left her.

This thought haunts her both when she's asleep and when she's awake. She knows it's useless to think it. There is no altering the past. All she can do is use her wish to ensure Sister Junius's soul will make it to Heaven. But she needs Saint Columba's skull if she is to wish for anything, and to get that back, she needs a convincing fake skull with red hair and glass eyes, which she doesn't have yet, at least, not the eyes.

Only the Venetians know how to make convincing eyes out of glass, and they guard their technique jealously, thus making such eyes expensive and rare. She has heard some very wealthy people wear them when accident or disease has robbed them of an eye, but she herself has only ever seen the dead adorned with them, like the saint's skull, and a waxen replica of Saint Stephanus in a church she visited when she was little and her mother still alive. That model had frightened her; it had looked like someone living, and no matter how much her mother had whispered to her that it was a statue, Sister Ursula wouldn't go near it. If only her own humble convent had a wax model like this, she and Elsebeth might...

Inspiration strikes her so forcefully, she sits up in bed, her hands pressed against her mouth so as not to laugh.

Her convent doesn't have a full wax model of any saint, but it *does* have a wax mask of one of her sisters, namely Sister Anna. The mask is supposed to be an accurate portrayal of her face when her tomb was opened a month after she had been interred. The nuns had begun to smell a sweet, delicious scent coming from it, which is a sign of possible sainthood. Upon opening the tomb, they had found the body still looked as fresh as if it had only just died, and so letters were written to the Vatican, and a wax maker commissioned to make this replica.

Sister Ursula has always avoided going near it, because she hasn't left that childhood fear of wax models entirely behind, and so she can't remember if it has glass eyes, but it is worth looking into. Where else will they find a pair?

Sister Ursula dresses hastily but quietly, careful not to wake Elsebeth. Her *Liebchen* is so endearing as she sleeps, her face all soft in a way it never is when she's awake, alert, and suspicious of the world. Sister Ursula represses the urge to press a kiss to her sweet, slack mouth. She lights a candle instead and slips out into the dark hallway. With the keys she has taken from Sister Junius, she lets herself into the crypt where they have hidden Sister Anna's incorruptible body to protect her from plundering soldiers. It has been placed carefully in a wooden box and stacked upon some other boxes to keep it safe from any damp rising from the stone ground.

Sister Ursula places her hands on the lid, but familiar fear stays her hands. She had hoped that her experiences of defleshing the head of the *Aufhocker*'s mother would have made this desecration easier, but perhaps there are some things you can never get used to.

Coward.

Only she promised Elsebeth that she would never call herself that again, didn't she?

"I am no coward," she hisses and pushes the lid to the side. From the box wafts a fusty old smell, not quite a stink but definitely not the sweet and rich perfume that alerted the nuns to the possibility of Sister Anna's sainthood, either.

She presses her sleeve against her mouth, then bends over the box and peers inside.

In the soft candlelight, the waxen mask placed over Sister Anna's face looks not like wax, but like flesh, slightly wrinkled at the eyes and forehead, gone soft at the cheeks and mouth, delicately veined at the temples and eyelids. The wax maker who labored over this piece for weeks even used real hair, all so that the mask would give the impression of life. It's fine and brown, and likely has been shorn from the head of a peasant in desperate need of money, or perhaps from an uncomplaining corpse.

But through that fine hair poke rough black hairs, hinting at something much darker and less palatable underneath. Sister Anna was incorruptible once, yes, but that does not mean she hasn't gone to rot since.

No matter. Sister Ursula isn't interested in anything but the mask. She stoops a little, holds the candle close to see better. If this mask truly is an accurate replica, then the eyes should be open at least a little. Death relaxes the muscles of the eyelids, leaving them half open unless something is placed on top to keep them shut, such as a coin.

Yes, the eyelids are not entirely closed, and through the lashes something glints.

Are those lashes real, too? Did that wax maker pay some poor wretch a few thaler to pluck out their lashes? Or are they merely animal hairs painted and shaped to look like something different?

Don't get distracted, she admonishes herself. She's here for what she can see shimmering between those lashes. Only glass could harness light like that, then throw it back all in sparkles.

Sister Ursula smiles nervously, touches the little crucifix at the end of her broken rosary, and offers up a small prayer of thanks to God for helping her so. Now, all she needs to do is extract the glass eyes from the mask, and she and Elsebeth will have everything they need to make a convincing replica of Saint Columba's skull.

Sister Ursula stretches out her hand, but she can't bring herself to touch the mask. A horrible thought has sprouted in her head that touching the wax will waken Sister Anna. There are no wax casts covering her hands, and though the light is poor, Sister Ursula can see the shape of them as they lie folded on her chest, the fingers thin and twisted like the legs of a dead spider. Sister Anna won't like to be wakened, especially not by a thief, and so those hands will unfold with hard, snapping sounds, and they will reach for Sister Ursula, and…

Stop it. You are not a child, afraid of the dead and the dark, Sister Ursula scolds herself.

Only those are not childish fears, now are they? The *Nachzehrer* was dead yet still moved and hunted for prey in the dark, and that poor *Aufhocker* boy hadn't known to die, either.

But they hadn't been buried properly, and Sister Anna has. There is nothing to fear. She wasn't scared of her dead sisters in the infirmary, nor of poor Sister Junius all corrupted, so why would this fellow nun frighten her?

Sister Ursula takes a deep breath, then forces herself to touch the waxen cheek with her fingertip. She shudders at the contact. The wax is not cool as she expected, but tepid, as if warmed by the body underneath. Only that can't be, because Sister Anna has been dead for thirty years, long before Sister Ursula came to live here.

Likely her hands are just cold, and that gives the impression of warmth when there isn't any. Yes, that must be it. Now she must get to work, for time is precious.

Sister Ursula's fingers hover over the left eyelid. Despite having touched the mask's cheek and felt that it is truly wax and not flesh, she still needs to conquer something within herself before she's able to touch it. It looks so lifelike, as if she is about to plunge her finger into a dead woman's eye.

She strokes it once, quickly and lightly.

Sister Anna doesn't stir.

of course not she's dead dead dead well and truly dead and even if she wasn't you have nothing to fear from her because you are on a mission of God and she must know that because she is likely a saint herself Sister Junius said so Reverend Mother Regina said so the Vatican said so and even if she's not a saint she's dead and so can't hurt you…

Sister Ursula presses into the eyelid with her nail. The painted wax is old and fragile, no longer pliable. It cracks under the pressure. She digs her nail in deeper, then brushes away the shards of wax, shuddering at the feel of the lashes against her fingertip and the soft, dry sounds the wax makes as it falls into the box. The glass eye underneath is cloudy, though no doubt it's just residue from the wax, and it'll come off with a bit of water and soap and a clean cloth.

She breaks away more wax until she can grip the eye and pull it out. When she holds it in her hand, she laughs softly, nervously, then quickly stops, because she still can't shake the feeling that Sister Anna is aware of her and won't appreciate being laughed at.

She tucks the eye into her pocket—not the one with her rosary, because glass eyes are fragile and she can't risk breaking it—then starts digging out the second eye. She uses both hands this time, working fast and recklessly, because the fear that has dogged her every step of the way is still breathing down her neck, ready to pounce. The sooner she can leave this place and be with Elsebeth again, the better. She shouldn't be alone right now.

But you're not.

Sister Anna is here.

Sister Ursula shudders violently. A great chunk of the waxen face breaks off, crumbles between her fingers. She only just manages to grab the eye; at least the little layer of wax coating it means it's not slippery in the way glass usually is.

The mask is ruined now, and underneath, speckled with crumbs of wax, part of Sister Anna's face is visible.

Don't look, Sister Ursula tells herself as soon as she realizes this, both because she fears the image will haunt her and because she remembers Elsebeth's warning to not look the dead in the eye because that will give them power over her. She hadn't heard of that before, but so far, Elsebeth hasn't steered her wrong, and even if this is merely superstition, it won't do any harm to heed it.

But it is already too late.

She is looking.

Unlike the mask, which gave the impression of soft, supple skin, Sister Anna's face looks like leather in various shades of brown and yellow, all tough and strangely shiny. Time has eaten away part of her nose and her eyelid, but not the eye.

It should have gone cloudy, then rotted. It should have sunken and shriveled as a raisin before disappearing altogether, but it hasn't. It's round, and wet, and clear, and it is looking right at her.

Something seems to leap from that eye straight into Sister

Ursula's mind. She stands frozen, her throat so small she can barely breathe, let alone scream.

She doesn't know for how long she looks into that terrible eye, pale and sharp as a chip of ice. It has no lid to blink with, and so there is nothing to break the spell. It's only when another piece of wax from the mask crumbles and obscures the eye that Sister Ursula finds she can move again.

She stumbles back, her breath coming in great gasping heaves. With the glass eye still clutched tightly in her fist, she runs up the stairs, taking them two at a time. She steps on the hem of her dress, stumbles, bruises her knees and scrapes her hands, but she doesn't drop the glass eye, and she doesn't stop, not until she is out in the light again.

Elsebeth is standing close to the door with their meager belongings packed and ready to leave. When she sees Sister Ursula, her eyes widen, and the tightness in Sister Ursula's chest and throat lets up a little. How could she ever think those gray eyes were harsh? Compared to those of Sister Anna, they are as soft as a pigeon's down.

"Where were you?" Elsebeth asks. "I called for you, but you did not heed me. What is wrong? You look sickly."

Sister Ursula sways. Relief has made her light-headed, and she can't feel her feet anymore.

Immediately, Elsebeth grabs her to steady her, then feels her forehead for any signs of fever, makes her stick out her tongue, sniffs her breath. She undoes the top buttons of Sister Ursula's dress and rubs her throat, then puts her fingers into the other woman's armpits. "No buboes, thank God, so what ails you?"

Wordlessly, Sister Ursula takes Elsebeth's hand, which the girl balled into a fist as soon as she was done using it to check Sister Ursula for signs of the plague. Her *Liebchen*, always ready to fight everything and everyone. She uncurls those beloved fingers and places the two glass eyes on her palm.

Elsebeth's own eyes grow large. "Where did you get those?"

But Sister Ursula's throat is still so tight, she can't speak. She just rests her head on Elsebeth's shoulder and allows herself to be comforted by the feel and heat and scent of her.

"Come," Elsebeth says after a little while. "I've looked at the map, and it's not so far anymore to the saint's grave, three days of travel at the most." Elsebeth takes hold of Sister Ursula's chin, makes the woman look her in the eye.

"It's almost over now," she promises, two lines of determination carved between her brows. "Let's leave this awful place behind and get you your wish."

27

ELSEBETH

URSULA AND I HAVE TO travel two more days before we find the necromancer and Otto. It's only through luck that we do, or mayhap through God. After all, it is said that nothing happens without Him willing it, and for One who made the world, making sure that Ursula and I find these two men must be a little thing indeed.

It's evening when we come upon them, and almost dark. They have already set up their camp for the night. Ursula and I hide ourselves in the bracken and study them as Otto cooks a rabbit they have caught.

When I was still Gottfried's whore, I was terrified of Otto, who seemed a giant to me, so strong, loud, and rough. I took care never to be alone with him, for fear he might rape or otherwise hurt me, simply because he could. Men like him take what they please whenever it pleases them, and though I knew he did not think me beautiful, for I have never been so blessed, I have found that beauty does not matter when men are possessed by lust. He might even have taken me just to spite Gottfried. Men so love to spoil and break one another's toys.

Now, Otto's hard face is much rotted. His nose has fallen off, leaving a dark hole, and his cheeks look gray and pulpy, like fruit threaded through with mold. If I were to push my finger against that rotted meat, it would go straight through. His broad shoulders have shrunken and are rounded, and his hand trembles as he lifts the spoon to his face to sniff the stew he's cooking. Some of his fingers are just bone and bits of stringy tendon now. A part of me pities him, this mercenary who once inspired terror but is now no more than a corrupting corpse.

A different part of me revels to see him brought so low.

Ursula and I retreat to a safe distance so we can discuss what to do next in low voices. Around us, the wind rattles the branches of the trees. With the fall of night comes this rich smell of damp earth and leaves; the fields will likely be studded with dew come morning. We shall have to travel far and fast, or the grass shall mark every step and make us easy to track.

But that comes after we have taken back the skull. With the gauze, the eyes, and some embroidery, we have managed to make our skull look enough like the saint's skull that the necromancer won't notice the deception if only he doesn't look too closely. "I shall creep into the camp when they are both asleep and switch the skulls," say I.

Ursula interlaces her fingers with mine, and I marvel once more at how perfectly our hands fit. "I shall come with you," she says.

"Why? Two women are more likely to make a noise than one."

"You might find that an extra pair of hands comes in useful, and I don't want to be a coward."

I squeeze her long lean fingers. "I know you're no coward. You needn't prove yourself to me."

"All the same, I am coming," she says, her forehead all lined with stubbornness. And because she speaks sense about an extra pair of hands mayhap being useful, and because I like her forehead best when unfrowned, I agree.

We wait for a long time after the necromancer and Otto have banked the fire and crawled underneath their blankets, for we want to be as certain as we can be that they are asleep. Then, Ursula and I creep into their camp, our muscles taut and our hearts beating in our throats.

The necromancer took the skull out of her box before he went to bed. It rests in the crook of his sleep-slack arm, his fingers tangled in the red hair. I wait for Ursula to lift it so I can replace it with the fake skull now tucked under my arm. She reaches for it, then suddenly grabs my arm, squeezes it very hard. I look at her to see what has upset her so, then follow her gaze to the necromancer's face. For a moment, I freeze, my heart bucking in my chest.

His eyes are open, and he is watching us.

It is all over. We won't reunite the saint with her body; we won't get our wish. Instead, we'll die here, in this field, where the ravens and the foxes will pick over our bones, and...

The necromancer doesn't reach for us, doesn't spring to his feet, shout, and work his black magic, and when my mind finally understands why that is, I almost laugh, it's all so silly.

He sleeps with his eyes open, I mouth to Ursula.

She briefly closes her own eyes, relief turning her mouth loose and sweet. When she opens them again, she takes hold of the skull. Slowly, carefully, she lifts it.

The necromancer twitches.

We freeze. My heart drums in my chest, and my hands are wet with sweat.

Ursula takes a shuddering breath, then slowly continues to extract the skull. Her hair brushes against his fingers, and he clenches them in his sleep, trapping a lock between them. I have no choice but to kneel next to him, our fake saint balanced in my lap. I daren't touch his fingers. Instead, I take a blade of grass and raise it to his face. Without looking into his animal eyes—I fear that, if I am to look into them too long, he shall trap me in his gaze until he wakes—I brush the grass against his cheek. He grunts as he lets go of the saint's hair to rub at his face.

Quickly, Ursula plucks the skull from his grasp. Again he grunts, his left leg twitching. I push the fake skull into the hollow of the necromancer's arm before he can wake.

Ursula's eyes meet mine, and I smile at her, for the hardest part is done now. All that remains is leaving these two behind and making our way to the saint's burial place as fast as our legs can carry us, for we know not how she has been buried. If she has been laid to rest in a stone tomb, for example, it shall likely be hard to get into, and...

When I turn around, I find that Otto is awake and watching me.

I expect him to run his sword through me, or to shout and thus wake the necromancer, and I instinctively reach for my little knife so I can cut him down.

Instead, he clears his throat, pain flickering over his face, and says, "Please don't take the skull. It isn't what you think it is, Elsebeth." His voice, too, is a weak thing now, all used up, as he soon will be, too; dead things rot down to bone within days in the summertime.

"Shut your mouth!" I hiss. I glance at the necromancer from the corner of my eye to see if he's stirring out of his sleep, but he lies unmoving.

Otto goes on as if he has not heard me, or mayhap he has but doesn't care. If he has ever heeded a woman's word, it must have been his mother's or his wife's, not a peasant girl's he deems no better than a whore. "It's not a saint's skull," he says.

"Hold your lying tongue, or I shall cut it out for you!"

"I'm not lying. The necromancer has told me so himself. It's the skull of his wife. She is like me: dead, and yet somehow not, because he brought her back to life."

Ursula dashes toward Otto, presses the blade of her own little knife against his throat. Otto tilts his head back, but lazily, as if Ursula is more likely to shave than to stab him, though mayhap it's because his muscles and tendons have hardened, and it's not so easy for him to move quickly anymore. He has a wound there stitched up with black thread. It's poor work, the stitches large and uneven.

"Elsebeth told you to hold your tongue," Ursula whispers.

Otto swallows, which makes his Adam's apple bob in his throat. It scrapes against the knife. "I mean only to warn you," he whispers back. "You are risking your life for nothing. If only you'd let me explain, I—"

He hisses, for Ursula has cut him with the knife. What wells up from the cut is not blood, but a clear fluid that smells strongly of alcohol and vinegar. Has Otto been pickled so that he may last longer? Laughter burbles in my throat, makes my face spasm.

"You lie," Ursula says. She is very calm, her hand very steady, and I find that I am a little afraid of her, for I have never seen her so. "I think you may not be able to help it. You are in league with Satan, after all, that lord of lies. All the same, Elsebeth and I won't be deceived by you. Now here is what will happen: Elsebeth and I will take this skull, you won't raise the alarm, you won't tell the necromancer what has happened, and you won't come after us. Understood?"

Again, Otto swallows. The nick Ursula made opens and closes as a baby bird's beak. "I can't," he whispers. "I am not free to make my own choices. I'm sorry."

He takes a shuddering breath. Then, quick as a snake, he rears back, out of reach of the knife, and smashes his fist against Ursula's face. She crumples without a sound, the knife tumbling from her hand. Otto catches the skull with both hands before it can smash to pieces on the ground.

Seeing Ursula lie on the ground with her eyes half-open but seeing nothing in the manner of a corpse, I run a little mad again.

I growl like a dog and rush at Otto. With his hands full of skull, he can't fend me off. With my trusty little knife, I hack at the back of his left leg, cutting through flesh, muscle, and tendon. Otto cries out as he falls to his knees. I kick him hard in the chest, so he falls to his back. Something inside of his rump crunches. Even before he's down, I sit on his knees to keep him from rising, and I plunge the little knife into his belly as deep as it can go. I pull it out, plunge it back in.

Over and over again I stab him in his belly, hard and fast.

He may be dead, but that doesn't mean he can't feel pain, and it doesn't mean he can't be destroyed, either.

Otto grunts and groans but doesn't let go of the skull to defend himself as I make a mess of his belly. The smell of rot, vinegar, and alcohol is so thick in the air, I can taste it with every breath, and though it makes me heave, it is good, and it is sweet.

I only stop stabbing him when the knife slithers out of my hand. It's all slippery with this stinking sludge made up of bits of rotting flesh and whatever juice the necromancer has used to pickle him.

Ursula has come around now. She gets to her feet, sways, presses one hand to her aching head. With the other, she reaches for the skull. Together, we take it from Otto. He struggles, but only a little. Mayhap he's glad to be relieved of it; this way, he can finally press his hands against his belly to try and keep everything inside.

For good measure, I spit in his face. "I told you I'd gut you like a pig if you touched Ursula. Should've believed me," I snarl.

When I stoop to pick up my knife, I see the necromancer is awake and sitting up. His goat eyes glow in the dark like two golden coins catching sunlight, and the sight is so unsettling, I drop the knife again.

"Otto?" he asks, the words sleep-slurred.

"Quick, quick!" I tell Ursula. I move the skull to the crook of my arm. It's all soiled, its red hair sticking to the mesh in great clumps as the fluid from Otto's belly begins to clot. I wrap my free arm around her waist so I can support her and keep her from falling. A blow to the head can leave a person sick and dizzy.

"What has happened? What have you done?" the necromancer asks, and there's nothing sleepy about his voice now.

We run.

28

OTTO

PAIN TEARS OTTO APART. IT eats him whole, possesses him completely. He wishes he could die, then somehow manages to remember that he is already dead. If he could laugh at the horrific absurdity of it all, he would, but he can't do anything but lie still as the pain consumes him. At some point, it wanes, almost becoming manageable, and then it waxes again, dragging him under.

Otto doesn't know how long he is a slave to the pain in his belly and leg. It feels like centuries, but then time is a funny thing. Blood-like, it can flow at different speeds.

The first thing Otto notices when the pain has receded enough to allow his other senses to seep back into his consciousness is the necromancer's eyes. They are like two bits of coal burning in their sockets, all orange and yellow.

The necromancer bends over Otto, fingers the wound at the back of his knee with the hand that isn't holding the skull. Otto roars with pain, but he daren't let go of his belly to beat away the necromancer's hands. Next, the necromancer ruthlessly moves Otto's hands away to assess the damage done there. He clicks his tongue when he sees the wounds.

"Please," Otto begs, his pathetic scrap of a voice raking his ruined throat raw. "Please just kill me."

"You are dead already, remember?"

Otto laughs, but only a little bit; it pains both his throat and his belly something awful. It's unfair, so insanely unfair, that he should be a walking rotting corpse and yet somehow still be forced to endure pain. "You bastard. You know what I mean. I want you to release me. Elsebeth cut some important tendons at the back of my knee. I will never walk again, so what use am I to you now?"

The necromancer sighs. "I suppose you are right. I could bind you to a different body, but where am I to get one of those on such a short notice? Time is of the essence now; the longer we stand here, the farther that peasant girl and her companion will take my wife's skull from me, and there's no saying what they will do with it when they discover there's no wish at the end of this journey."

Otto swallows. He is frightfully thirsty, which is stupid because his body's digestive functions have long since ceased to work. "You're holding your wife's skull in your hand, aren't you?" he asks weakly.

"Not at all. How silly of those girls to think they could trick me. I'd know my beloved anywhere simply from the curve of her jaw, the blue opacity of her teeth, the way the wind lifts her hair. Besides, my wife was missing a tooth. This skull isn't. It belongs to another, and as such means nothing to me." The necromancer looks at the skull, his eyes cold as wet autumn leaves. Then, he lets it fall. Before it can hit the ground, he kicks it hard. It explodes into shards and dust so fine that it passes through the silk mesh and floats for a moment, pale, ghostlike, until it disperses to the point of invisibility.

"You needn't have done that. She might have been someone else's beloved," Otto whispers.

The necromancer bares his teeth at Otto. It's a grin, but only barely. "You knew this was not my wife's skull, so tell me, Otto Donatus Kreuzler: Why do you lie for a girl to whom you owe nothing, now that she has so brutally savaged you with her knife?"

Otto swallows again. It's like swallowing a piece of glass. "Because I don't want you to hurt her. I don't want you to hurt anyone. There's been so much pain and violence already...it has to stop sometime."

"If I don't release you, insects, birds, and rats will come for you and eat the flesh off your bones, and once those are picked clean, the wind, the sun, and the rain will scatter and destroy them slowly. You shall still be conscious then, yet helpless, and all because of Elsebeth and her little knife. Just a few weeks ago, you would've killed her methodically and as slowly as possible for far less."

It's not because of Elsebeth I am like this, but because of you, he thinks but doesn't say, for if he wants to avoid this grim fate, he must stay on the necromancer's good side. "I'm not the man I was a few weeks ago. I no longer want to torture, rape, and murder. I just...I just want to go home and be with my wife," Otto says quietly. Softly, he begins to sob, but the pain in his belly is so atrocious, he can't keep it up for long. He wipes at his eyes with his gore-streaked hands.

The necromancer smiles, but there's no mirth to it, no sly mockery, just a kind of sadness. "That I can understand. Do not cry; who knows what might happen when I release you? God alone knows all the secrets of the universe. You might fly to your Frieda's side, and she might know you anywhere, as my wife would know me and I her," he says.

Otto would like to think so, too.

The necromancer places his fingertip against Otto's forehead as if he is about to bless him. "You have served me well. Farewell, Otto Donatus Kreuzler."

Finally, blessedly, there is no more pain then, and no more thoughts.

29

URSULA

SISTER URSULA AND ELSEBETH RUN.

Sister Ursula has the almost irresistible urge to laugh; the only reason she doesn't is because she can't spare the breath. Already her lungs are aching, and that stitch in her side is back. A lifetime in the convent has hardened her to most discomforts, yes, but it hasn't made her a strong runner.

Soon, Elsebeth is taking the lead, dragging Sister Ursula along. Her hand is sticky. She smells so strongly of decay and vinegar that Sister Ursula only occasionally catches a whiff of this wet, clean night scent that is all around them, cutting across their faces in wild, cool shafts.

They stop running only when Sister Ursula slips in the wet grass and falls down, dragging Elsebeth with her, who instinctively curls her body around the saint's skull to protect it.

"Are you well?" Sister Ursula asks as soon as she has breath to speak. "Are you hurt?"

"I'm fine. Fret not. The skull is well, too, just a little dirty with Otto's fluids."

Sister Ursula sits up, clasps Elsebeth's dear face all speckled with gore. "Did he hurt you?"

"No," Elsebeth says. "No, but I hurt him. Do you think he'll die? Truly die, I mean?" She shudders suddenly, causing her teeth to clack together with a hard, clean sound. "Do you think it's still a sin to kill someone if they were already dead?"

She squeezes Elsebeth's face. "No. 'Thou shalt not kill' doesn't apply when you defend yourself and others from a sorcerer of Satan. Do you understand? This was not a sin! And if you don't believe me, I shall drag you to the nearest river and scrub you all clean again."

Elsebeth laughs. "What a papist thing to say, and with such fire! If you had been born a man, you would have made a fine priest. I can see you in a pulpit, preaching love, kindness, and charity."

"Do you not like that?"

"I like it very much. Before Otto hit you, you scared me a little. You were so cool, calm, and collected, it was like you were another, not my Ursula at all. I like you best when you are true to your own self."

Now it is Sister Ursula's turn to laugh. "Cowardly, afraid, and quite useless, you mean?"

Elsebeth frowns. There's a dark smear on her forehead drying into a crust. Her frowning causes the crust to crack. Flakes rain down, catching in her lashes. She blinks hard. "You are not useless. You are kind, and you are careful, and those things have served you well thus far. Why would you mislike being that?"

Sister Ursula shudders, then laughs, then shudders again; she can't help it. "You forget I tend to freeze when I am scared, which I am often. I couldn't let that happen, not tonight, so I pretended I wasn't my own drab little self, but a saint. Saints so often were both mighty and meek even when martyred. But when I had my knife at Otto's throat, I didn't feel meek at all. I felt like Judith must have just before she cut off Holofernes's head: powerful and full of righteous anger." She touches the side of her face where Otto punched her, which is hot with pain and swelling swiftly. "Though Otto knocked all those feelings clean out of my head in the same manner David felled Goliath."

Elsebeth has pulled her handkerchief from her pocket and moved it through the tall wet grass so that it is now sodden. She presses it against Sister Ursula's bruised eye as she says, "And like Goliath, I thought for a moment that you were dead. That is why I went a little mad, and I stabbed Otto so…"

Sister Ursula presses a kiss to Elsebeth's mouth. She tastes of vinegar, wine, and salt, of violence, anger, and greed, but the longer Sister Ursula kisses her, lapping up that taste and taking it inside herself, the more her *Liebchen* tastes sweet and true again. After a while, she stops, takes Elsebeth's handkerchief, and uses it to wipe away the worst of the gore from Elsebeth's face. Her hands are trembling with excitement.

"Come," she says. "I don't know if the necromancer realizes we took the skull, but we mustn't assume we are safe. Better to keep going and only stop once we've had our wishes."

They reach the point marked on the map as the sun is setting.

It is a crossroads.

Had it not been for the map, they would have walked past it without a second glance. It is, after all, just a place where two roads meet, of which there are many in this world. There is little that sets this particular crossroads apart from all those others: no chapel, no shrine, not even a simple marker telling those who can read where the road will take them if only they walk a certain number of miles farther. All it really has are a number of rough black rocks the size of sheep that look as if they have been thrown down haphazardly by a giant who no longer wanted to play with them.

The wild, almost ecstatic joy that possessed Sister Ursula those first moments after they stole the skull, already somewhat dampened by their hours of frantic rushing through woods and fields to get here as fast as they could, is now extinguished almost entirely. She rubs her eyes. They are sore with tiredness. "This can't be right. Are you sure this is the place on the map?"

"I am. Look." Elsebeth shows her the piece of fabric. "This thread is the road, and these clumps of dark wool must be those stones. There's seven of them on the map, and I count seven here in front of us."

Bewildered, Sister Ursula looks from the crude embroidery of the map to the stones and back again. "How do we know those clumps are meant to be stones? They could be anything, really, the embroidery being so poorly done."

"What else could it be?"

"But this can't be it! I don't see a crypt here, or a shrine, or some other place we could reasonably expect to find a saint's sacred remains!"

Elsebeth stuffs the map back into her pocket without bothering to fold it neatly first. "Mayhap Otto was right, and there is no saint. There never was. We have been tricked," she says, her voice flat.

Sister Ursula shakes her head so fast, her hair lashes her cheeks. "No, no! Saints do exist, as do miracles."

"No, they don't, and if they did, they wouldn't happen to the likes of me. Good things are rare in life. This was too good to be true." She falls to her knees, the heels of her hands pressed hard against her eyes. She moans, this animal sound, rough and full of pain.

Sister Ursula stands stricken, trying not to cry. There is a pain between her breasts, a soft, pulsing ache that radiates up her throat. She tries to swallow it down, but it remains, hard as a pit.

What if Otto was right? What if this is no saint's skull, but just the skull from one of the ordinary dead?

Only the ordinary dead aren't usually buried at crossroads. That's a special kind of degradation saved for suicides, criminals, and all the others who are deemed not worthy of being buried in consecrated ground.

But no, it can't be that the skull in her hands belongs to such a sinner. No ordinary skull could travel into her dreams to instruct her. And not just her dreams, either; twice, Elsebeth dreamed of the skull speaking to her, too. Three dreams. Three is the number of the Lord.

Three makes it true.

Sister Ursula kneels next to Elsebeth, moves the girl's hands away from her eyes. "Don't despair," she says.

"Why not? We have come so far, suffered so much, and for what?" Elsebeth growls.

"Not all is lost yet, *mein Liebchen*. I think—"

"And for *what*, Ursula? I'll tell you for what. For a fairy tale that I knew in my heart of hearts to be false, and yet I let the promise of a wish seduce me into cutting off a dead woman's head, and stabbing a man, and countless smaller sins besides!" With each word, Elsebeth's voice becomes louder and shriller, and Sister Ursula's heart aches for her.

"Listen!" she says sharply, clasping Elsebeth's wrist with her free hand and digging her nails into the thin skin to snap the girl out of her grief and anger. "You are tired, and you are hurt, and I understand, but just because there is no church or chapel or crypt here doesn't mean there is no saint. Think about it. If you had to hide a sacred relic to keep it safe from soldiers and plunderers, where would you hide it?"

"Somewhere people wouldn't think to look," Elsebeth says.

"Exactly. Would you think to look for a saint's body at a crossroads like this if you didn't have a map to tell you she lies buried here?"

"No."

"And that is why I think we are in the right place after all. Have some faith, *mein Liebchen*. There is always hope. Now let's hurry." Sister Ursula loosens her grip on Elsebeth's wrist. Her nails have left little marks that are flushing almost purple now that the blood comes rushing back. If she had more time, she'd bring the wrist to her mouth and kiss it to soothe the flesh she has marked. Instead, she places the skull on one of the black stones at the side of the road, so it is safe and out of the way.

"Oh, but we are truly blessed! More digging!" Elsebeth sneers as she follows Sister Ursula to the middle of the crossroads. They have no shovel, but the earth is still wet with dew and thus soft. With their bowls, spoons, and hands, they set to digging.

It doesn't take long this time. Whoever buried the saint's body must have been in a hurry and didn't dig deep; Sister Ursula and Elsebeth are only two handspans in when Sister Ursula's bowl strikes something hard.

"Oh dear Lord!" Sister Ursula exclaims. "I think I found something, Elsebeth!" She puts her bowl aside and digs with her fingers, carefully removing crumbs of black earth until she reveals rough, cheap cloth that falls apart when she tries to lift it. Inside lie small bones, some long and lean, others round as pebbles.

No, some of those *are* pebbles. They are white, yes, but speckled or banded with pink, blue, and gray. Sister Ursula removes them. With cloth this poor, it's not to be wondered at that some stones have gotten mixed in with the bones. "What do you think these bones are?" she asks.

Elsebeth bends closer to look. "Methinks those are the bones of the hand. They look a little like the sheep knucklebones my sister and I used to play with, only smaller."

Relief makes Sister Ursula feel all weak. It's only now that they have found bone that she can admit to herself that she was, for a moment, truly terrified that they weren't at the right place, or worse, that there was no saint's body to reunite the skull with, no wish.

"They're a little damaged," Elsebeth remarks, picking up one of the little bones. It has a large crack running through it.

Sister Ursula sits up, looks at the skull as it stands grinning on its piece of rock, winces. "Do you think I did that? That I broke her hand when I struck it with my bowl?"

"If you did, it's nothing the good Lord won't know how to heal, I'm sure. How were you to know they had placed her in such a shallow grave? Though it's a good sign for your theory that she was moved here not so long ago, when she was already a skeleton. Else, an animal would have dug her up and eaten her, and the bones would be scattered."

They quickly exhume the rest of the body, flinching at every sound, their nerves stretched almost to the point of fraying by the knowledge the necromancer might reach them at any minute. The cloth in which the saint's remains are wrapped has rotted to the point where they can tear it off with ease; even a ripe apple on a bough offers more resistance to being plucked than this cloth does. With every bit of cloth they rip off, they uncover more of the skeleton: a femur, an ulna and tibia, a rib cage. All of them are that same chalky white, unnatural for bone so old. The skeleton has been buried lying on its belly, and that is odd, but as soon as they uncover the place where the head should be and find it missing, none of that matters anymore.

Sister Ursula begins to laugh with joy. "It's her! It's really her, Elsebeth!" she says.

Elsebeth sits frightfully still, her hands at her mouth. Then, she jumps up, throws her fists into the air, and shouts, or maybe laughs; it's hard to tell. When she is done, she flings her arms around Sister Ursula's neck and draws the other woman so tightly to her, she could clasp her own elbows. "I am sorry I doubted you," she whispers.

Sister Ursula's arms are pinned to her sides, so all she can do is rub her cheek against Elsebeth's head. Her cap is filthy. When all of this is done, and such everyday concerns as laundry will start to matter again, she will scrub at it and beat it until it is as clean as it can possibly be. For now, she says, "I doubted myself, too."

Elsebeth lets her go. "I am sorry for it all the same."

"What does it matter now? Let us be glad!" Sister Ursula places a light kiss on Elsebeth's nose, then gets up to go fetch the skull. In the dying light of day, the skull's red hair seems to have harnessed the sun's fire and glows various shades of red and orange. It is not at all like the dry, brittle hair they took from the *Aufhocker*'s mother; that looked dead. This looks alive.

Sister Ursula carefully picks up the skull. "I am sorry my hands are not any cleaner and that we have dirtied you so," she says. Otto's blood has set in the fine mesh. Their rubbing has only seemed to spread the stains.

Maybe the saint won't mind, though. She had to wait a long time to be reunited with her body. The fulfillment of a wish that big and held for so long would leave anyone in a good mood, especially someone already filled with godly grace.

Sister Ursula brings the skull to her mouth and gently plants a kiss on the forehead. The mesh feels cool and slippery against her lips. "Time to bring you back where you belong," she whispers.

"Ursula, look out!" Elsebeth screams.

Sister Ursula whips around, allowing the necromancer to plunge Elsebeth's little gore-streaked knife into her throat.

30

ELSEBETH

I WATCH THE NECROMANCER DRIVE a knife into Ursula's throat, destroying all that beautiful white flesh, and something snaps inside of me. It's not my heart, though that feels as if it is being mauled, but something inside of my head. I can actually hear it, this crunching sound, not at all the swift hard snap of bone, but the slow crack of a branch that won't break cleanly.

No, not a branch, a dam that can no longer stand tall and strong against the beating of the water. After the snap, I am filled to the brim with feelings, anger, hurt, disbelief, guilt, hatred, grief, sadness, and many other things besides, ones I have only seldom felt and others I know not the names of, and they all tangle together like rope, and the rope rises inside of me and binds me fast so that I cannot move; I cannot speak; I can only stand and watch as the necromancer moves the knife to the side, slowly and with clear intent, ripping that beloved flesh threaded through with pale veins.

Blood spouts from the wound.

And all the while, Ursula stands with a little frown on her face, as if she doesn't understand what is happening. She raises no hand to her throat, and the blood pours down in an unbroken stream so that, for a moment, it looks like a sheet of dark silk shifting in the breeze.

But there is only so much blood in the body, and Ursula's seems in a hurry to gush from her throat. By the time the necromancer pulls out the knife, she is swaying on her feet. It's only a few fevered heartbeats more until she staggers to her knees. The necromancer plucks the skull from her hands as she falls.

Ursula is dead before her dear face hits the ground.

She is dead.

She is dead.

She is dead deaddead *SHE IS DEAD sheisdead*

she is she is sheisheisheis she is DEADDEADdeaD SHE IS DEAD

SHE IS *DEAD* SHEISDEADSHEISDEADSHEIS SHESHEsheShEsHe my *BELOVED* she is dEAD she is dead I watched her *die* I stood and watched ithappen isawher DIE and did naught to save her AND NOW SHE IS dead she is she is she is

she

is

dead

Someone is laughing.

The sound is so offensive, so wrong and horrible, that it snaps me back into sanity. I look at the necromancer, and he looks at me, and I see it was not him who laughed, but me. Horrified, I clap my hands over my mouth. I taste grave dirt, and I gag, and then I am crying, or mayhap laughing again. It's hard to tell. I am not fully sane, not anymore, mayhap not ever again, for madness is truly a kind of place, and once you wander in too deep, you can't find your way out again.

The necromancer does not laugh, does not grin, smirk, or gloat. In fact, he looks both disappointed and disgusted, and that is worse. "Now look at what you have made me do," he sighs and kicks Ursula's corpse with his foot, and for that alone he deserves to be skinned alive, then thrown into a pot of boiling oil. "I told you I didn't want to hurt you, but that I would if you forced me to."

"Don't touch her, you bastard!" I growl. "Touch her again, and I'll kill you."

That dour expression flees the necromancer's face. He throws back his head and laughs, a high girlish sort of giggle that suits him poorly. "Oh, Elsebeth," he sighs, and with the hand he isn't using to hold the skull, he wipes tears from his eyes. "You are such an angry little thing, aren't you? A feral cat in human form. Poor Otto discovered that to his detriment, when all he did was try to warn you that you were wrong. I fear that this whole situation could have been prevented, had you only listened."

He looks at the skull, sighs again, tenderly brushes some hair away from the forehead. "And if you hadn't tricked them in the first place, you naughty thing. Filling people's heads with the idea that you can grant wishes to trick them into taking you here!"

"You lie," I hiss. I wish to fall upon him, or mayhap to crouch down to Ursula and touch her, but I must not let hot rage cloud my mind, so instead I keep standing, my hands balled into trembling fists.

"For all my many faults and sins, I am no liar, Elsebeth, and neither was Otto. This here is the skull of my wife. If you are quiet, I shall tell you everything in a way you can understand. Once upon a time," the necromancer begins, and for a moment a finger of fear strokes my spine, for how does he know that I have many fairy stories in my head and that they help me make sense of the world? But then he is a witch, and it must not be wondered at that he can do many dark things.

"Once upon a time, there lived a simple man who wanted nothing more from life than to serve God. This had been the most fervent wish of his heart ever since he could remember. He had no eyes for women, or riches, or any other worldly thing that so many others covet. All he wanted was to read his Bible and instruct those around him, that they may live in a manner pleasing to the Lord. For twenty years, the man lived in perfect contentment. Then, the man fell in love."

The fear that flicked up and down my spine vanishes, for this is a boring story so far. I have heard half a dozen others like this, and those my grandmother told with far more skill. But what can I do but stay still and listen? It's not as if I have anywhere else to be, not now, not anymore.

"She was no great beauty," the necromancer goes on, "and her garb was simple, her hands and hair unadorned, yet she touched something within the man that had never been touched before. Though the man had prayed, and fasted, and flagellated himself, worn horsehair shirts, and placed sharp pebbles in his shoes in the hope that his thoughts would turn to God once more and drive her out, she would not be exorcised from his heart. He knew then that he was not merely lusting after her, for temptations may be strong, but they are also fleeting. He thought about it long and hard, and decided then that he should marry her, if she was willing. She was, and so they married, and the man rejoiced and praised the Lord for sending him this precious miracle of a woman."

I look at my precious miracle of a woman, who lies so still and pale at his feet, that little frown still on her face. I wish I could rub it from her forehead like one can rub out a mark in the sand, but I can't, and my heart tears into pieces, and I wish I could rip it out so I need not feel this, not again.

For a moment, I go mad, and I hear see smell taste nothing, only feel a sickening pain in my chest, my eyes growing so heavy, I fear they might drop out of my skull if I bend over, and this scratching in my throat as if something wishes to be let out.

When I come to myself again, I have missed part of the necromancer's tale, though he talks in such a long-winded way that it hinders me not in understanding what he wants me to know.

"But the bite was fatal, and she died in his arms. The man called on God and the angels and saints to please return his beloved, but no matter how he ranted and raved, his wife remained dead. Then, in a fit of madness and desperation, the man called out one final time, not for God or an angel or saint, but for anyone, anything, to please have pity on his sorry self and help him. This time, something answered, something dark, foul, and unclean."

"So you conjured up a demon and sold yourself to Satan to get your wife back," I snarl, for I do not want to hear him talk of death at length, not when my Ursula lies at his feet with her throat ruined by his hand.

The necromancer frowns at my interruption. Methinks he has a love of hearing his own voice. "I did. I signed my name in Satan's book, and in exchange he lengthened my life long beyond what is common, and he gave me the power of necromancy. Satan takes great pleasure in the perversion of holy miracles, and what miracle better to defile than that of resurrection? So you see, I did not sell myself cheaply."

I wonder if he means for me to clap, as if it's somehow admirable what he has done, when really, it's sad. "So he made you a necromancer, and you brought your wife back from the dead, but you did it wrong, or she wouldn't be just bones in the ground now."

The necromancer's face becomes tight, as does his grip on the skull, and won't it be funny if he squeezes her so hard in anger that the brittle bone breaks, so that everything will have been for naught? "I didn't do it wrong."

"Then why are we here?"

"Because my wife did not appreciate being brought back to life by dark forces and fled from me, you rude little *bitch*!" the necromancer screams, spittle flying from his mouth like venom from a snake's fangs.

I am quick to anger, yet when another rages, it makes me feel calm, and so I do and say nothing but stare at him.

Two spots of color burn on the necromancer's sallow cheeks. The sun has set by now, darkness falls swiftly over the land, and the spots look not like blushes but like smears of grave dirt.

"Forgive me. I did not mean to lose my temper," he says after a while, his voice restrained. He wipes at his mouth with a handkerchief, clears his throat. "What I meant to say before you interrupted me is that my beloved wife's soul was pure and clean, and when she discovered what had happened and how I had restored her to life, she was appalled and disgusted. I discovered that we had… different interpretations of what I had done and what that meant."

His face becomes tight again, as if he is in great pain. He looks at the skull, strokes it with a fingertip. "I felt I had been selfless. I had sacrificed my soul and the chance at eternal bliss in Heaven just so I could be with her again in this vale of tears, because I loved her more than anything in this world. She, however, felt that I had been rash and selfish. Our separation had been temporary, because, upon my death, I would have been reunited with her in Heaven, where we would live in joy for eternity. By selling my soul to Satan, I had instead ensured our separation was final, and in that way, I had taken away her chance at happiness, too."

The necromancer raises the skull to his face, rests their foreheads together. His quick, gulping breaths stir her coppery hair.

When he speaks, his voice is soft and pained. "She no longer wanted to be with me, because necromancers are an abomination unto the Lord, and since she was God-fearing and God-loving, I was an abomination unto her, too."

He lowers the skull, presses it against his chest over the place where his heart beats. "I told her she was still my wife and had promised to love and obey me. She said we had taken our vows until death do us part, and that it had, and so she was no longer beholden to me. I argued death hadn't parted us, because here she was, alive and well. At this she laughed in a manner most cruel and mocking, and showed me her hands, which had begun to blacken at the fingertips."

"So you did do it wrong," say I.

Through gritted teeth, the necromancer says, "I did not. The art of necromancy means the conjuring of the spirits of the dead. I had recalled her spirit to the land of the living, and what is more, I had bound it to her body. The problem is that I desired resurrection rather than necromancy."

I find myself growing both bored and angry with this man. I wish he'd speak plainly. All this babbling when my little love lies in the dirt all wet with her blood makes a mockery of my grief, and for that he deserves to be punished in the manner of traitors: pulled apart by horses, but not before his privates have been torn from his body with hot pliers.

But I've no horses, no pliers, only my tongue, and so I say, for I know it will madden him, "I suppose you shall tell me now what the difference is between necromancy and resurrection?"

"Yes, I shall," he snaps, and it's a glorious thing to see his usual smug smile wiped from his evil face and the giggle scraped from his voice. "I shall, for how else will you understand what you have gotten yourself involved with? Necromancy means bringing back someone's soul into their body so that you may speak with it. Resurrection means returning a soul to its body *and the body to its prime state before death.*"

I laugh, though without genuine mirth. "So you are telling me your wife's soul was bound to a rotting body, all because you did not bother to tell Satan what, exactly, you wanted?" His mother must not have told him many fairy stories, or he'd know that you must always be precise and leave no room for loopholes when dealing with elves, fairies, and demons.

"True resurrection can only be achieved by the Lord."

"Then why did you bother with Satan in the first place?"

"Because the Lord didn't answer my pleas! Have you not been listening, or are you stupid?"

I glower at him. "I am not stupid, but I am bored by you. All this talking, and for what? I care not for your story. I only care about Ursula, and the skull in your hands, and the wish that was promised me."

The necromancer looks at Ursula with disdain. He spits on the ground next to her, and I imagine what it shall be like to pull his tongue out by the root, cut it up in little strips, fry them, and then feed them to him one by one. It shall take a while. It's a difficult thing, to swallow without a tongue. Mayhap he'll choke on it.

"I am trying to tell you there is no wish," the necromancer

snaps, and it's a joy to see him so frustrated with me. "My wife fled from me. I tried to find her, but I had not yet learned how to divine truth with bones and teeth, and so by the time I finally discovered where she was, it was too late. People did not see a devout and godly woman, but a walking corpse, and thus something foul. A group of peasants led by a priest tried to kill her, but they could not. Only I could, for I had called her back to life."

"Your poor wife must have suffered something horrible before they discovered that."

The necromancer's long fingers tense again, making tendons stand out like roots. "I made them pay for that. Oh, how I made them pay! But yes. They decapitated her, and when they found that still did not kill her, they buried her. Not her skull, though. That, they gave to a group of pilgrims traveling to Rome so that it might be exorcised. I have to admit this plan was not entirely without merit. It's much harder for a body to get up and make mischief without its head."

I am not laughing, jeering, or mocking now, for I believe he is speaking true, and it is terrible. The pain in my chest grows, and it's as if I have a hole there, gaping, aching.

The necromancer giggles. "I see you are finally grasping what I have been trying to explain to you."

I curl around my pain, as if it can be tamed, if only I hold it tight. Two tears fall from my eyes, dripping dimples in the raw dark earth of the saint's grave.

No, not a saint.

Just a woman brought back from the dead against her will by a man who could not let her go.

I gasp, and it's as if a knife is driven between my ribs. "But the skull, she is all done up like a papist saint," I moan.

"Something can look like one thing and be another."

"But why would anyone make her look like a saint?"

The necromancer shrugs. "They likely thought she was one. She has been with so many people, the story of how she came to be was lost. If a skull was entrusted to you, wouldn't you think it was likely a holy relic? Besides, the longer the dead linger here, the stronger their powers grow. After a few decades, they know things, can spin illusions, and can influence the mind in various ways… like through dreams."

I feel as if I've been dropped from a great height and all the air has been knocked out of me.

The necromancer sees, and his smile widens. "She came to you in your dreams, didn't she? She did; I can tell. Naughty thing." He lovingly sticks his finger in the hole where her nose used to be, as if tickling her.

"No, no! This makes no sense!" I groan. "Why would she compel Ursula and me to bring her skull here if she is just an ordinary woman who cannot die?"

"I thought that must have been obvious even to a humble peasant girl such as yourself. How would you like for your head to be in one place and your body in another?" he says, and now it's him who is mocking me, but I care not, or at least not nearly as much as when it's Ursula he defiles.

"That is not what I meant!" say I.

"Then what do you mean?"

"She warned me about you. She warned me, and when you had taken her away from us, she told Ursula how to steal her back. Why would she do that? Why would she care so much who brought her here if she is no saint, honor-bound to fulfill whatever the person who reunites her skull with her body wishes for?"

The necromancer sighs and pulls his finger out of the skull's nose, then traces the curve of her socket. "She doesn't care who brings her here, as long as it isn't *me*. I suppose she is still angry with me and does not want to see me. I can't quite fault her for that, though I had hoped the past few centuries would have made her more amenable to me. I am her only hope, after all."

"You are lying about all of this. You *must* be lying." For if he is not, if he is speaking true and there is no wish, then Ursula has died for nothing, and she and my family are lost to me forever, and I am alone, alone, alone…

I scream.

I scream, I pull out hanks of hair, I beat my brow against the damp ground, and I scratch at my throat, arms, and the back of my hands, anything to stop these feelings inside of me, but no matter how I hurt myself, the bodily pain is a mere grain of sand on the beach of my hurt.

When I return to myself, blood is dripping from my scalp and running into my eyes, making them sting. I sob and rub at them with my knuckles, which are bleeding also.

"Poor thing," the necromancer says, and I know not whether he speaks of me or his wife.

"I will kill you for this," I say, but with my voice all hoarse from screaming and my face all bloodied by my own hands, I know I look pathetic rather than frightening.

"I don't think so. But I shall tell you what will happen now, Elsebeth," he says, and he speaks in that calm and sad voice that makes me want to rip apart his throat so I may plunge my hand inside and pull out his vocal cords until they snap. "You are going to get up, and you are going to move away from my wife's body so that I can collect all that remains, because I need every last bit of her for this to work."

"For what? To take her out of her misery?"

"No!" the necromancer says, appalled. "To bring her back to me! I know so much more now than I did when I revived her. I can bind her to a new body, a fresh one, and if that goes to rot, we shall find another body, and another, and so on."

I look at Ursula at his feet, and I know then why he killed her when he really didn't have to.

The necromancer follows my gaze. "Careful now, Elsebeth," he says, voice low and dangerous. "If you value your life, you will not interfere or do anything else rash or stupid."

"I don't value my life if it has no Ursula in it," I say, and then I interfere and do something else rash and stupid. I plunge my hands into the grave and grab all the bones I can, a rib and all these little shards.

I straighten, and I look into the necromancer's demon eyes. "Does your wife still feel everything that happens to her body, I wonder? If so, I think it will be painful if I swallow some of these small bones and my stomach burns them all up, what say you?"

I can see the necromancer's pulse in a vein on his forehead, which wriggles with every heartbeat. "That's not a charitable thing to do, Elsebeth. Do you think Ursula would like for you to be uncharitable?"

"Take her name out of your filthy mouth, you bastard," I say, and I place one of the little bones on my tongue. I taste the crumbs of earth clinging to it, but the bone itself seems oddly flavorless.

The necromancer's jaw tenses. "Don't do it."

"Or what?" I ask, the words coming out all strange, for I have to talk around the bit of bone in my mouth. "You shall punish me slowly, like you did those who hurt your wife? Now that Ursula is dead and I am all alone, I fear neither pain nor death."

"'Now that Ursula is dead,'" the necromancer mimics me, and laughs in a way I'd find humiliating if I still cared about that sort of thing. "You forget, you bold bitch, that I am a necromancer." Without taking his eyes from my face, he squats down and touches Ursula's forehead with a finger long and white as a twig stripped of its bark, and for that he deserves to be bound to a wooden rack and have his limbs shattered with a hammer over the course of days, and…

But I can think no more of how to punish him. I even forget the bone on my tongue and its nothing taste, for Ursula is stirring.

31

ELSEBETH

URSULA JERKS, AND SHE GROANS, and then she sits up. Her head lolls, causing the terrible wound in her throat to gape open. Her eyelids are at half-mast, her eyes like that of a sleepwalker, all empty.

"I regret I have to do this, I really do," the necromancer says, "but if you insist on being difficult, then I see no other way."

He makes Ursula stand, and it's all wrong. She never held herself like this, so stiff and strange.

I almost gulp down the little bone still in my mouth; I had forgotten it was there. I spit it back into the grave for fear I might choke on it otherwise. "Don't," I beg, though I know not whether I am talking to Ursula or the necromancer. "Don't do this, please. It's not right."

"We are beyond that now, Elsebeth," the necromancer sighs.

When Ursula moves toward me, it's in the manner of a child who has scarcely learned how to walk, but it is fast, and it is terrible.

Those beautiful hands of hers, which have brought me such pleasure, grasp for me, and I sob with the horror of it even as I dash out of her way. "Don't, don't, don't," I moan as she comes at me again with her arms outstretched.

Widdershins, she chases me around the grave. Although I am close enough to the necromancer for him to grab me and pluck the bones from my hand, he does nothing but stand back and watch, giggling all the while.

With every jarring step Ursula makes, the tear at her throat widens and then closes again like a mouth. There's this horrible gurgling sound that comes from it.

It's only when I stumble and the gurgling intensifies that I realize it's laughter.

Ursula—*no not Ursula only her body it's just her body being moved about like a puppet for Ursula would never not ever ever*—straddles me. She wraps her cool white hands around my throat and squeezes.

I have often felt pain, and yet there's nothing that compares to the horrible ache of having your throat pressed shut.

Instinctively, I try to push her away from me, but she is much taller than I am, and the way she is sitting on me makes it hard to buck. I grab her hands instead, try and pry them loose, but her grip is iron.

The only way to stop the restless dead is to behead them or set them on fire. I have no means to make a fire, though mayhap if I grab Ursula's hair and pull hard enough, her head will tear away from her neck; the wound the necromancer made is awfully deep.

I don't want to hurt her, but what choice do I have? The blood beating in my head is loud as a drum of war. My lungs are burning, my throat is aching, and black spots float in my vision.

I let go of her wrists. My fingers have gone numb and feel more like sacks of needles than meat and bone.

"I am sorry," I try to say, but I've no breath to spare and can hear naught but the desperate pumping of my heart.

With all my strength, I punch Ursula's chin.

Her head snaps back. The wound at her throat widens, a spurt of fluid that may be blood or something else entirely shooting out and only narrowly missing my face. Her hands loosen, and that is all I need. I flip on my belly and wriggle out from under her. I gulp in the air, drinking it the way a drunkard does wine, eagerly, quickly, and as much as I can, and it matters not that each breath is liquid fire that scorches my throat and makes my eyes tear.

And then Ursula is coming for me again, and I am not fast enough to crawl away from her, not when there's still flecks of dark in my vision and I am coughing and choking.

"Please!" I gasp. "Please, God, help me. Save me!"

"God won't come for you," the necromancer sneers.

Ursula grabs me by the hair and drags me back. She kicks me in the belly, and it drives all the air from my lungs once more. I curl around the pain, try to make myself small as she keeps kicking me. One of her kicks catches me in the face, and my mouth instantly floods with blood.

"Please," I choke, blood dribbling out between my lips. "Please, God, help me."

If He exists, He must help me, for it's not right that I, who have suffered so much already, shall be pummeled to death at the hands of my beloved's corpse.

"Please, God, please, *please*," I babble.

The necromancer's voice whispers in my ear, "Save your breath, you stupid girl. Look around you. Do you see God here? He has forsaken us. He won't aid you."

And I believe him, for nothing happens without God willing it, and so if God did not will this, then He would have stopped it by now.

Mayhap this is punishment for falling in with papists, or being so greedy as to think I could get my family back when God has called them to Him. Mayhap I deserve this for all the filth that stains my soul, for I am a sickening sinner, aren't I? I know I am.

Yes, mayhap the best thing to do is to lie back and take it; there's a good girl.

Or mayhap there is no reason for any of this, for there is no God, and I am no more than a stupid peasant girl being beaten to a pulp by someone bigger and stronger than me just because they can.

Those soldiers who raped my big sister, Margarethe, to death were bigger and stronger than me, as were Gottfried, the *Nachzehrer*, and the necromancer.

They are always bigger and stronger than me.

Why are they always bigger and stronger than me?

I am sick of it.

It's as that witch said, the one I saw burned when still a girl:

this is a cruel world, and poor women such as she should grab any crumb of power they can get their hands on.

Poor women such as I.

As I dance at the edge of unconsciousness, which feels a little like flying, I whisper through my broken and bloodied mouth, "Satan, help me, please."

There is a sudden drop in the air of the kind that normally heralds a thunderstorm.

Ursula stops beating and kicking me.

I lie very still for a moment. In places, my skin feels too tight for the flesh underneath. My legs, back, belly, chest, neck, throat, and head all ache, throb, and burn, and I am afraid I have been hurt in some way that won't heal and might worsen if I move now. I breathe out slowly, letting a little blood dribble out of my mouth. I tongue my teeth carefully. None have been broken, but the molars in my left upper jaw are sore and feel loose, so I shall have to take care not to chew on that side.

Something cool and smooth touches my cheek.

I open my eyes, or try to. The left one has almost swollen shut, and blood has leaked into my right one. It paints the world red.

The necromancer and Ursula stand frozen, he with that smug, gloating look on his face that I dearly desire to peel away with something small and sharp, she still looking like a sleepwalker.

I sit up and look around to see what brushed my cheek so tenderly, and I find it only a few feet away from me. I thought Satan would be a dark and handsome man with cloven feet and the horns of a ram, or mayhap a red-haired woman with broad hips and full breasts. But to me, as he did to Eve, he comes in the guise of a large snake, black and gleaming like oil. The snake has raised itself, and now that I am sitting, we are of the same height.

Its eyes are orange and intelligent, and they are looking at me expectantly.

I make to spit out the blood still in my mouth, but I don't want to give offense, so I swallow instead, wincing at the pain. Say I, "I have conjured you here, that I may barter with you. Tell me: Do you understand me, and are you Satan?"

"I am he," the snake says. It doesn't open its mouth, but I hear its voice clearly in my head, not the harsh hiss of a snake in distress, but a soft, sweet whisper, so cool and slippery it makes me shiver, though from fear or delight, I know not.

There are many questions inside of my head, but the one that makes it into my mouth and tumbles out first is this one: "Have you power over time? Is that why the necromancer and Ursula are so still?"

The devil says, "I have made it so they cannot move, but time still flows onward."

"Can they hear and see us?"

"The necromancer can. The nun is just a corpse devoid of its soul, and so neither hears nor sees."

That makes my heart flutter. "Where is Ursula's soul now? In Heaven or Hell?" For if it is in Heaven, I shall leave it there, no matter that the loss of her ravages me and we shall not meet again, for if a papist can get into Heaven, I think that a lapsed Calvinist sinner such as I stands not a chance.

The snake says, "She might be, and she might not."

I frown, but it pulls painfully on the swollen skin of my face, so I try to smooth my brow once more. "What sort of answer is that?"

"The only one you shall get from me. I know many things, but not all, and some of the things I do know I cannot share." The devil's snake head bobs this way and that. It's strangely soothing to look at. "Now tell me, child, what is it you desire?" he asks in his whisper voice.

"What can you give me?"

"I can give you pretty dresses and ribbons for your hair. I can give you butter, cream, and bread every day of your life. I can give you a pretty wench to dally with who will pleasure you with her hands and mouth until you forget even your own name."

"What care I for that?" I may be a sinner, but I am not vain, I am not greedy, and though I may at times be lustful, it's only Ursula I lust after.

"Then what is it you desire?"

I take my time to answer, for I know from my grandmother's stories and the necromancer's tale that I shall only have the one chance, and I must be both polite and precise, and thus give Satan no way to cheat me. "That man over there is one of your servants. He sold his soul to you in exchange for power over death, that he might return his wife to the land of the living and keep her there until he gave her leave to die."

"What is it you desire?" the snake repeats.

"That man killed my Ursula. She was..." I choke, for how can mere words ever properly explain all she was, and all she was to me?

Better not to try. I take a deep breath and go on. "If she resides not in Heaven but in Hell, I want her returned to me as she was before, when she was still living."

"I cannot meet the first condition of what you ask. I told you: That information is not mine to give, and you shall not get it, not even by trickery."

I must gamble then. To rip her out of Heaven would be cruel, yet she may return there once she dies again, surely. And if she is not there, but is burning in Hell, then my deal shall offer reprieve.

I take a shuddering breath, which causes a fiery pain in my ribs, and manage to choke out, "I want her either way. I want her whole, and I want her well. I want the power of resurrection, not necromancy."

"The power you seek is not mine to give."

Almost I say, "Then you are weak indeed," but I want not to make an enemy out of Satan and so must tame my waspish tongue. After all, he came to me when I asked, when God did not. Instead, I ask, "Then what can you give me?"

The snake seems to smile at me, letting me look into its soft pink mouth. "I can return her soul to her body and bind her to it."

I shake my head, but the movement causes a sharp pain in my neck, like a knife being driven between the bones of my spine. I cry out and almost vomit. By the time I can speak again, I am covered with a fine sheen of sweat. "That is what the necromancer did to his wife, but her body was still that of a corpse, so she rotted, and now she's just bones in the ground, yet she somehow still lives. I don't want that for my Ursula."

"I cannot return her body to how it was when she still lived, but I can make it so that her body doesn't rot. It shall remain as it is now."

"For how long?"

"For as long it would please you."

But I am not the necromancer, who played God with his wife. "Can you make it so that it is Ursula herself who decides?"

"Yes," the snake says, drawing out that *s* into a pleased hiss.

Say I, "And will you give me the means to kill the necromancer right here and now?"

The snake nods.

I lick my lips. Despite the blood, my mouth and throat feel dry. "If I kill him, will his wife die also?" I am still angry with her for having crept into my dreams and lured me here, but I also know that she was desperate and knew not what else to do. From the moment her husband dragged her back from death, she must have lived in hell.

"No. Curses like that endure beyond the grave," Satan tells me.

"But how is that fair?" I ask, distress making my voice shrill. "It's not her fault her husband cursed her!"

"Life is unfair, and a good thing it is, or my job would be a lot harder."

I ball my battered hands into fists. The skin over my left knuckles has split, I know not how, and the movement tugs the flesh wider apart, making it sting. "Then how am I to help her?"

I am not a selfless creature, and I traveled this far mainly because I thought the skull would reward me for it, but I know what it is like to suffer, and I shall be damned if I let this poor creature suffer any more at the hands of a man.

You'll be damned either way, I think. I snort. It's strange, what things become funny when all is bleak and awful.

"I am sure you will find a way," Satan says. He sounds bored now. "Besides, what does it matter? You did not conjure me for her sake."

"Very well. I shall seek an answer to the skull's problem elsewhere," I say. "Let us discuss the terms of our deal some more. I want the power to bring Ursula back to me, locked in a body that shall not wither, rot, or else change, a body she is free to leave whenever it pleases her. I want to be able to do this to others also, and I want to kill the necromancer. What will you have from me in return? I have not much to give. I have no gold, no land, no maidenhead, but name your price, and I shall do whatever I can to pay it."

Satan slithers around me, as if appraising me. His scaled body in the sand makes this sweet, silky sound. "Ursula is much beloved, isn't she?"

Tears leak from my eyes. "She is most precious," I manage to say.

"So precious that you shall sign over your soul to me? That you shall turn away from God and be forever bereft of His love, all so that she may walk the earth again?"

My throat feels small and tight. "I love Ursula more than God," I whisper, and though it's a terrible thing to say, I know it to be true.

Satan laughs, this burbling, watery sound. "Very well. Sign your name in my book, and I shall make you a necromantic witch." The snake slithers toward a book that I hadn't noticed before. It's very large and bound in skin. I know not how to read, but even I can see that there are many names in this book, all written in different hands.

"I cannot write," I say and feel the familiar prick of shame.

"I shall help you," Satan says. He slithers into my lap and up my arm, and he is heavy as a coil of tarred rope. Once he reaches my hand, he sinks his fangs into my finger, and I jerk; then I scream. Unbearable heat rushes into my bloodstream and up, up, up my veins, through my lungs, my heart, and my brain, searing, scalding, scorching.

When it ebbs away, I am sweating, and my throat and mouth feel parched, but I also find that the scratches on my hands have disappeared, as has the swelling in my eye, the wounds on my scalp, and the pain in my neck.

"You made me whole again?" I ask as I marvel at the smoothness of my skin, the supple movements of my joints.

"I may not be able to heal the dead, but I can still heal the living."

"But why?"

"What use is a sick servant to me?"

"I am not yours, not yet, not unless I sign."

Satan looks at me with his large eye round and orange as a setting sun. "And would you go back on your word?"

"No. Lying is a sin," I say without thinking.

Satan laughs, this rumbling chuckle. "Indeed. Now place your finger on the page, and I shall guide your hand."

I do as I am told and feel as if another has laid their hand on top of mine and is moving it this way and that, using my nail and my blood to write out what I suppose is my name.

I look at the letters forming on the yellow parchment, and I feel sick and strange.

There is no going back now.

I worry not for my own self, but for Ursula. Mayhap she will hate me like the necromancer's wife did when she found out he had sold himself into slavery to Satan. Mayhap she'll denounce me and flee from me. But it seems to me that it's better to live in a world in which she hates and reviles me than in a world in which she feels nothing at all. And it may not come to that. She is kind, and she is forgiving. It's one of the many things I love about her.

When we are done, the book slams shut of its own accord.

"What now?" I ask.

"Now, you are mine. The spell that keeps the necromancer and your beloved's corpse from moving shall last until midnight. That gives you more than three hours. Use that time as you will. This is another one of my gifts to you. Let it never be said that the devil is ungenerous." Satan smiles at me, again showing that wet pink mouth with the ribbon tongue, then slithers from my lap and into the darkness.

I come to my feet and saunter over to the necromancer. The knife he used to slay Ursula lies not far from his feet. I pick it up. The heft of it is familiar and comforting. The necromancer still smiles smugly.

I stand on tiptoes and whisper in his ear, "I told you I'd kill you.

It's a pity you didn't believe me. Now, let's see how long you can keep up that smile."

A long time, it turns out.

I should have known.

After all, a skull's grin is eternal.

32

URSULA

ONE MOMENT, THERE IS ONLY the stinging pain in her throat, and the cold creeping into her limbs, and the wetness of her dress as the blood soaks it. The next, she is lying on the ground, and she is weak, and the world is dark.

Is she dying? Is that why she has gone nearly blind? Her hands fly to her throat. Someone has bound fabric around it, very tight, as if trying to strangle her. She whimpers, tries to work her fingers underneath the folds.

Rough hands take hold of hers, pull them away. "Don't, my love. The necromancer slashed open your throat. Do you not remember? I sewed the wound shut, then put some fabric around it so the threads won't catch on anything. I would have done a better job, had I silk or catgut to sew with, but for now, it'll do."

She knows that voice. It is sweet to her.

Elsebeth, she remembers, and with that, all her memories come flooding back.

She sits up, feeling sick with fear, and grabs Elsebeth's shoulders. "The necromancer! Elsebeth, quick, quick!" she babbles.

Elsebeth loosens her grip, brings one hand to her mouth, kisses it tenderly. "Fear not, my love. I have slain him. No, don't look! It's a sight I wish to spare you, for I made his death long and hard. He shan't ever hurt you again. We are safe."

Sister Ursula can't reply, not now that she has looked into Elsebeth's face. Her eyes have changed. There is no white anymore, just an orange color, like the yolk of an egg, and a large round pupil.

They are the eyes of a snake.

"What is it?" Elsebeth asks, a little frown on her face.

"Your eyes," Sister Ursula manages to say. "They are not your own anymore."

Elsebeth grows still. "What do you mean?"

"They are snake eyes. *Mein Liebchen*, what have you done?"

And Elsebeth tells her. She tells her everything, the whole sordid story. When she is done, Sister Ursula presses the heels of her hands hard against her eyes, which she hopes are still their usual human brown. The pressure makes fantastic colors bloom. She feels sick and strange, knows not whether to laugh or to cry.

If she can still cry.

Can a corpse cry? For that is what she is now: a walking corpse, not living, not yet quite dead, either.

An abomination unto the Lord.

And for what? All because Elsebeth could not stand to be alone. A selfish girl, she, and now damned for all eternity…

"Say something, my love, please," Elsebeth begs. She touches

Sister Ursula's wrists. Sister Ursula recoils violently. Intense pain flickers over Elsebeth's face. It shines in her new eyes, no longer gray, that beautiful color of storm clouds and slate, of a pigeon's down and a dog's fur, but orange as the fires of Hell, in which she will burn until the end of time and maybe beyond that, for what is time but another thing the Lord made and can thus undo?

"Is it so bad you can't stand for me to touch you?" Elsebeth asks in a small voice.

"I don't know," Sister Ursula confesses. "Your soul is the most precious thing you possess. You shouldn't have sold it for anything in the world, but especially not for me. Oh, Elsebeth, how could you?"

"My soul is mine to do with as I please. And it pleased me to sell it so that I could have you next to me again."

Sister Ursula laughs bitterly. "You sold yourself cheaply then."

"I did not!" Elsebeth says hotly, her hands balled into fists once more. "I love you above all else, and so I sold my soul, and sold it gladly, to have you back."

"You're supposed to love God above all else."

"But I don't. I love you more than Him, and that may well be why I am damned now, yet I care not for any of that as long as I have you at my side!"

"You have saddled me with a debt I may never repay," Sister Ursula whispers.

Elsebeth rakes her hands through her hair in frustration. She has lost her cap. "There is no debt. I don't expect anything from you in return, though I would like for things to go back as they were before, when you gave me your love and affection freely. Please, Ursula, won't you understand?"

"How can I? It's a wicked and selfish thing you did, Elsebeth. Why do you demand my compassion and understanding when you have none for me?"

Elsebeth throws herself at Sister Ursula then. She wraps her arms around the other woman, holding her fast. Sister Ursula doesn't know what to do, so she stands stiff and still, not reciprocating but not pushing her away, either.

"I do have compassion and understanding for you," Elsebeth murmurs. "I know I am wicked. You need not tell me. But I sold my soul not solely for my own sake. Had I been sure you were in Heaven, I would have left you, but I wasn't sure, for Satan would not tell me. Were you? In Heaven, I mean? Or were you in Hell? Tell me, my darling. Tell me, that I may know whether I have chosen wrong."

But Sister Ursula can't say. Whatever has happened to her after she died has been snipped from her memory. Nothing remains. Instead, she says, "Elsebeth, you must let me go."

"How cold you are! Why, my beloved? You were never so with me before."

"You weren't damned then."

Elsebeth laughs, a horrible, low sound. "What a papist thing to say! I believe I have been damned from before I was born." She presses her cheek against Sister Ursula's sternum, rubs it as if she is a cat marking Sister Ursula as hers. "But just because I am damned does not mean I have no feeling. My breast is aflame with it. When the necromancer cut your throat, and the blood spouted from it and drenched the earth, it broke my heart and mutilated my mind. That is how much I love you. I love you, I love you, I love you. Mayhap it's a selfish thing, this love of mine, but I cannot help this. Don't you see? Will you not understand?"

Sister Ursula does, if not with her mind, at least with her body; she feels that phantom pain in her belly and hips again, that ache of gathering another's suffering to her and feeling it as if it were her own.

"God wouldn't…" she begins.

"Damn God!" Elsebeth screams. She raises her face so she can look at Ursula. Her cheek looks all bruised from having rubbed it against the rough fabric of Sister Ursula's dress. A button has been stamped just below her eye like a brand. "He took everything from me. My home, my family, even you. What right did He have to do that?"

Helplessly, Sister Ursula says, "Every right. He is *God*." Her voice is hoarse and soft now; Elsebeth's embrace is like a winding sheet, tight and choking.

"But why would he do this to me? What have I done that would warrant such a correction? Nothing, nothing! I do not claim to be free of sin, but I am no worse than many others, yet I do not see them suffer as I do. Or do you deny this?"

"I can't think right now. Please, don't hold me so tight. It hurts."

Elsebeth groans, this deeply animalistic sound full of pain, and tightens her grip, her hands clawing at Sister Ursula's dress.

Fear takes possession of Sister Ursula then, an instinctive terror at being suffocated. She can no longer stand still but begins to buck and writhe.

They struggle then, an awkward moment of shoving and grabbing, pushing and pulling that only ends when Sister Ursula bites Elsebeth's cheek.

Shocked, Elsebeth recoils, her hand pressed to the seamed line left behind by Sister Ursula's teeth.

Sister Ursula flees.

"No, don't go! Please don't leave me!" Elsebeth wails, but Sister Ursula doesn't stop. It seems that all she has done lately is run. It has strengthened her legs and lungs, and so she keeps running for a long time. When she can't go on anymore, she crawls into a thicket that will obscure her from anyone on the road. It's not unlike that place where she and Elsebeth hid from those soldiers. It even smells the same, of bitter earth and green sap.

Shall such scents now forever recall Elsebeth to her?

She finds that corpses can cry after all.

Something gently nibbles her earlobe. Sister Ursula sits up and discovers she is in back in her cell. It smells of incense and damp stone, and is cool as a cup of fresh water.

On her pillow lies the skull, coppery hair spread around like a halo, eyes keen behind the silk mesh.

"I am dreaming," Sister Ursula says, her heart sinking inside her chest. For a moment, she believed she was home.

She resists the urge to grab the skull and hurl it at the wall, or shake it till the glass eyeballs spin in their sockets. "You have quite a lot of nerve, invading my dreams after all you have done to me and Elsebeth."

Immediately, the skull shoots into the air and rages, "How dost thou dare call thyself a Christian when thou art so uncharitable to a poor creature such as me? If thou hadst suffered as I have, thine head and body in two different places, thy poor self betwixt death and life, thou wouldst not dare speak to me thus! I have no other way to speak anymore but through dreams."

The skull's anger and self-pity feed the flames of Sister Ursula's anger. "And how well you used that ability to manipulate Elsebeth and me into doing everything you wanted!"

"What else was I to do? Wouldst thou have undertaken the dangerous journey to give me back my body, hadst thou known there was no reward for thee? Thou wouldst not. Thou art selfish, like all the rest."

"We shall never know what I may or may not have done had you not lied to me."

"I did not lie. I never claimed I was a saint," the skull says petulantly.

"But you knew Elsebeth and I believed that, and you did nothing to correct us. That is a kind of lie." Sister Ursula touches her throat. In her dream, the skin is still smooth and uncut. "I suppose I shall understand why you did it soon enough. We are alike now after all, you and I."

The skull laughs. It's a mean sound, harsh and mocking. "Thou art not like me! That peasant wench was cleverer by far than my husband in the deal she made with the devil. Unlike my poor body, thy body shall not rot or alter. No peasants shall see thee and know thee as a walking corpse, and stone thee, and rip off thy flesh, and cut off thine head!"

"That is a kind of blessing, I suppose," Sister Ursula says.

"And dost thou also forget that thou art free to leave whenever it so pleases thee, or didst thou not heed the girl when she told thee so?"

"What?" Sister Ursula asks. Elsebeth told her so much at once that she now fears she may not have understood her fully.

"Thou canst shuck off the burden of living as if it were no more than a shift clinging to thy skin. Not I. I may only die with my husband's leave, and now that the devil has dragged him home to Hell, I am as cursed as the wandering Jew, who mocked poor Christ and must now walk the earth until the Second Coming. Yet what crime did I commit?" the skull laments.

"Surely it won't come to that. God's love for us is endless." Despite everything that has happened, Sister Ursula still believes this. She feels the truth of it like a flame in her chest.

"'Tis not. Thine Elsebeth has damned herself and is beyond His love now."

"No one is beyond God's love, or His love wouldn't be endless."

"Then why has He not called me home?" the skull asks, and for once, she doesn't rage; she doesn't sneer or spit. Her voice is small now, yet contains infinite sadness, and Sister Ursula sees her not as a holy relic, but as what remains of a woman abused almost beyond endurance, all because her husband could not let her go.

Elsebeth has a seed of that possessiveness inside of her, yes, but even at the depths of her despair, she has not been blind to the fact that Sister Ursula is her own person, and has ensured that Sister Ursula is free to leave her, even though that would mean she sold her soul for nothing.

Sister Ursula feels her own sadness rise in her veins like sap. To the skull, she says, "I don't know why you are still alive. It's not up to us to understand His ways, now is it? All we can do is trust in His love and hope for the best."

"I know not if I have any strength left in me to hope," the skull confesses.

"Then I shall hope for the two of us," Sister Ursula says and opens her arms. The skull hesitates, then floats over, lands on Sister Ursula's lap, and presses her face against her belly. Sister Ursula strokes the long red hair as the skull moans and shakes.

When the skull grows still, Sister Ursula picks her up so she can look her in the eye. "I will help you. I don't know how, but I will try. But there must be no more lies between us, do you understand?"

"How wilt thou help me? I am with Elsebeth still."

"That's all right. I shall return to her as soon as I wake. There are some things I must say to her."

Come morning, Sister Ursula finds Elsebeth is still at the crossroads. She is gathering the skull's bones and placing them in her pack. When she sees Sister Ursula approach, she stands, holding a rib as if it is a knife, her dear face scowling. The flesh around her snake eyes is red and puffy.

For a while, they don't say anything, just stand and look at each other. Then, Sister Ursula takes the dew-damp hem of her skirt in hand and raises the cloth toward Elsebeth's face.

Elsebeth briefly closes her eyes, whimpers. Then, her face hardens, and she steps out of reach, her grip on the rib so tight that her knuckles are almost the same color as the bone. "You left me," she says. Her voice is ragged; how long did she weep and scream after Sister Ursula ran?

Sister Ursula takes a shuddering breath. "I did. But I have come back now."

"Why?"

Sister Ursula puts her hand in her pocket and winds her fingers through the strands of her rosary; the beads feel cool, hard, and pleasant, giving her strength. "One of the hardest things to do in this life is to maintain your faith in God when this wicked world is full of horror and suffering. I choose to believe that God is kind and good, even if I can't always see it. His love for us, His imperfect children, is endless. But I was also taught that there are some sins God does not forgive. Adultery. Murder."

She rubs the rosary beads until they feel hot and rough against her fingers as she searches for the right words to express what she feels so keenly. "This has always chafed at me. If God's love is endless, then how can He condemn someone to suffer in Hell for all eternity? There must be a chance at redemption and forgiveness, because if there isn't, then His love is conditional and thus not endless. It seems, then, that I have to choose once again what to believe."

"And what do you believe?" Elsebeth asks, face half fear, half hope.

"I choose love, always. And if God's love is unceasing, then He must still love you, Elsebeth, no matter that you turned your back on Him. And if He still loves you, then He shall offer you a way to come home to Him once more. It shall be hard, because infinite love does not mean no correction or punishment, but I believe you are not beyond salvation, and I…I want to help you on your search for redemption."

"Why?"

"It's because of me that you have sold your soul, and so I share in your sin."

Elsebeth bares her teeth. "I told you that it's not like that. If it's only for pity's sake that you came back to me, only to soothe your sore and sorry conscience, then—"

"How can you think that?" Sister Ursula cries out. "Do you not feel that I love you terribly? Had you been anyone else, your damnation would not have affected me so violently. I love you so much, I can scarcely speak of it. You have crept inside my heart and taken root there, and unlike a dandelion, I cannot rip you out."

"*Taraxacum officinale.* The common dandelion," Elsebeth murmurs.

Despite everything, Sister Ursula laughs a little. "Yes, indeed."

For a moment, there is silence between them, charged and awkward. Then, Sister Ursula reaches for Elsebeth, because it is agony to stand so close and yet not touch her. She pulls the girl close to her, dropping kisses on her mouth, her cheek where Sister Ursula's teeth have left a purplish mark, her nose, even those hated eyes.

After a while, Elsebeth gently cups Sister Ursula's face, stopping the gentle rain of kisses, and asks, "What about your sisters, the ones who still live? Would you abandon them for my sake? Do your vows even allow it?"

"I am loyal to God alone, and what He wants now is for me to aid you as you find a way back to Him."

"How can you be so sure?"

"Why else would He have put you in my path? If everything happens for a reason, I see no other one that makes sense."

Elsebeth's flaming eyes brim with tears. It's a strange sight, like an ember burning underwater. "What if I am beyond saving?"

Sister Ursula brushes away the tears with her thumbs. "Then I am likely Hell bound too, and we shall be damned together. But first, we live."

"But first, we live," Elsebeth repeats. Her dear face cracks into a smile, which only disappears when she kisses Sister Ursula deeply.

Epilogue

ELSEBETH

When I was a little girl, I saw three witches burned. As the flames fed on the third witch, she managed to wrench loose from the ropes that bound her to the pyre and jumped in the air. She caught my eye as she hung there for a moment, suspended, and she smiled, as if she saw something within me that pleased her. At the time, I knew not what that might be. I knew only fear.

Now, I know she saw that I was already damned and would one day be as she was.

For I am a witch now, my soul pledged to Satan. In return, I have been given the power of necromancy, which I have used so far only once: to bring Ursula back to me.

Ursula believes she may yet save me. For this reason, and because we have the care of the bones of a woman who wishes to die but cannot, we have taken to the road again. Ursula says we must visit every shrine, every church and chapel, that she may be aided by the power of the reliquaries there as she prays for my sorry soul and for that of the necromancer's wife. Mayhap there is a saint who will intercede for us.

I cannot enter these holy places anymore. It's as if there is a wall between them and me, and for all that I have powers now, I cannot move through brick. When Ursula goes inside to pray, bringing the bag of bones that is all that remains now of the poor necromancer's wife inside with her, I sit at the border and wait for her, my eyes bound with a bit of cloth. Those who see us think that I am blind, and that Ursula prays for me so that my sight may be restored. The truth would scare them: My sin is writ in my eyes, there for all to see.

Yet I mind these snake eyes of mine less than I thought I would, for they keep me safe, and Ursula also. No one will try to harm a girl who so clearly enjoys Satan's protection. Even bands of marauding soldiers, their names written in Satan's book as well as mine, even if they don't know it yet, will run in fear when I turn my gaze upon them.

Three years Ursula and I have been on this quest for salvation and found none. Still the war rages on around us. I wonder often if it will ever end.

Mayhap ours is a fool's quest, and mayhap it is not. But even if I shall be damned for all eternity, I cannot feel sorry for selling my soul, not when I have my Ursula. For as long as I am with her, Earth itself is Heaven.

I love her.

I love her.

I love her.

A NOTE ON THE HISTORICAL CONTEXT OF THIS NOVEL

If you have come here after reading the entire novel: Thank you for reading it all the way through. I hope it has been a good read. If you have come here at some earlier point (relatable; I often read authors' notes before finishing a novel, too), please be aware that there will be spoilers within the following pages, so be warned!

In *Bone of My Bone*, I have taken certain liberties with the truth in order to tell a compelling story. I think it is clear that I am most interested in the lived experiences of the common people during this conflict rather than the political and military aspects of it; the lack of these within the story is therefore a conscious choice. I readily admit that geography and topography are not my strongest points. Any mistakes in distances traveled and the landscape Elsebeth, Sister Ursula, Otto, and the necromancer traverse are therefore definitely not a conscious choice.

As for the lesbianism: Sodomy, which did not exclusively refer to same-sex relations but rather to a whole host of sexual practices considered deviant, including oral sex and bestiality, was illegal in Bavaria and indeed throughout (most of) early modern Europe.

Those convicted of sodomy were burned alive at the stake. This novel already deals with lots of heavy topics. I did not wish to add homophobia to the list as well; it is partially for this reason that I have refrained from having Elsebeth and Sister Ursula fret (too much) about whether their relationship is sinful.

The other reason is that the bringing about of an orgasm to cure certain maladies is historically accurate. Chlorosis, also known as "green sickness," *morbus virgineus* ("virgin's disease"), or *febris amatoria* ("lover's fever"), was a real disease that women and girls could be diagnosed with from the Middle Ages up until the nineteenth century. It seems to have been a combination of anemia and anorexia. Its symptoms included paleness, swollen ankles, palpitations, difficulty breathing, and an aversion to food, especially meat. In 1554, the German physician Johannes Lange argued that it was a disease caused by celibacy; the only way for girls to recover was therefore to get married (the only social construct in which sex was allowed) and become pregnant. Other early modern doctors argued that the act of sex itself, specifically a female orgasm, was enough. If marriage was not an option, a midwife (or, in the case of Sister Ursula, an infirmarian) could manually stimulate her patient until orgasm occurred. Apart from treating anemia, issues related to the womb, and hysteria, midwives sometimes also brought about an orgasm to help women give birth; we find this recommendation in several midwifery handbooks. According to Harriette Andreadis, the female orgasm was not seen as sexual in these contexts,* which has given me all the leeway

* Harriette Andreadis, *Sappho in Early Modern England: Female Same-Sex Literary Erotics, 1550–1714* (University of Chicago Press, 2001), 17.

I needed to incorporate a romantic and sexual relationship between two women into this book without feeling as if I did much (if any) violence to historical truth.

Apart from historical and religious horror, I would categorize *Bone of My Bone* as folk horror as well, since it includes several creatures from German(ic) folklore. *Nachzehrer* are traditionally a kind of vampiric revenant, and although the word didn't come to be in use until the nineteenth century, the belief in such an entity is much older. Your average *Nachzehrer* is a pretty passive monster: They just lie in their grave and suck the life force out of their unfortunate victims from afar until they, too, perish. The Kashubian version, however, is much more active and much stranger: According to legend, they eat their own feet, hands, and arms before crawling out of their grave. It is said that if they manage to clamber to the top of a church tower and ring the church bells, anyone who hears that sound will perish (as to how, exactly, the *Nachzehrer* is supposed to do so without any arms and feet, the legend doesn't specify). As for how someone can become a *Nachzehrer*: Those buried with fabric touching their lips run this risk, as well as people who committed suicide or died a violent death. My version of the *Nachzehrer* is a blend of both the passive and the Kashubian version.

Aufhocker are another kind of folkloric revenant. They jump on the back of an unsuspecting passerby and demand that that unfortunate passerby return them to their grave. In the original stories, they usually grow heavier and heavier with every step until they crush their victim to death. I have changed this for obvious reasons.

Apart from revenants, this book also deals with witchcraft.

Germany had some of the largest witch trials of the early modern period, such as the Fulda witch trials (1603–1606), the Würzburg witch trials (1625–1631), and the Bamberg witch trials (1627–1632); it is no coincidence that two of these occurred during the Thirty Years' War. This is not the place to go into this topic in great depth, but I think it is worth pointing out that, although the stereotypical image of the witch as an old lady derives from these trials, men could also be accused of witchcraft. Indeed, in the Middle Ages, it was more common for men to be accused, and in the Scandinavian countries, ultimately more men than women were convicted on witchcraft charges. For this reason, I have made my antagonist a male witch.

The dark arts that the devil offers to the witch who Elsebeth saw immolated as a little girl—being able to spread sickness among cattle and people, killing babies by driving a needle through their brains so they can be turned into a salve that allows witches to fly, etc.—are all things people genuinely believed witches did. It must, however, be noted that such witch trials, let alone executions of suspected witches, were rare in Bavaria. Contrary to what some may believe, plenty of people in early modern times did not believe witches existed, or at least not in the way a number of books such as the *Malleus Maleficarum* claimed they did. The idea that men and women who made a deal with the devil had animal eyes is my own invention.

A LIST OF RECOMMENDED FURTHER READING

I read various books and articles to help me write this novel. Here is a selected list of recommended further reading.

- For what caused the Thirty Years' War and how it progressed:
  - Harrison, Dick. 2018. *De Dertigjarige Oorlog: de allereerste wereldoorlog 1618–1648*. Translated by Ger Meesters. Omniboek. Unfortunately, this book is only available in Dutch or Swedish, but if you are able to read one of those languages, I highly recommend it.

- For what life was like for the common people and soldiers during the Thirty Years' War:
  - Haude, Sigrun. 2021. *Coping with Life During the Thirty Years' War (1618–1648)*. Brill.
  - The diaries of Peter Hagendorf, a miller's son who became a mercenary and kept a diary from 1625 until 1648. The diary was written in German, but various English translations exist that are available for free online.

- For understanding the attitudes toward crime, sin, and salvation in early modern Germany:
    - Stuart, Kathy. 2023. *Suicide by Proxy in Early Modern Germany: Crime, Sin and Salvation*. Palgrave Macmillan.

- For the skull, catacomb saints, and other Catholic relics:
    - Koudounaris, Paul. 2013. *Heavenly Bodies: Cult Treasures and Spectacular Saints from the Catacombs.* Thames & Hudson.

- For understanding lesbianism in the early modern era:
    - Andreadis, Harriette. 2001. *Sappho in Early Modern England: Female Same-Sex Literary Erotics, 1550–1714.* University of Chicago Press.
    - Traub, Valerie. 2002. *The Renaissance of Lesbianism in Early Modern England.* Cambridge University Press.

A LIST OF TRIGGER WARNINGS (ALPHABETIZED)

This book contains discussions and/or depictions of the following:

- Abduction
- Assault
- Blood
- Cannibalism
- Christianity
- Corpses
- Death and dying
- Forced exile/being forced to flee your home
- Gore
- Human remains
- Looting
- Loss of a loved one, specifically a grandparent, a parent, a sibling
- Madness
- Mental illness
- Misogyny

- Physical violence
- Religion, specifically Christianity, specifically losing your faith, struggling to maintain your faith in the face of the horrors of everything mentioned on this list, grappling with feelings of overwhelming guilt and shame, and religious persecution
- Sexual violence, including rape (mentioned but not explicitly described)
- Sickness
- Suicide
- Torture
- Trauma
- Violence
- Vomit
- War

READING GROUP GUIDE

1. Elsebeth says early on that she is no longer certain that she believes in God, but she does believe in Satan. Why does she say that? What did you make of it?

2. If it were you who had found the saint's skull, would you have taken it? Why or why not?

3. Describe the relationship between Elsebeth and Sister Ursula. What draws them together? How are they similar? Different?

4. Why do you think Sister Ursula's chapters are in third person and Elsebeth's are in first? What does that say about them as characters? What does it add to the story?

5. Why does Sister Ursula teach Elsebeth the Latin name for dandelions? What role do dandelions play in the novel and in Elsebeth and Sister Ursula's relationship?

6. What did you make of Otto's character? Why does the necromancer use him the way he does? What perspectives do his chapters add to Elsebeth's and Sister Ursula's story?

7. Why, when Elsebeth calls out for God, does Satan appear? Does God ever make an appearance?

8. Why might Satan take the form of a snake?

9. Discuss the deal Elsebeth makes at the end of the novel. Was it justified? How does it compare to the deal the necromancer made? Would you have done the same?

10. Even after war, torture, and death, Sister Ursula continues to believe in the love of God. Why do you think that is? Is there anything that causes her to waver in her belief?

A CONVERSATION WITH THE AUTHOR

What inspired *Bone of My Bone*?

A lot of things! My interest in the strange and the macabre, my fascination with religion and religious people and their relationship with death and corpses, my desire to write about the early modern period, my wish to try something a little different from my previous two books... The list truly goes on and on!

What was your process like writing a book steeped in real history and religion? How much research did you have to do?

I already had a good understanding about the religious conflicts between Protestants and Catholics in the early modern period because of my MA in Book and Digital Media; for my thesis, I created an annotated edition of several letters written by a group of Puritans, which required quite a lot of research into the topic. After completing my MA, I wanted to do a PhD and wrote a proposal about Christian comfort literature (which is exactly what it sounds like: literature written from a Christian perspective meant to comfort those who are suffering). I ultimately ended up joining the workforce instead because of financial reasons,* but my MA and this research did mean I had a good grasp on the topic already. Additionally, I have completed two years of the BA in German Language and Culture; one of my courses was about seventeenth-century literature and history. I still had to read quite a bit before writing *Bone of My Bone*, especially about the specifics of the Thirty Years' War and how ordinary people experienced it, but all of this is to say that I already had a good basis to start from!

Elsebeth and Sister Ursula are so different in personality and beliefs. What is it that you think draws, and keeps, them together? How do they reckon with their differing religious beliefs?

Opposites attract! I believe both can provide the other with what they need. Sister Ursula isn't very world-wise; she's inside her own head quite a bit and tends to freeze in dangerous situations. Elsebeth is pragmatic and a fighter and as such can help Sister Ursula survive physically. At the same time, Elsebeth is also pretty pessimistic and deeply traumatized; she needs Sister Ursula's warmth and optimism to survive mentally. As for their different religious beliefs: Unless one of them converts, I don't think they can resolve them. There is, after all, no proving either one right or

---

* Perhaps it's useful to point out here that PhDs work differently in the Netherlands (and, by extension, most of Europe) compared to the U.S. In the U.S., you can get a PhD after you have completed your bachelor's degree. The programs last about five to six years and are relatively easy to get into; getting tenure, though, is hard. In the Netherlands, you can only get into a PhD after completing your master's degree. These programs take about three to four years. It is very difficult to get into a PhD program, but once you have, getting tenure (or a high-paying job) is relatively easy.

wrong (as my sixth-grade teacher would say: "It's called believing, not knowing for sure."). Fortunately, they can agree to disagree!

This is your third novel—after *My Darling Dreadful Thing* and *Blood on Her Tongue*. Did writing this story feel different from the others? Why or why not?

With both my previous novels, I had written a failed first draft before rewriting them from the ground up. Although I don't necessarily recommend this approach—it is *brutal* to write about eighty thousand words and then realize that the novel isn't any good—it did have one advantage: I was already deeply familiar with the characters and the setting when I set out to write the story anew. For *Bone of My Bone*, I didn't have that. I like to think that's because I am a better writer now (those first failed drafts for *My Darling Dreadful Thing* and *Blood on Her Tongue* were written many years ago when I was still very much learning the basics of the writing craft), but it did mean the writing process felt different. I think the fact that this book is a bit different from the other two (folk horror as opposed to gothic horror, set in Germany rather than in the Netherlands, three POVs) added to that feeling.

Among many other things, this is a story deeply about the lives and struggles of women and is driven in large part by the relationship between two women. Why add Otto's chapters into the mix?

There are two main reasons for this. Firstly, from a technical perspective, I needed a third point of view to keep the tension high. There is a big difference between the saint's skull telling Elsebeth and Sister Ursula that a necromancer is after them and the reader experiencing that directly through Otto's chapters.

The second reason is that I felt it would be good to explore a male perspective within this conflict. Otto's chapters allowed me to explore a matter that I think is still extremely relevant today: How can someone whose entire life has been war and violence (re)learn empathy and humanity? Can such people be rehabilitated? I don't ask readers to forgive Otto—he is still very much a war criminal—but I do hope that his chapters add an interesting perspective.

From the beginning, this story features a lot of gruesome scenes and dark themes. What is it like writing details like that? Is it difficult being in that headspace?

It is quite difficult, yes. The Thirty Years' War was exceptionally cruel and bloody. The details included in *Bone of My Bone* are all accurate. As a matter of fact, I have actually opted not to include some of the horrors I encountered during my research because I feared the book would become too bleak if I did. Luckily, I have enough good things in my life to counterbalance the darkness within my books. That being said, I did have to watch plenty of comedies and read some fluffier things as I was writing!

This novel deals with many themes, including religion, love, witchcraft, and the consequences of war. Is there anything in particular that you hope readers take away from this story?

I think there is always hope, even when things get very, very dark.

ACKNOWLEDGMENTS

If you regularly spend time on social media, you may have come across funny pictures drawn in the margins of medieval manuscripts called marginalia: cats working the fields as peasants, knights battling giant snails, nuns harvesting penises from trees and shrubberies. You may also have seen photographs of the beautiful capital letters at the start of a page known as Lombardic capitals, or of jewel-encrusted covers. The amount of work it took to create one such manuscript is truly astonishing; it would take multiple years to complete.[*] If we also take into account the many craftspeople involved—the bookbinders, the goldsmiths and silversmiths, the parchmenters, among others—then it is safe to say that dozens of people were involved in the creation of one book.

The invention of the moveable-type printing press by Johannes

---

* Small wonder, then, that apart from funny pictures, we also find complaints about cold hands and painful fingers in the margins as well as curses at cats urinating or stepping on the pages and prayers of thanks that the blasted book is finally done.

Gutenberg in 1440 gradually changed this.* Today, books can be printed in mere hours, and although there are plenty of gorgeous special editions out there, we don't usually involve actual gold and gemstones anymore. One thing has remained the same, though: It still takes many people to make a book.

In the case of *Bone of My Bone*, the following people were involved in addition to yours truly:

My editor, Jenna Jankowski, whose feedback greatly improved this novel. Any author out there knows that, if they should ever get their hands on a true saint's skull that shall grant them a wish, it wouldn't be a half-bad idea to wish for an amazing editor. Luckily, I don't need to spend any wishes on that because I've already found mine!

My copy editors, who made sure every comma is where it should be and there are no typos left. (We hope! It's a truth universally acknowledged that, no matter how many people look at a book before it goes to print, there's usually at least one mistake that somehow escapes notice. Maybe, with some divine intervention, this book shall be the exception.)

My sensitivity readers. I believe that good art should disturb the comfortable and comfort the disturbed; these readers help

---

* The coexistence of manuscripts and printed books in the early modern period and the different attitudes toward both is absolutely fascinating and well worth looking into if this is a topic that interests you. Scribe Filippo de Strata, for example, wrote that "writing indeed, which brings in gold for us, should be respected and held to be nobler than all goods, unless she has suffered degradation in the brothel of the printing presses. She is a maiden with a pen, a harlot in print."

to ensure that I do not traumatize either the comfortable or the disturbed.

Dawn Xintong Yang, who did the art for the cover and the sprayed edges of the deluxe edition. If everyone who picks up this book judges it by its cover alone, I foresee only five-star reviews!

Erin Fitzsimmons, who did the cover design. Look at that font! Look at the placement of that text! That's symbolism and good design, baby!

Kristina Pérez, my agent. It's wonderful to have someone who is always on your side and who handles all the nitty-gritty administrative and financial stuff so I have time to read books about macabre historical practices that then make it into my novels. Did you know, for example, that the Vatican shipped out a whole bunch of bedazzled skeletons to Germany after the Thirty Years' War was over to reward and comfort the Catholics there? They are called catacomb saints and well worth googling because they are likely the most stylish skeletons you will ever see. If I should fall during the skeleton war, I hope it's at the hand of a catacomb saint.

Isabel Lineberry, who is a junior agent and helps with all the audio and foreign rights and probably some other important things that I am not aware of, which I think is a good thing because, again, her tireless work behind the scenes gives me time to read and write.

Less directly involved, yet vital to the process, were the following people:

My wife, who listens to my endless ranting about interesting things I read and the plans I have and plot problems I must solve.

She also keeps me alive with all her delicious cooking and baking. I don't think it's true that I couldn't have written this book without her, but I know for a fact that the experience would have been less pleasant and the end result less good.

My sisters, who always read my work and give thoughtful feedback even though they claim not to like horror (but they do like my work, so at this point, one has to doubt the veracity of this statement).

My parents, who, although they aren't religious themselves, did send me to a Christian primary and secondary school.* According to the butterfly effect, I wouldn't have written this book if they'd sent me to a public school instead, so for that alone I must thank them, and then we haven't even touched upon all the ways in which they are awesome. I'm still not sure what I would wish for, should I ever get my hands on a wish-granting saint's skull, but different parents certainly isn't among the possibilities.

Lastly, there is you, dear reader. Regardless of what you think of this book, I'd like to thank you for picking it up and reading it all the way through (unless you're like me and you read acknowledgments at the start or halfway through, in which case: I hope you'll like the rest of this novel!).

* I should probably clarify that both schools were rather liberal and relaxed; no religious trauma for me!

ABOUT THE AUTHOR

Johanna is a bestselling and award-winning author of queer spooky books for both adults and children. She has received an MA in English Literature with a specialization in early modern literature and an MA in Book and Digital Media with a specialization in early modern book history, both of them at Leiden University.

When she isn't exorcizing herself of the visions that haunt her by turning them into macabre tales, she enjoys spending time with her wife, her sisters (they're triplets!), and her dog, though not necessarily all at the same time.

BURY YOURSELF IN MORE HORROR FROM JOHANNA VAN VEEN